# Two Sailor Lads
## A Story Of Stirring Adventures On Sea And Land

*by*

Gordon Stables

Double9
BOOKS

# Two Sailor Lads
## A Story Of Stirring Adventures On Sea And Land
### by Gordon Stables

ISBN: 978-93-68093-26-8

**Published by**

# DOUBLE 9 BOOKS

2/13-B, Ansari Road
Daryaganj, New Delhi – 110002
info@double9books.com
www.double9books.com
Tel. 011-40042856

# ABOUT THE AUTHOR

Gordon Stables become a 19th-century Scottish creator and a multifaceted discern who made great contributions to literature, mainly in the style of adventure tales and maritime memories. One of his terrific works is "The Cruise of the Snowbird." "The Cruise of the Snowbird" is a compelling maritime adventure novel that takes readers on a thrilling adventure throughout the high seas. Set towards the backdrop of the overdue nineteenth century, the story follows the bold exploits of Captain George Vesey as he embarks on a tremendous voyage aboard the Snowbird, an imposing yacht. Gordon Stables' writing fashion is characterised by way of its vivid descriptions, meticulous attention to nautical information, and a profound love for the sea. His narratives offer a glimpse into the demanding situations and triumphs of seafaring lifestyles, from dealing with the elements to exploring uncharted territories. The book not best serves as a captivating adventure but also imparts precious life instructions and values of courage, camaraderie, and the indomitable human spirit. Stables' storytelling resonates with the essence of maritime exploration and the appeal of the unknown. Gordon Stables' contributions to adventure literature have left an indelible mark.

# CONTENTS

# CHAPTER I
# "HUSH! DO YOU HEAR THAT CRY? WHAT CAN IT BE?"

There is no more beautiful bay than that of Methlin on all the wild west shores of Scotland; there is no quainter or more old-fashioned little town than the fishing village that clusters around its shores, its wee little whitewashed cottages half hidden in the green of waving elders and drooping silver birch trees. Behind the village is a wealth of woodland, stretching for miles away up the valley, between hills so high that at sunrise they cast their darkling shadows far across the sea.

But our story opens at eventide. The sun has already gone down behind the waves, leaving a sky and sea of such gorgeous and startling colours—such a mad mixture of crimson, orange, purple, and grey—as never surely was seen on artist's canvas.

And not only from the water, but even from the wide expanse of wet sand, are these colours reflected.

The sea is very calm, yet the Atlantic Ocean, that swells and heaves and breaks along this coast, never falls quite asleep; and if you glance to-night across the sands at the far-receding tide, you may note long moving lines of orange, and hear the gentle boom of the breaking wavelets.

Right in the centre of this mixed mass of radiant light and colour—darkling against it, and throwing long shadows on the wet flat beach—are two figures. How tall they look! Yes; but they are but boy and girl. Even the sea-gulls that run across the sands appear gigantic birds in that painted haze. Children both they are; he but ten, and she but six.

In looking seaward there is something else one will not fail to note; namely, a long dark wall of rocks, forming the southern horn of the bay, and running straight out into the ocean a mile and more.

There are a few fishing-boats drawn up upon the beach, and this is all the view.

Young though they are, both Fred Arundel and his foster-sister Toddie must be impressed by the solemnity and beauty of the scene, for they are unusually silent, as hand in hand they come homewards across the soloured sands.

But suddenly they start, and stop and listen.

"Hush, Toddie! Did you hear that cry? What can it be?"

"Only a Tatywake, Fled."

"No, Todd, it was no Kittywake. It was no bird at all Hark! There it is again."

Yes; borne towards the beach on the evening breeze, and falling on their listening ears, comes once again a faint but plaintive cry, that anyone less a child of the ocean than Fred, might well have mistaken for the scream of some sea-bird, a gull, or tern, or skua.

Toddie clung fearfully to Fred now.

"O Fleddie," she cried, "I is so flightened. What is it? Some poor man dlowning out there all by his self. Yun home, Fled, and tell daddy. O Fleddie, yun, yun!"

"No," said Fred boldly. "Whoever it is, must be clinging to the rocks. The tide is rising fast, Todd; but the little cobble is handy, and I'll pull out and see."

"And I must come too," insisted Toddie.

"All right," said Fred. "I'll ship the tiller, and you can steer."

"Yes, I'll teer, Fled. Oh, be twick!"

Fred was quick; no boy could have been quicker; and in less than five minutes, impelled by his strong young arms, the cobble was bounding over the rising tide.

Fred had got wet to the waist in launching the boat, but he did not mind that. Something told him there was a precious life to be saved, and he could think of nothing else.

For fully half a mile straight out to the sea ran the rocks and cliffs, ending in a bold and rocky promontory nearly seven hundred feet in height.

Bight along by the rocks rowed Fred, Toddie grasping the tiller in her tiny hands, her anxious, pretty face strained with listening.

Every now and then Fred rested on his oars for a few moments to listen, and ever as he did so, rising high over the screaming of the gulls, they could hear that piteous cry for help.

Quicker and quicker now rowed Fred. He was a good oar, and was warming to his work. No extra finish was there about Fred's rowing, no feathering of oars or any such folly, but a long pull and a strong pull, dipping his blades into the water deep enough to get good purchase, but not an inch deeper, and bending well to every stroke. Right steadily too the lad rowed, so that verily there was music and rhythm 'twixt rowlock and oar.

The clouds had lost their gorgeous colours, and from a rift of blue on the eastern sky one single star looked down.

Night was coming on apace, and there was not wanting evidence that it would be a stormy one. The swell was rising high out here, the surging seas broke white against the cliff foot, and little angry catspaws were already ruffling the water.

Fred rested on his oars and listened once more.

All was still. The wandering sea-birds wheeled near and shrieked their dismal shriek, but no human sound could the children hear.

Fred himself began to get frightened now. The silence was like the silence of death, and even the voices of the birds had a ghostly ring in them. Was it all over then?

No; for even at that moment Fred's quick ear caught the sound of something moving in the water.

"Look! look!" cried Toddie. "A seal, Fled, coming this way all by his self."

Yes, there was a black head yonder, coming rapidly on towards the boat.

Fred quickly shipped his oars now, and stood by to give assistance; for he soon discovered that the black head was human, the face pale and startled-looking.

Presently the swimmer stopped, and trode water not four yards away from the boat's bow.

"Please were you co-co-coming for m-m-m-me?"

"Of course," cried Fred. "What else? Swim nearer and I'll help you up. Mind, Toddie, we don't capsize."

Toddie held the helm grimly amidships, and sat on the gunwale, and in a moment more Fred had pulled a lad apparently a year or so older than himself in over the bows.

A tallish, gentlemanly-looking boy, dressed in a dripping kilt, and with a strongly English accent.

"It's awfully go-go-good of you," he began. "Oh," he added, "you have a li-li-little la-la-lady on board. Good evening, m-m-miss. The tide was r-r-rising over the rocks, and soon would have drowned me."

Then he raised his hand as if to pull his cap off, but there was no cap there.

"I do-do-don't s-s-stutter, mind," he said, "it is only the co-co-cold."

And Toddie felt she could have cried for this handsome boy, whose teeth were chattering in his head.

"Mammy Mop will soon wa'm oo," said Toddie consolingly.

"Oh, thanks! And may I take an oar? Thanks awfully."

Before the boys had beached the boat and hauled her up the stranger had quite recovered his speech.

"I can never thank you enough," he said, "for rescuing me from what would have been a watery grave."

"Give me oo hand now," said Toddie. "We will all yun home, and oo can tell the stoly to Mammy Mop."

"But really I mustn't— —," began the boy.

There was nothing else for it, however; for Fred had seized his other hand, and between Toddie and him they ran him right up the beach, along the road a little way, and through a bonnie garden, towards the door of a cottage, the light from which was streaming out into the gloom of the falling night.

Half an hour afterwards, had you peeped in through the four-paned window of the fisherman's cottage, this is what you would have seen: A bright and cheerful fire of peat and wood burning on a low hearth, a pot with a steaming and savoury stew in it hanging from a soot-blackened chain above it; in one corner, sitting in an old-fashioned high-backed chair, a tall and elderly man, with finely-chiselled features, long hair floating over his jersey, an almost wild look in his eyes, but kindness in every lineament nevertheless. This is Papa Pop, and on his knee sits Toddie, one arm round his neck, but her great wondering blue eyes fixed on the face of that handsome English-looking boy, who, to her way of thinking, seems like the prince of some fairy tale, suddenly dropped out of the clouds. In the other corner sits Fred himself, and at his feet a sonsy cat and a dachshund dog.

Standing on the floor behind this group is the fisherman's wife, tall and bony, rough, but kindly-looking withal, and in front of her, with the firelight streaming on his strangely uncouth face, is Bunko, the fool of the village.

But "fool" is too harsh a word to use; for although but half-witted, there is a deal of sense and shrewdness under that towsy mop of his. Bunko holds in one hand a rough stick or pole higher than himself. This is his rod of office; for Bunko takes all the village cows away to the hills every morning, and besides this he does all kinds of odd jobs that few save he could accomplish.

"Weel, Bunko," the fisherman's wife is saying as she crams his pocket with buttered scones, "you'll tak' the road right over the hills."

"Umphm!" says Bunko.

"And ten miles and a bittock will bring ye to the hoose o' Benshee. Knock at the door—d'ye understan'?"

"Fine that."

"And tell the laird's folk that Master Fielding is safe for the nicht at——"

Bunko strode across the floor and laid a huge red hand on the young stranger.

"Master Fielding—that's this wee blinker, isn't it noo?"

The lad laughed, and put something in Bunko's hand. Bunko looked at the coin.

"A bonnie white shillin'!" he cried. "Hurrah! Noo I tell ye, sirs, the grass winna grow aneath poor Bunko's feet till he's at Benshee-house and back again. Keelie, laddie, whaur are you?"

A wall-eyed collie dog sprang up at the summons. Bunko struck his pole once on the floor, then he and Keelie went out into the darkness, and were seen no more that night.

"I really ought to have gone with Bunko," said Frank Fielding, for that was the stranger's name. "But it doesn't matter much," he added, "only mamma will be quite pleased to hear of our adventure. Fred, you will be a hero, and Miss Toddie a heroine. For mamma is very romantic. And I'm sure, Fred, I'll never forget it. I had been fishing, sir"—he was addressing the old fisherman now—"and was overtaken by the tide. It was very dreadful with the night coming on, and the sea birds moaning and screaming around that cold grey rock, and the water rising, rising, rising. Heigho! it would soon have covered me; so you see, Miss Toddie, you saved my life."

"Well," replied little Miss Consequential, "when oo says oo players to-night, of tourse oo'll thank the dood Lord?"

"Yes, Toddie, I must," said Frank with a little sigh. Well might he sigh! Prayers in the family circle were unknown at Benshee Hall.

Frank was already strangely interested in the inmates of this little cot, and when Mammy Mop, as the children called her, handed down the great old Bible, and when this brown-faced fisherman read a portion, and afterwards prayed more earnestly and in loftier language than ever the parish minister used, Frank looked at him in reverent wonder not unmixed with awe.

Then they all sat round the fire again.

The wind had now risen and was moaning round the cot, and the rain rattled dismally against it.

Fred shuddered a little as he listened to the wind.

"I'm so glad," he said, "that we went down to-night to our aquarium, to feed the blennies, and a new pet of Toddie's that she called Tom."

"Tom has been naughty," said Toddie, "so Tom has been sent home."

"Yes, that is true," said Fred, "very naughty, and we had gone down to the rocks to put Tom away, else we never should have heard your cry."

The children's aquarium, I may tell you, was a marine one in a cave down by the sea. The cave was a shallow one in the south side of the ridge of high cliffs that ran out to sea, but far removed beyond the avaricious clutch of a rising tide unless something out of the common should occur. Bodily the sea had never risen so high as Fred's cave in his time, although in days of storm and tempest, when great green waves broke and thundered on the beach, the spray was often carried far along the face of the cliffs with force enough to drench anyone to the skin who ventured as far as the cave; once inside, however, one was safe enough. Not more than ten feet in depth or width was the cave, though more than nearly twenty feet high, and a very pleasant place to spend an hour or two in by day during the summer months. At noon the sun shone right into it, and penetrated the water of Fred's aquarium at the end. This latter was a natural basin in the rock, a kind of hollow shelf about three feet above the floor, which these children kept filled with water, and stocked with many curious creatures, that they found upon the beach, such as shell fish, tiny medusæ, sea anemones, and little fishes of many kinds. Toddie delighted in droll, weird-looking water things, and used to shout aloud for joy when she found any new form of youthful marine monster left in a pool of the rocks when the tide went back. She never went seawards without Fred, and he carried a little hand landing-net, and whenever a fresh specimen was discovered ugly enough to commend itself to Toddie, she peremptorily ordered her chaperon to fish it out and convey it to the cave aquarium.

Things throve here very well indeed, owing perhapa to the fact that they kept the water constantly changed and carefully removed any wee creature that died. Singularly enough, however, soon after the arrival of Tom, specimens began to disappear in the most mysterious manner.

But it is time to explain who Tom was. Watching the fishermen drawing in their nets one day, in which was a goodly quantity of bonnie silver herrings, Toddie noticed one of the men pull a strange-looking fish out of the net and throw it inland to die. Toddie went straight away after it. The creature had fallen among a lot of dry seaweed, so it was none the worse, though it wriggled alarmingly when the girl lifted it up and put it in her apron. In ten minutes' time she had placed it in Fred's cave aquarium, where it rested on its side a short time, then began a tour of inspection much to Toddie's delight. A long stone-grey, light-spotted thing, with a semicircular mouth away under its chin, and a tail with one half of it much longer than the other. In fact it was that species of small shark that abounds round British coasts, called the dog-fish.

Toddie and Fred had determined to make a great pet of it, so they fed it on sand-hoppers and earthworms, and bait generally. Tom ate everything they gave him greedily enough, and seemed to look for more.

But since his arrival the other specimens began to disappear, and the pretty little sea-minnows, as Fred called them, that had been placed beside Tom to keep him company, had gone also.

On this evening when Fred and Toddie had gone to the cave they found Tom waiting expectantly.

I'm afraid Tom was a very sly fish.

"Just look at me now," he seemed to say, as he gazed at them with that slit of an eye of his, "you see before you one of the most innocent and kind-hearted trouts in all creation. To be sure my shape is rather against me, and so is my colour; but for all that I'm the most gentle and— —"

It is a pity that at this very instant the last newcomer, a sea-minnow, should have darted out from under a bit of sea-weed, and sailed to the front.

All Tom's virtue and goodness were forgotten in a moment. He quivered all over from stem to stern, his very eyes appeared to flash fire. Next moment he had thrown himself on his side, the water rippled, the sea-minnow was gone at a snap.

Toddie threw up her hands and screamed. Fred stood firm.

"What do you think of that, Todd?" he said.

"Oh, Tom, Tom," cried Toddie, "you naughty dolly fish!"

"It was all a mistake I assure you," Tom seemed to say. "I opened my mouth to yawn, you know, and— —"

"Fred! Fred!" said Toddie, "tatch that naughty Tom and put him in the sea."

So Tom's doom was sealed at once.

He was caught, therefore, in the landing-net, carried away to the deeper water close by the rocks, and dropped into the sea.

And that was the last Toddie saw of her "dolly-fish."

"And now," said Frank, addressing Eean, "I know you have a story to tell. Do tell it, sir, and make it as dreadful as possible."

The fisherman laughed as he looked at Frank.

"I don't think," he said, "I must tell you anything very terrible; but if I tell you a story, I promise you it shall be a true one. And a true story is better than a terrible one. Ahem!"

# CHAPTER II
## "BUT LOOKING BACK, BOYS, IT IS ALL LIKE A DREAM"

Was it a gleam of pleasure, or the flush from the firelight, that spread over old Eean's face as Frank Fielding made his quiet but ingenuous request, to be favoured with a story?

The fisherman smiled, and now the rugged lineaments of his face softened wonderfully. He did not answer directly, however.

Eppie, his wife, had drawn near to the circle round the fire with her great black spinning-wheel, and it was towards her that Eean turned. Surely too it was for her that smile was intended.

He stretched out his left arm, the one that was nearest to his wife, and laid his hand on her lap. There was something very touching in this simple act, and in the tender look that accompanied it. For a moment or two the birring of the spinning-wheel ceased as Eppie took her husband's hand in both of hers.

He had really asked a question, though not in words; but it was in words that Eppie replied.

"Yes, Eean, yes," she said. "What for no tell the story?"

"Our story, Eppie."

"Ay, ay, our story, Eean."

Birr—rr—rr went the spinning-wheel again; and I'm not sure there was not some moisture in Eppie's eyes as she bent once more over her work.

It was a very old-fashioned pipe of clay that Eean now lit with a morsel of burning peat, and when he got it to go he placed over the bowl the white iron lid which was attached by a tiny chain to the stalk. Then he leaned back in his chair, and for a time seemed intent only on watching the blue rings of smoke, that went curling up towards the blackened rafters of the humble cottage.

"Boys, boys," he said slowly at last, "it is a long, long time ago since my real life-story began. Thirty years and over, lads. Is that not so, Eppie?"

Birr—rr—rr! went the spinning-wheel.

"Imphm," assented Eppie.

"But go on, Eean," she continued; "and if ye ravel in the thread o' your discoorse, I'll try to pit ye straight again."

Thus encouraged, Eean took a few more pulls at his pipe and went on.

"Thirty years seem a long time to look forward to; but looking back, boys, why it's all like a dream. Yet, my lads, life has no business to be a dream. 'Life is real, life is earnest,' as the hymn says; and if your eyes don't open before you are out of your teens, I tell you this, it is a poor look out for you in after-life.

"I notice a weary kind of a light in your eyes, young Master Frank. I know what you're thinking: 'The old man is not telling a story, he's only preaching.' But the ways of old men must be borne with. So patience for a moment, boy; patience!

"I was born with a silver spoon in my mouth. Oh, not a big one, I assure you! But I knew right well that when twenty-one I should have a few thousands to begin life with; and it was this very knowledge, I believe, that made me careless and a dreamer.

"My father was a Highlander, like myself. He *had* been rich, but he had also been a soldier, and squandered all his own money, though he retired on half-pay with fame and glory; for on many a blood-red field in India his sword had rang and clashed, and his slogan been heard wherever the battle raged the fiercest.

"That was my father, and I was his only son. I had a dear mother that doted on me, and could scarcely bear to have me out of her sight. She would have me to be a child even when I was seventeen years of age. I tell you that up till that age I did nothing on earth but dream my life away. I was to be something great *in futuro*. There was a castle building for me somewhere, in which I should live when a man. The good fairies were building it, I suppose; but woe is me, boys, fairy promises are but like soap-bubbles that rise and float on the soft summer air, all glitter and beauty, then—burst.

"I was a poet in those days—they tell me I am a bard still—but I fear my verses have lost the fire and frenzy of youth. Never mind, in those dear foolish days I learned nothing that was not pleasant, I did nothing I could not find pleasure in. With gun on shoulder I used to start for the hill. Too often my gun was thrown on the heather, and I lay down beside it in the sun to versify and dream. Or I might take my fishing-rod, and with my dog Kooran at my heels, set off for the lonesome tarn or mountain burn; but, ah, me! the fish seldom rose to my flies, and the streamlet sang to me, and I to the streamlet—there was music in everything around me, in the sailing clouds, in the waving broom, the drooping birch-trees and dark solemn pines themselves.

"Did my conscience never tell me I was doing wrong? It did at times. There were moments when the stern realities of life used to force themselves upon my thoughts. Surely man was made and meant for something better than to be an idle dreamer. Then I would start and awake as if from a lethargy. I would look around me, and even blush to see all men busy but myself, all creatures toiling, yet all, all happier even than I.

"What should I be? What should I be? How often the question would keep recurring to my mind. Be a soldier like my father? No, I cared not for camps and fighting. Be a sailor, and go sailing over the world. Yes, that was better; but the work, it was the work I feared. To sail on, on, on, for ever over sunlit summer seas would have suited me. But seas are not always sunlit, and storms arise, and—no, I would not be a sailor.

"Why not live to sing as Byron, Ossian, and Burns had done? But I must have some one else save the birds and streams and trees to sing to. Then a gloomy spell came over the spirit of my dream, and I thought myself the most miserable of all created beings. The linnet that sang among the golden furze, his nest not far away, seemed to laugh at me. The linnet had love. The wild deer in the forest shook their antlered heads, and appeared to despise me in my forlornness, they were as happy as the summer's day was glad and long. The eagle that floated high above the clouds mocked me. He could soar. Oh, how I wished and wanted to soar! Everything too about me was so lovely, I had a poet's eye for beauty. Even the metallic lustre on the beetles that crept through the grass shot rays of pleasure to my heart. 'Was it possible,' I said to myself one day, as I lounged by a river side. 'Was it possible for me to transfer some of the beauty I saw around me to canvas? Why not? Others have done so. I had been to the great city of London, I had revelled in picture-galleries, all the memory of pictures I had seen came back to me now with a force I had never felt before. Hurrah!' I shouted, starting up, 'I will be an artist. I will build my own castles. Away, fairies, away I'll dream no more. I'll be a man. I am a man.'

"My poor dog must have thought I'd gone mad. I broke my fishing-rod across my knee and flung it far into the dark brown stream, and once more shouted till the wild coneys fled into their holes on the cairney hill sides.

"No, my mother did not object; I should have the best of teachers; the best of teaching; I should go to London; go to Rome. My pictures should be hung, I'd make wealth and fame, her darling boy should be— —"

Here old Eean paused for a moment. He shook the ashes from his pipe with a gesture almost of anger.

"Dreams! Dreams! Dreams!" he muttered.

"Boys, I had not learned the art of application early enough in youth, I was thoughtless, my dear mother said in excuse for me, and thoughtlessness was natural to youth.

"But, oh, lads, listen! Thoughtlessness is not, should not be, natural to youths. Life's stern battle is all before them; should they be thoughtless or careless as they gird up their loins to meet the foe? Life's stormy ocean is rolling resistlessly on towards their frail barques; how shall they mount those heaving seas, how fight against wind and tempest, if they trust all to blind chance? I tell you what—and he who tells you knows—that thoughtfulness must be your guide to every good in life; ay, and to the world beyond as well, Oh, my dear lads, grasp these truths, and never, never forget them! Act on them too, and they will make you men, yes, heroes.

"But I am preaching now. Forgive me, and my tale—alas! it is an all too common one as far as it regards myself—shall soon be told.

"I was not by any means what is called a wild youth, while pursuing my studies under masters in London, and elsewhere: the ordinary and sinful frivolities of youths about town had no charm for me. I loathed them, and despised the empty-headed fools who gave way to them. I did not quarrel with these men, I simply avoided them. I preferred my own company to theirs, and my own thoughts. I was often to be seen alone at the play, or opera, or alone in the picture galleries. It was a pity for me I did not visit the latter in company with art critics, but I had found out that some of these were lacking not only in knowledge but in honesty, so I avoided them all, as a child who has been burned fears flame in any and every form.

"Did I work well? I worked fairly well. My fault, and it is a radical one, was, that I was in too great a hurry to be a painter—the rudiments of drawing were to me a weary task. Like a boy I gloated over colour and effect. But I had one picture hung. Oh, bless that day for just one reason—it made my poor dear mother happy! When she received the letter in which I announced my success, she shed more tears over it than if the missive had been one announcing the death of a dear friend. Yes, they were tears of joy.

"Did my single success have a good effect on me? Alas! no, the very reverse. I fancied myself—fool that I was—upon a mountain top of fame and glory. High up among the rosy clouds of sunrise, with all the world at my feet. I determined to do no more work for a time, not genuine study at least—I should set out on a grand walking tour! What a happy idea I thought this was! Mind you, I still was the poet at heart, and Nature in every form still appealed to me. I had come to hate my sky-high studio in London, the dusty winding stairs that led to it, its furniture and furnishings, and even the outlook from its windows.

"I was like a boy while preparing for this grand tour. For more than a week my time by day was occupied in shopping. All my purchases might soon have been made had I been content with the ordinary outfit of a walking artist. But this would not suit my vanity. I believe I was a rather handsome young man then. Was I not, Eppie?"

Birr-rr-rr went the wheel. No word came from Eppie, only a smile lit up her face for a moment.

"So," continued Eean, "I determined to take heavy baggage as well as a knapsack and cudgel. This I would arrange to be sent on by train or coach. Guns, fishing-rod and tackle, books, the best of novels, the best of poets, I even took dress suits. Yes, boys, I feel ashamed now when I think of it, but my vanity led me to believe that I should be fêted and feasted at the houses of the wealthy.

"Away I went, and for many weeks of wandering I was truly happy. I worked too by fits and starts, and my portfolios were getting filled with pretty bits that I culled upon my rambles. I had not yet found out, nor could I have believed, that rural England was so charmingly sweet and pretty. No great wonder that I lingered therein for months and months. True, my dress suits were never once taken out from the trunk that contained them, nor was any squire or nobleman ever likely, I began to think, to invite the wandering artist to dinner or give him even a day's fishing or shooting. Was this fame then? Surely everyone had heard of the rising artist who had had a picture hung. And prettily criticised too. Well, I did not break my heart. I ate my humble meals and slept at village inns, and if I was taken for anything at all by the villagers, it was either for 'a kind of surveyor,' a 'strolling sign painter,' or 'something in tea.'

"But during these long rambles there had been the glamour of spring, and the glory of summer, over all the land, and I was contented and happy.

"I hardly ever thought of writing even, wicked that I was, to my mother. But when at last the summer commenced, and I saw one day a pale yellow splash of foliage on a green ash tree, as if some tint of last night's sunset had fallen on it and lingered there, I bethought me of the purple and crimson heather on the bonnie Highland hills of my wild native land. And in a week's time I was home at my father's house.

"Oh, I had been working hard, I told my mother.

"'I know,' she said, 'and I expected to see you wan and pale, dear boy, instead of rosy red.'

"Then I told her all—where I had been, and spread out before her my portfolios of crude unfinished bits.

"'They will work up, and work into noble pictures when I return to town,' I said.

"It was thus I deceived myself and her.

"I next set out to study the beauties of hill scenery of straths and glens, of loch and stream and torrent, of weird pine forests, far in the depths of rugged mountain passes, of sheep and shepherds' shielings, and of everything that makes up the stern silent grandeur of the Scottish Highlands.

"One day I found myself seated high up the glen here with the reek of this same wee village rising blue above the birchen trees, with the great Atlantic Ocean sobbing on the sandy beach, or breaking into whitest foam against that long ridge of darkest rock that runs westward yonder to meet and welcome the rolling seas. There were white clouds afloat in the sky's blue, there were white sails dotting the blue of the sea, there was the buzz of insect life in the heather all around me, and the afternoon was warm and soft. Had I fallen asleep I wonder? I know not. But I started up at last inspired with a new idea.

"It was an idea that made my cheeks tingle with pleasurable emotion.

"I should write a book, a book that would make me famous. I should in this book wed together the harp and the easel, the thistle and the rose.

"Let me explain to you, boys, for I can see you hardly catch my meaning. The book, then, was to embrace both poetry and painting, the wild songs I should sing of my own mountain land; the illustrations all from my own pencil and brush, hence *The Harp and the Easel*. But the scenery should be touches from Nature in both Scotland and England, hence the title of *The Thistle and the Rose*.

"I went down the mountain side at the rush, vaulting as vaults the deer, so strong, so well, so happy was I that my very feet seemed to spurn the turf on which I trode.

"But was it turf? No, surely it was air. So filled with the inspiration of my grand idea was I, that I appeared no longer on earth or even belonging to it.

"Boys, these last words of mine contain a grim kind of a joke which you will at once see. I made just one vault too many, then I was indeed walking on air, and no longer on earth. I was falling, falling, falling! Oh, it did seem such a long, long time ere I reached the foot of that rocky cliff! Then all was a blank.

"I had fallen as it were into sudden darkness, and but for a pine-tree on which I bad luckily alighted, and which lowered me earthward all torn and bleeding, it might have been the darkness of death.

"Eppie, wife, heap more peats upon the fire and stir the blazing drift-wood. Listen, lads, to the moaning wind; surely that is hail that rattles so against the panes. Frank, it is well you haven't to make your way through moor and forest to-night with Bunko."

"I shouldn't have minded being with poor Bunko, sir, I assure you, because I like to be out in storms; but then I could not have heard the conclusion of your story."

"And must I conclude to-night?"

"Oh, sir, yes! You're just coming to the best of it."

"Well, boys, well," said the old bard, "you must be humoured."

# CHAPTER III
## AN AIMLESS LIFE—PEACE AT LAST

"The darkness seemed to lift at last, and I gradually became sensible. Everything around me was hazy for a time—a kind of a gauze curtain seemed to hang 'twixt me and as pretty a rustic picture as I ever yet had seen.

"I was not lying at the cliff foot, I was in a soft, warm bed, all hung round with snow-white curtains. It was so near the gloaming hour that I could see the firelight dancing on the plain deal furniture, and on the pictures of ships and boats that hung on the whitewashed wall. There was a stuffed sea-gull in a case, and the model of a fishing-boat also under glass, and on a little table a big ha' Bible and other devotional books, surmounted by a vase of freshly-culled wild flowers. Then I turned my aching eyes towards the little window, prettily festooned with curtains of dimity, and on the sill of which pot-flowers were growing, the red radiance of sunset lighting up and strangely altering the green of their leaves. But my eyes fell on a picture of a different sort at the same time: a young girl seated by the window sewing, her head bent towards the white seam, her dark hair half hiding a face that to me was as lovely as an angel's.

"Some movement on my part caused her to glance towards the bed, and seeing me awake she put down her work and came towards me.

"'Where am I?' I asked faintly.

"She put her fingers on my lips.

"'You are where ye maun lie,' she said, smiling, though I'm sure there were tears in her eyes; 'where ye maun lie till well, but ye must not speak.'

"Poor, simple lassie! I knew then as I knew after that she was doing her best to talk in English, though far dearer to me was the expressive language of Burns the poet.

"She now put something to my lips in a spoon. I drank, and slumbered again.

"When once more conscious, there stood the village doctor, and an old, white-haired, pleasant-faced dame in a fisher's cap.

"'Will he live, doctor?'

"'Live! yes, if he has plenty of good nursing.'

"'He'll want for naething here, puir laddie, that we can gie him. Ech, sir, but I'm thankful.'

"My young nurse was not there, so I slept for a time, and when I awoke she sat there again.

"'May I talk just a little?'

"'Yes, just a little,' she said. 'Tell me,' she added, 'who your people are, because ye ken they must be told?'

"'Plenty of time. Plenty of time,' I murmured.

"Then bit by bit I told her all my story.

"'I would rather,' I said, 'my mother knew nothing till I am up and about.'

"'But will she not be— —'

"'No, no, child,' I said. 'She is used to my wandering ways, and oftentimes I do not write for months.'

"'Isn't that unkind?'

"'I fear so,' I said.

"'Are you *good*?' she asked pointedly.

"'Not too good I fear.'

"'D' ye say your prayers nicht and mornin'? Had ye said your prayers on that day ye fell o'er that fearfu' cliff?'

"I was silent.

"Only a simple Scotch lassie would have preached to me thus. But she looked so saint-like as she sat there, gazing almost mournfully at me with her calm, tender grey eyes, that really I was thinking then more of painting her in a subject than anything else.

"'No,' I said at last, 'I am not good as you understand it, but you shall teach me.'

"'The way of transgressors is hard,' said the little Puritan; 'but oh, sir, the plan o' salvation is sae simple a bairnie can understan' it. What's your name, sir?'

"'Eean.'

"'I'll pray for ye, Eean, and so will mother.'

"It was a month after this conversation ere I could stroll about the beach, and paint rock and cloud effects. The girl was seldom with me. She would be away out at sea casting nets with her father, and in her simplest attire, to my eyes, she always made the prettiest picture.

"Boys, this story of mine is in some measure a confession. I have at all events confessed to you already how idle and how vain I was, and now I am going to give you another illustration of my vanity I made up my mind then to make this girl my wife. I positively thought I had only to go in and win.

"I was well now, and it was only for her sake I still lingered in the village. I had taken up my abode at the village inn because, though they had nursed me back to life, those kindly fisher people positively refused to accept of anything in the shape of pecuniary reward. All that I was permitted to do was to paint the old couple sitting together Bible in hand on the stone dais in front of their little cottage door.

"So one day I called on the mother, but was not displeased to find the girl there too.

"I soon stated the object of this particular visit.

"'I *intended*,' I said, 'to make her daughter my wife.'

"A quick flush came over the girl's face. She glanced just once in my direction, then bent again over her white seam.

"'You intend,' said the old lady, 'to make my daughter your wife. O, sir, do you think sae little of us, that ye imagine ye hae only to command? We are only poor fisher-folks, sir, but we have the pride of honesty in our hearts. Na, na, na, sir, there is a great gulf fixed 'twixt you and us. Gang awa', sir, gang awa', and marry some gentle dame, that ye can introduce to your dear lady mother. May every blessin' on earth he yours, sir. We're nae insensible to the honour ye would do us. Dinna think us ungrateful—' here the good old soul broke down and cried—'but gang and leave us to our poverty and our honest toil.'

"'So be it, madam, so be it,' I said. 'I have yourself and daughter to thank for my life, but it was not to show my gratitude I made the proposal, but because I am wise enough to discover sterling worth and goodness even beneath a humble garb. Good-bye. I'll never think of marriage more.'

"I shook the mother's hand warmly. I but touched the girl's. To have looked even once in her sweet tearful face would have unmanned me, so I all but fled.

"I left the village long before daylight. I went home. Then I told my mother all.

"My muse was now my only comfort, for months went by before I thought again of painting.

"Then the same old idea recurred to me that had so nearly cost me my life on the mountain side.

"The book, *The Easel and the Harp. The Thistle and the Rose!*

"I commenced work in earnest now. But, alas! misfortune befell me. My soldier father died. He died in debt, and one short year afterwards I laid my darling mother in the church-yard beside him.

"I was alone in the world now—alone and with only a few thousands of pounds betwixt me and want, should I fail with my brush.

"I was awakened at last to the reality of life, and tried hard to do my best to face its storms.

"My great book! I laid my plans before publisher after publisher. Some of these received me kindly, praised the idea, but did not see their way.

"One told me that the people were not educated yet up to such a work, and it was to the people he had to look for success.

"I laid my plans before great artists. Each and all of these dissuaded me from any such undertaking. I called this envy. O the vanity of young manhood!

"I visited printers and lithographers next, as well as engravers. Each and all of these assured me the world was ripe for such a work, and by publishing it myself I should not only secure fame, but all the profits.

"I went home rejoicing, and at once commenced to work out my scheme. I soon after retired to a quiet rural village, and here I lived like a recluse for a whole year, working but dreaming as well.

"My work was finished.

"My book was published. *The Easel and the Harp. The Thistle and the Rose!*

"It did *not* go like wild-fire. The critics hardly noticed it, not even to revile. I wished they had. Hardly a copy was sold, and I was all but ruined.

"I saw my vanity when it was too late. How bitterly now I felt the truth of the scriptural text, 'Pride goes before a fall, and haughtiness before destruction.'

"I had not been like the moth that seeks glory by courting a too close acquaintanceship with the candle, and falls groundwards with singed wings; but like the moth that set out to fly to the evening star, when, lo! clouds arose and rain fell, then down came the all too ambitious flutterer, every gossamer featherlet in its downy body draggled and wet, to lie in the grass and suffer sorrow.

> "In pride, in reasoning pride, our error lies;
> All quit their sphere, and rush into the skies.
> Pride still is aiming at the blest abodes,
> Men would be angels, angels would be gods.

"I hardly cared now to meet my old associates, much less my old masters. They had warned me in my overweening pride, I spurned their warning, and now I was crushed and hopeless.

"I believe to this day that I took my punishment like a man, I did not even pretend to laugh and treat my discomfiture lightly; so many of my friends would have stuck to me, and assisted me up again once more. But I shook the dust of London from my feet, and went away once more into the country to meditate and think. There still was hope for me. I was young, why should I mourn?

"The moth that tried to reach the star was able to fly again next evening, though it never could be the same moth as before. I had aimed at a too high ideal. I thought I had almost reached it. I fell. But I should rise again. Yes; but never the same man.

"I should leave this country, however and begin life anew in some far distant clime, and—so I vowed—endeavour to climb the ladder of fame one step at a time, instead of foolishly trying to rush it as I had done.

"And now I did the only wise thing I had yet done in my life. I took the little remains of my fortune—it consisted only of hundreds now—and placed it in a bank, keeping but enough to last me with economy a year. Then I left my native land, taking ship for the Antipodes as a steerage passenger. I even changed my name, so determined was I to forget all my past life.

"There was one portion of it, however, I never could forget, and that was the short but happy time I had spent during my convalescence in the little village, and the humble fisher lassie's last tearful looks of adieu. That would be the loadstone that should draw me back to Britain if anything ever could.

"But I became strangely enamoured of a sea life and of ships and sailor men. We had a long, dreary passage out around the Cape in a sailing vessel, and before I had been out a fortnight I asked permission of the captain, and obtained it too, to go before the mast.

"Perhaps I had found my vocation at last. I almost believed I had, for in a month's time there was scarcely any part of a seaman's duty I could not perform, and before we reached Australia I was dubbed a sailor.

"I had been a favourite with my messmates, and even with the few passengers aft, and I believe all were sorry to part with me.

"But the gold fever was then at its height, and what more natural than I should catch it? Not all at once, however. I stayed around Sydney for a time. I managed to beat up several newspaper men and artists like myself. But this work was all too slow, the remuneration too small, for me.

"One day I found myself standing alone in the street in the drizzling rain, without hope, without a home, and nothing belonging to me except the somewhat tattered clothes I wore. I was near a newspaper office, and was about to enter to beg—not for money, boys, I'd have died sooner—but for work, when I found myself face to face with a man who was, like myself, an artist.

"'Off to the diggings!' he cried merrily. 'Join me, old fellow, join me. We will return as rich as Croesus.'

"'I'd go,' I said, 'but I'm——'

"I turned out my empty pockets.

"'I'll wait for you a week,' he said, 'and you shall work. Come in here.'

"He pulled me inside the very office I had been about to enter; and in a fortnight's time we were both marching away to the diggings, with hopes as high as the fleecy clouds and hearts as—well, as light as our purses.

"Did we succeed? At last we did, after ten years of a life of back-breaking slavery. We stuck together all this time, and our adventures would have filled a lordly volume. We found time, too, to write to the papers, and send many a sketch of life at the diggings.

"We made a pile at last, and gladly agreed to leave this rough-and-tumble life and settle in some town, or come back—this was my idea—to Scotland.

"Fools that we were, we gave what was called a 'glorification' to our friends the night before we were to start on horseback with our pile away through the bush.

"I hate to dwell on this part of my story. But there came that evening to our camp two Irish strangers. They seemed green-hands, and I and my friend took them in and treated them well We talked too freely about our wealth of gold, and we lived to repent it.

"We bade all the camp good-bye next day, and with our convoy started for Melbourne.

"Day after day, day after day, through forest and bush, living on damper and wretched tea, and sleeping by night under the stars, but light-hearted and happy.

"'Hold! Put up your hands!'

"It was a shout of command, given by two men on horseback as we rode through a beautiful gully one day.

"We had no time to draw and defend ourselves, and our servants were paralysed with fear.

"The robbers were the self-same Irish green-hands we had entertained in camp.

"Of all our pile they left us barely fifty pounds a piece, and this, they told us, they gave us out of charity.

"Two months after this I was serving as a common sailor on a merchant ship bound for San Francisco.

"During the long, hard years in the Australian bush I had not quite forgotten my art, and I hoped to make it pay in a new land.

"Once more I was partially successful. Once again, boys, I began to dream dreams of greatness, and once again my dreams worked my ruin.

"My art was praised by some, my verses were said by others to have about them the ring and rhythm of the born bard. I forgot or neglected art for poesy, and soon found myself penniless and without work itself.

"Ambition, lads, is a grand thing; but it must be guided by a steady hand at the tiller, or it is a ship that will never sail into the haven of success.

"I need not tell you all, nor any of my wild adventures for the next eight years of my life by sea or land. You have heard the mythological tale of the man who prayed that everything he touched might turn into gold, and how the gods granted his prayer, and how his very food became gold as he tried to lift it to his lips, so that he died of starvation. Nothing I touched turned to gold, but, like Dead-sea fruit, every scheme of mine turned to dust in my attempt to grasp it.

"At last, in a fight with lions in the forests of Africa, I was seized and carried away by a man-eater. The monster was wounded, and, though he lacerated me fearfully, he laid down and died at my side. My companions soon followed and found me, and after a weary time I recovered a tithe, but not more, of my former life and spirit.

"The adventure had made almost an old man of me, and in my weakness and debility I had but one wish, one desire—to return to my native land and die!

"I did return. Providence was good to me, and the sea had in some measure restored me a portion of my pristine strength.

"I visited my Highland home and my mother's grave. Then an irresistible longing stole over me to visit this little wild glen.

"I stood one day on the very hill-top where well-nigh twenty years ago I had dreamt of nought save glory.

"All seemed the same on this sweet summer's day, the sea, the hills, the rocks, the wee whitewashed houses standing among the greenery of the waving birches, and the blue smoke trailing over the trees.

"Then I went quietly down the hill. Alas! where now was the bounding fire and fury of my youth? I almost shuddered when I saw the precipice over which I had fallen, and the pine tree still denuded of branches that had saved my life.

"In a few minutes more I stood at the door of the village inn. There were new people here now, but the old folks could scarce have known me, so changed had I become.

"While I munched my morsel of bread and cheese, washed down with milk, a tall figure passed the window leading a child. I knew her step at once, though she too was sadly changed. But I wondered to notice that her hair was sprinkled with gray.

"All my heart seemed to go forth to her.

"'That,' said the landlady, 'is the kindliest creature in all the parish.'

"'Her name?' I almost gasped.

"'Miss Elspet Deane.'

"'Miss? Ah, then she is not married?'

"'No; there is some sad story about her—about an artist she ought to have married, but who went away and was drowned at sea.'

"'And you say she is good and kind?'

"'Good and kind, sir! What would the clachan do without her? We all call her auntie. I don't know why. Some bairnies began it, I suppose. Ah! don't the bairnies love her, sir! And she lives all by herself, and that wee laddie in the house where her parents died. Never a child is ill in the village, sir, that she doesn't attend. She gathers the herbs and simples on the moors, and mixes them with her own honest hands, and little toddlers will take physic from her who would spurn it from the doctor.'

"'Dear sir,' continued this somewhat garrulous landlady, 'death itself doesn't seem so dreadful when she is in the room. And she has aye a word of comfort for poor wives, when their boats are detained at sea or blown far, far away by the raging storm. On that terrible Tuesday, sir, and all the dark drear night that followed, when the wind blew louder and the sea was wilder than anybody ever remembered it before—when out of eleven boats and their brave crews but only five regained the shore, Miss Elspet was everywhere, directing, sir, and comforting, praying with the widows and the fatherless bairns, and sometimes even scolding the women for their want of trust in the Maker—like a very angel in the midst of the great grief that wailed around her.'

"'The boy, sir? He had no mother, and his father was drowned on that stormy night——"

"I stopped to hear no more,

"In ten minutes' time I was in the well-remembered wee room in Elspet's house, and she stood before me.

"I thought that, hardy and strong as she was, she would have faulted.

"'Eppie,' I said, 'it is *me*!' Yes, boys, I forgot my grammar just then. 'You could not marry me when I was rich and young, now I am old—though not in years—and I am poor and ill. You nursed me once, Eppie. Will you nurse me again?' Ah! lads, it has been a new life to me since the village bells rang on our wedding morn. I have found peace and contentment at last, and after the fever of life I can rest me here. Are we not happy, Eppie?"

He did not give Eppie time to reply.

"Yonder sits the drowned fisherman's son, Fred, who saved your life to-day, Frank Fielding."

"And the wee thing who has gone to sleep on my lap," said Frank Fielding, "she is?"

"A shipwrecked waif; a stray from the sea. But now, lads, to bed."

Then the birr-rr-rr of the wheel ceased, and Eppie, rising, took wee Toddie from Frank to carry her off to bed.

But Toddie was wide awake now, and all dimples, smiles, and yellow hair.

She pointed a fat little forefinger at Frank as she was being borne away on Eppie's shoulder.

"Be a dood boy, Flank," she cried, "and mind oo say oo players."

# CHAPTER IV
## SITTING UP TO THINK—THE DIGNITY OF LABOUR

Frank Fielding wondered where he was when he awoke next morning, and found the sun shining in through the window of the little cosy room in which he had slept so soundly after his adventure, the night before.

Fred's room was in a back wing of the cottage that looked right away out to sea. But Fred had not slept so well, and the reason was not far to seek. He had often before heard his Daddy Pop, as he called the old fisherman, tell snatches of his life story, but never had listened to its complete recital. And when he retired that night to his little chamber he was as full of thought as any boy of his age can be. The feeling uppermost in the lad's innocent mind was one of sorrow for Daddy Pop's sadly wasted life. The old man had made it so plain to his listeners what the cause of his failure had been. He had been a dreamer instead of a student and a worker. Would there, he thought, be any chance for a humble lad like himself doing well in the world if he worked and studied? The question kept him awake half the night, and even then he hadn't half answered it. But long before this he had made up his mind that he would work and study, and he really felt thankful he had the chance, for the parish church school he attended was excellent—in other words, it was thoroughly Scottish—it sent at least half a dozen lads every year straight from it away to the University, and more than one of these had become senior wranglers at Cambridge or double first classes at Oxford.

But what, thought Fred to himself that night, was the good of being a wrangler? whatever the somewhat pugilistic word might mean. He supposed, however, it meant that the wranglership opened the way to one through the thorny jungle of life, and softened many a difficulty.

He thought, nevertheless, he shouldn't care much to be a wrangler. One wrangler, he remembered, had come back to his own Highland parish to die. That was what wrangling had done for him.

Fred did not care a very great deal for either Latin or Greek, both of which languages he was already well versed in. But then Daddy Pop had told him—and didn't Daddy Pop know everything?—that learning and study made one active-minded, clever, and bright; that, in fact, it wasn't so much what anyone actually did learn as the actual learning of it, that did the good, and increased the size and fertility of the brain just as—and these were Daddy's own words—the ploughing and harrowing of a field fitted it to receive any sort of seed that might be sown therein. "But," Daddy Pop had added, "it is as well to learn what will be useful in after life, and the so-called dead languages would be so."

Fred perhaps ought to have gone to sleep as soon as he went to bed; but having once commenced to think he could not. He thought out all Daddy Pop's story, first lying on one side, then he rolled over on the other, and thought it all over again. Then, as it was getting late, he rolled over on his back and determined to sleep. Pah! he might as well have tried to fly.

"Well," he said to himself, "I don't see any good in lying here tumbling all the bed. It is hard work, and nothing good to show for."

So up he jumped, and drew aside his little window-blind. The window was in shadow; but he could sea that the moon was shining brightly over the sea, so he quietly dressed himself, opened wide the window, and sat down beside it.

Toddie's dachshund was out there under a bush, and coughed a low enquiring sort of a bark at him.

"Down, Tippetty, down!" said Fred.

Tippetty did lie down, but not without a little growl of displeasure.

"You ought to be in bed, you know," the little wise fellow appeared to say; "and I'm responsible for the safety of this establishment after nightfall."

Fred gave himself up to thought now, just as heartily as in bed he had tried to avoid it. Of course there was a little castle-building mixed up with these cogitations of his. And I would not care much for a boy who did not build a few castles in the air at times, and inhabit them too; for what, after all, is castle-building but a kind of budding ambition?

Now Fred Arundel's father had been drowned when the boy was far too young to know the meaning of the sacred word "parent," while his mother had been taken away quite in his babyhood. But he had come to love and respect his foster-parents very much indeed. They were all in all to him. Fred was a good-natured lad, and there was nothing he would not have done to give the kindly old couple an hour's happiness.

Well, but for them he might have been running about in rags and wretchedness a "mitherless bairn,"

"When a' other bairnies are hushed to their hame,
By auntie, or cousin, or freckled grand-dame,
Who stands lost and lonely, wi' nobody carin'?
'Tis the poor doited laddie—the mitherless bairn,

"The mitherless bairn gangs to his lone bed,
Nane covers his cauld back, or haps his bare head;
His wee hackit heelies are hard as the iron,
And litheless the lair o' the mitherless bairn."

But Fred could not have been called "a mitherless bairn." And indeed if you were to have asked the lad confidentially he would have told you he was not a "bairn" in any sense of the word, but almost a man.

"Daddy Pop is old," thought Fred, "but he may live for twenty years and more yet, and so may Mammy too. Twenty years, what a long time! Why I shall be getting old myself in that time. Now although Daddy had some money in the bank before he went away on his long wanderings, and found when he came back that it had grown into a heap more; and although he had enough to build this cottage, and a fine fishing-boat also, still I know he isn't rich. His bed is not a very soft one, he doesn't live so well as I would like him to; he says he can't afford an easy chair, and that his Sunday coat is good enough. Well, if I had money, Daddy would have such a lot of comforts, and so would Mammy Mop. Why shouldn't Mammy have a silk dress as well as farmer Grigg's wife? She shall have it.

"Why shouldn't Daddy have an easy chair and a better pair of specs, and an easier seat in the cave among the rocks in which he writes his beautiful poetry? My Daddy shall be comfortable when I am older. But what shall I be? I can't be a fisher lad. Oh, no! I must travel and see the world, and—but, dear me! common sailors don't get rich, and Sandie Davis told me, after he came back from being all round and round the world, that often and often he was not allowed to put a foot on shore even in some of the prettiest places on the face of the earth. Sandie told me this because he likes me. Sandie wouldn't tell everybody, I'm sure of that. It wasn't for the half crown I lent Sandie that he likes me. Oh, no!

"But what does Sandie do? He comes home wearing his best blue clothes, and a dandy tie, and silver rings and things, and to hear him talk anybody would think he had been first officer of a ship. He smokes and takes beer—not that he pays for it, except by the stories—yarns he calls them—that he tells those who treat him. No, poor Sandie never has a penny to bless himself with after he has been two weeks at home. That isn't the kind of sailor I'm going to be, if ever I'm a sailor at all. Sandie's mother has a lot of 'curios,' as he calls them—some wonderful Japanese boxes, bottles of *eau de Cologne*, a funny-looking tea-caddy made out of a nut, an ostrich's egg, a savage's spear, and an old bow and arrow; but nothing she can eat or wear. She can't even eat the ostrich's egg, and funny she'd look going about with that dirty old bow and arrow.

"He's not a bad fellow, though he boasts and brags, and talks through his nose, and says words I never heard before, and don't wish to hear again, for sailors like Sandie would make me sick of the sea.

"No, I'll be something—something. I'm going to study and work to begin with, and then — —"

Only the moonlight lying clear on the sea, only the lisp of the waves on the shore, only the whisper of wind in the trees, only—why, it can't surely be daylight already!

But it is though, and has been for hours, though Fred still sits there, his face and his arms, and his bare head exposed to the morning breeze.

"Oh, you naughty Fred!" cried Toddie, discovering her foster-brother, and pulling his hair to wake him. "Oo has never been to bed. I declare oo'll bleak my heart; and Flank and I has been all wound the beach and at the atwalium (aquarium) too. Flank's a dear, dood boy. Tome to bleakfast at once, I tell oo."

Fred looked up, smiling sleepily, then he gave himself a shake, as a dog would, jumped right through the window, and patted Toddie's head.

"I'll be back in ten minutes, Toddie, old woman," he said.

Then straight for the rocks he ran, and divesting himself of his clothes in a little recess, sprang in, had a good swim, and returned home singing, and quite as happy as the skylark that was lilting high above the woods.

Frank came out of the cottage to meet him, and the two lads shook hands heartily.

"You're none the worse for your ducking," said Fred.

"No, all the better. Ha! ha! I wonder what mother will say? But tell me, are you always so late of coming down to breakfast?"

Fred laughed.

"It isn't coming down," he said, "because, you know, we haven't any up. Yours is a big fine house, I suppose?"

"It's a fair size. Two story, you know, and all among woods and gardens. Oh, I'm sure you'll like it!"

It was time for Fred to laugh again.

"Very likely I shall see it," he said somewhat ironically; "but come in till I sup my porridge."

"I've had mine long ago, and so has Toddie, and we've had such a game of romps. But of course you'll come often to Benshee House. I have a Shetland pony and a little trap, and can come over to you."

"Oh! but, Frank Fielding," Fred said solemnly, as he dipped his spoon in a basin of creamy milk, "don't forget I'm only a poor working lad, and you are a young gentleman."

The tears sprang to poor Frank's eyes in a moment but he manfully kept even a single one from falling. He stretched out his hand and grasped that of Fred, even though he had the spoon in it.

"There," said Frank, "I've made you spill the milk. But never mind. Now, Fred, just listen. Don't be a fool. I'm not a cad, mind. My father is a Scotchman, though my mother is English. My father made his money in stocks, and might lose it to-morrow."

"*Avertit omen*," murmured Fred.

"I don't know Chinese, Fred; but I do know this, you and I are going to be fast friends, and bother the rank and riches. My father makes me learn Burns's poems. My mother thinks they are not *bon ton*."

"Bong tong," said Fred. "Well, I don't know Japanese."

"Never mind. Just listen to this. I'm going to recite. Father makes me do it. Now here is the scene. You are a baronet and I am Bobbie Burns. I have been visiting you, you know, staying a few days at your mansion, when a nobleman—a downright cad—comes also to visit you, and you ask him if he would object to the ploughman poet dining with him.

"'What!' cries this ignoble nobleman, 'a ploughman singing fellow dining with you and me! How very absurd to be sure!'

"Then you, Sir Fred, are awfully put about, and you come to me sheepishly, and explain matters, and I bite my tongue and don't say anything.

"Well, after dinner his lordship says, 'Now, pon honour, I'd like to hear your singing fellow just for five minutes, don't-cher-know?'

"And so I—Robert Burns—am asked in.

"Of course I'm in a boiling rage at being treated thus. So I strut in and bow to you and his lordship, that is Toddie yonder.

"'Singing fellow,' says the lord, 'give us a specimen of your poetic powahs.'

"And this is the specimen I give:

"'Is there, for honest poverty,
   That hangs his head, and a' that?
The coward-slave, we pass him by,
   We dare be poor for a' that!
      For a' that, and a' that,
         Our toils obscure, and a' that,
      The rank is but a guinea's stamp,
         The man's the gowd* for a' that.

"'Ye see yon Birkie,† ca'ed a lord,

(Frank points at Toddie.)

      Wha struts, and stares, and a' that;
   Tho' hundreds worship at his word,
      He's but a coof‡ for a' that:
         For a' that, and a' that,
            His riband, star, and a' that,
         The man of independent mind,
            He looks and laughs at a' that.

"'A prince can mak a belted knight,
   A marquis, duke, and a' that;
But an honest man's aboon his might,
   Guid faith he canna fa'§ that!
      For a' that, and a' that,
         It's coming yet, for a' that,
      That man to man, the warld o'er,
         Shall brothers be for a' that.

* Gold.

† Proud, silly fellow.

‡ Blockhead.

§ Manage.

"Oh!" cried little Toddie, clapping her pink hands, "oo is a pletty boy when oo speaks like that."

"Now," said Frank, laughing, "I think like Burns, Fred, and if you don't come and see me and be friendly it will be all your own fault."

"I'll come," said Fred, laughing, "and if I happen to be carrying a creel of lobsters, I suppose you won't set your dogs at me?"

"Oh, no, because father talks about the dignity of labour, and that would be the dignity of labour. And you know—'a man's a man for a' that.'"

"Bravo! Frank Fielding," cried the old fisherman, entering the room, "How I love your sentiments, my boy. Why they are noble—noble. Shake the old bard's hand."

"Now," said Toddie, "evelybody must hold his tongue, I'se goin' to 'cite a piece."

And this little waif and stray that the Atlantic waves had tossed up on the beach as if she had been seaweed, stepped boldly into the arena, that is, into the middle of the sanded floor.

She was a beautiful child, this Toddie, with large eyes, delicate features, and such a wealth of glossy hair that one could not but wonder how it could have grown on a head so young.

She held one wee arm aloft, and in slow and measured tones, with many a brief but impressive pause, spoke as follows:

"There once was a leetle, leetle dirl,
    Who—lived—in a shoe,
And she had so many tsilden,
    She—didn't—know—what to do.

But the Dood Lord sent a wild, wild stolm,
    An' the waves wose—mountains high.
An lightenin's dleamed acloss the hills,
    An' sunders shook the sky.

An' a dleat big whale dot vely sick,
    Wi' the wobblin' o' the sea,
An' so he tumbled on the beach,
    As dead as dead tould be.

But Bunko took the dleat whale's bones,
    As none but Bunko tould,
And set them up adainst the rocks,
    And lined them all with wood.

And when the whale was all tomplete,
    We named it the Ig-loo,* And there the little dirl lives,
    And all her tsilden too."

* The hut in which Eskimos live.

Frank looked much amused, but quite puzzled; the old bard patted his foster-daughter, and smiled not a little proudly; while Fred roared with laughter because Frank looked so enquiringly droll.

"Is there any meaning in all that?"

"Yes," cried Fred, "and it's all true; at least the last of it. Toddie and I, and Toddie's children, that is her pets and things, do really live in a whale."

"Oh, shouldn't I like to see it!" said Frank. "Hullo!" he added, as the rattling of wheels ceased at the cottage door, "here is mother in the pony chaise, and—why look, there is Bunko himself driving my pony carriage with the Shetland in it! I wonder how the pony allowed him."

"Why not?"

"Oh, because if anybody but myself drives him he nearly always lies down to roll."

Frank ran to meet his mother, who lovingly embraced him. She was a very handsome lady and Toddie really stood in awe of her at first.

"Oh," Toddie said to Fred in a kind of stage whisper, "Oh, Fred, I don't like her much, I weally must suck my fumb."

And so she did.

# CHAPTER V
## AT THE FISHERMAN'S CAVE—
## FRED'S AQUARIUM

"And where," said Mrs. Fielding, "are the dear brave children who saved my darling's life?"

"Here is Fred, mamma, and yonder is Toddie, hiding behind her daddy's legs."

"Toddie," said Fred, "take your thumb out of your mouth."

"Come to me both of you. Dear, dear, it was quite an adventure I'm sure. What dear children! I'm sure they ought both to have the Society's medal. Very poor, aren't they? I must do something for them."

These last words, though addressed quietly to Frank, were loud enough for all to hear.

"Oh, ma!" he said.

But the lady heeded not.

"And you are the fisherman poet, are you not, sir?" she said, turning to the bard.

The old man was standing as erect as a statue, his bonnet in his hand, his hair streaming over his neck, and his face somewhat set and stern. He really looked noble. Mrs. Fielding must have felt he did, or she would never have added that little word "sir" in addressing him.

"I've heard of you so often, in really good society too. You write those beautiful verses in a cave, do you not? Why they are in every good magazine. Do you know I *should* like to see your cave. So romantic! Might I, Mr.——A——."

"Arundel. My cave is a very humble place, Mrs. Fielding; but if you will come with me you shall see it. The road is rough though."

"Oh, I'm very strong!"

Away along by the top of the cliffs he led her for quite a quarter of a mile. Here some bushes grew, and among them was a half-hidden staircase leading downwards into the very bosom of the rocks. The steps had been cut a hundred years ago perhaps by smugglers. No one ever yet found out the mystery of Talbot's cave.

The lady condescended to take the bard's hand, and he led her down. It was almost dark at the bottom, but once in the strange cave it was light enough. Here were two windows, or rather ports, and one of these the bard threw open. Right down beneath was the deep sea, with clear water over shining yellow sand, so clear you could see the beautiful medusæ or jelly fish floating about like splendidly-jewelled parasols. Between the ports was the poet's rough deal table. Here was a bench of deal, and a tall-backed deal chair. The floor was laid with wood, and a great ship-lamp swung from the roof.

The irregular walls were the rough rocks, but much to Mrs. Fielding's amazement, these walls were adorned with water-colour and oil-colour paintings, that to her seemed priceless.

I had almost forgotten to say that there was a fireplace in this cave, and evidence enough too that Eean often had tea here.

But it was the pictures that most attracted the lady's notice.

"These," she said, "are not mere copies?"

"Yes, madam," said the bard, smiling somewhat sadly, "every one of them, but copies from Nature. Mostly things I daubed when travelling abroad, they serve just to remind me of scenes I have passed through during a somewhat chequered career.

"I don't know," said Mrs. Fielding with innocent candour, "which to admire the most, yourself or your surroundings."

"Round every one of these picture things, madam, I have to weave a tale for my foster-children, who come here in the summer and even winter evenings.

"How enchanting. Might my dear boy come sometimes too?"

Eean stretched out his hand as if by sudden impulse, and Mrs. Fielding clasped it cordially.

"Now you do delight me, madam. I love children and your boy is a gentleman."

"I'm so pleased."

Then turning to the windows.

"You will observe," he said, "that the glass in these ports is of very great thickness. Green seas have often dashed over them, yet we have never been flooded. Only on stormy nights I lower great wooden ports."

He untied a chain as he spoke, and down with a thud came a shutter of wood and iron.

"Safe you see against the mightiest gale that ever blew."

"How interesting. The sea too looks charming to-day from your windows. Was it out yonder my poor darling was nearly drowned?"

"Yes, madam."

There was a moment's surcease of talking, during which nothing could be heard but the gentle lap-lapping of the waves on the black rocks beneath.

"Are you fond of animal life, madam?

"Will you be startled if I introduce to you one or two of my pets?"

"But they won't hurt?"

"No, they are good-mannered crabs."

As he spoke the bard took from his pocket a piece of string to which was attached a morsel of fish. This he lowered into the sea through the open port, then slowly drew it up again.

A moment afterwards there came crawling up two immense crabs, and they positively appeared to enter arm in arm, side by side certainly. They paused for a moment on the outside rocky ledge, and gazed at the lady with their stalky eyes.

Seeming perfectly satisfied, they then advanced, and Mrs. Fielding noticed that each had a red cross painted across his dark shell.

The bard quietly spread before them their dinner, and they ate it greedily, rolling their eyes about as they did so with an appearance of great satisfaction.

"Shall I make them dance?" said the poet.

"Oh, do, sir!"

The poet held a morsel of white meat of some kind above them, and in a moment they were standing on one end, hand in hand, or rather claw in claw, dancing round and round and all about in the most comical manner.

The lady laughed till the cave roof rang again.

"Of all things I have ever seen," she said, "that is the most ridiculous."

Then one more morsel was given to each, a red handkerchief was waved, and away the strange performers shuffled, and slowly disappeared over the ledge.

"Now, Mrs. Fielding, what do you think of my red cross knights?"

"Delightful! oh, delightful! But pray, Mr. Arundel, what are the red crosses for?"

"Oh! so that they shall be known by fishermen. They have often been captured in the lobster creels, but no one would think of killing them."

"I have to thank you for such a pleasant hour," said Mrs. Fielding, as they once more emerged upon the cliff top. "Oh, look! Yonder comes my boy with your dear mite on the Shetland pony."

Toddie waved her hand to Daddy Pop.

"Daddy! Daddy!" she shouted as soon as near enough to be heard, "I'se a weal lady now. All I wants is a widing-habit."

"My dear," said Mrs. Fielding, "a riding-habit would hide the beauty of those shapely legs and feet."

Toddie looked at her, and at once commenced to suck her thumb.

"Why do you suck your thumb, dear?"

"Oh, I always suck my fumb when I'se finking!"

"And what are you thinking about, child? What makes you look at me so?"

"Is oo Flank's mammy?"

"Yes, pet."

"Oh-h! Well, I likes Flank mostest. Flank," she added, with the air of a young princess, "we will wide back adain, please."

And away they went at a mad trot, Frank shouting and Toddie screaming.

"Mamma," said Frank when they met at the cottage, "this is a school holiday with Fred. Please may I stay till evening?"

"Did ever I deny you anything, child? But be sure you're home in time. Good-bye, Mr. Arundel. Good-bye, dear children. Drive on, John."

"Dood-bye," shouted Toddie, so gleefully that it must have been evident even to Mrs. Fielding herself that Toddie was glad to be rid of her.

"Now," cried the little madcap, "I feels full of joy up to my mouf. Tippetty and I is off for a wun on the beach. When Tippetty and I has our wun we'll come back for you boys, and to-night we'll have tea in the whale. Tippetty! Tippetty! oh, here tomes Tip!"

And off bounded Toddy and Tip, and no one seeing the two scampering across the level sands would have cared to say which was the wilder or which the defter.

Toddie's little arms and legs were bare, she had pulled off her red fisherman's cap to wave it above her head, and as she dashed on to meet the roaring sea her hair floated straight behind her in the breeze. And Tippetty, the dachshund, barking with all his might, came just a little in advance.

This spoke volumes for the strength of Tip's lungs. Though lovely and hound-like in head, like all dachshunds, he was bandy in legs, very low to the ground, and of tremendous length. So long and low indeed was he, that when at the gallop his black body wriggled like an eel. So long was he that he could not jump on a chair. He could put his two paws and head up, but if asked to spring, he looked about him wisely at his tail end, as much as to say,

"I would jump up willingly with my front part, don't you know? but then the other end of the procession wouldn't come along."

Tippetty was one of the wisest and kindest-hearted wee dogs that ever lapped milk.

He was the pet of the village, and no wonder, for Tippetty dug bait for everybody.

"Is Tip at home?" a fisherman would say to Eppie as he passed seawards.

"Tip, Tip," Eppie would cry, "you're wanted." And off he would go. He knew the worms' holes in the sand, and none could go too deep for Tip. With his little mole's feet and his wee bandy legs he would throw the sand up behind him as if he were a living mitrailleuse, and soon expose the coveted bait.

The first visit of the children to-day was to the aquarium, and Frank listened with delight to the terrible story of Tom, the naughty dolly-fish.

"But what a good thing," said Frank seriously, "that you were there putting back the dolly-fish. Else I should have been drowned."

"Oh," said Toddie, nodding her demure morsel of a head, "that was Plovidence, Flank. Oh, yes I 'ssure oo, Flank, it was Plovidence, 'cause Daddy Pop told me. Now then."

After they had seen all the queer creatures in the aquarium, and every creature's life history had been told to Frank by Toddie, they went off to the woods. "Dood-bye, dear, dear blennies," said Toddie, stroking these marvellous wee fishes with a morsel of seaweed, "be dood tsilden and oo mammy won't be long away."

Three of these were lying on the centre island of the aquarium, like so many miniature walruses, and so tame were they that they never moved when Toddie stroked them.

This children's aquarium had been got up by Daddy Pop, and he explained the nature of every new pot that was put into it. But he had never seen the dogfish Tom.

Daddy Pop believed, and rightly too, that letting children have a hobby keeps them out of many a danger, and when that hobby was the keeping of living pets in a condition of nature, it became in itself an education, and brought the bairnies into direct communication with the Creator, who loves all things He has made.

What fun they had in the woods, but they went to show Frank the terrible cliff over which Daddy Pop had fallen when a young man.

The tree beneath was marked by a cross deeply cut in the bark.

By the time they got back, Daddy was ready to accompany them all to have tea in Toddie's whale.

# CHAPTER VI
## TAKING TEA INSIDE A WHALE—THE STRANGE STORY OF THE STRANDED LEVIATHAN

There were two persons who on this particular afternoon considered themselves of the very greatest importance. One was Bunko, the other Tippetty. And the most perfect understanding existed betwixt the two. Next to his little mistress, I feel certain that Tip loved Bunko above all people, and Bunko loved Tip, and admired him too. Like many peasants of his class, Bunko was fond of adorning his conversation with Biblical phraseology, always, however, with the greatest reverence and veneration. Half-daft Bunko might have been, but the Scriptures were indeed to him the Book of books, and the beautiful and simple stories of the New Testament were not beyond his childlike comprehension.

Therefore Bunko was really paying Tip a compliment when he told that doggie he was more "subtle than any other beast of the field," and like the serpent in the book of Genesis.

Nevertheless, although Bunko made a companion of "Tippie," as he called him, whenever he could get him to make a companion of, he would not have permitted anyone to say the dog had reason.

"I have na muckle reason mysel'," he told the old fisherman one day, "but poor Tippie's only a breet" [brute].

Then he scratched his head as he looked at his four-footed friend. "Ma! conscience though," he added, "just look at they bewitchin' brown een [eyes] o' his. What a lot o' wisdom the Good Lord *has lent him!*"

The fisherman thought this was certainly a new light in which to view the controversy of Reason versus Instinct.

Well, both the friends went to the igloo, as Fred called the whale-house, early that afternoon, for Bunko had caught Tippitty and carried him off in triumph. It was no easy matter either, to carry Tip; for if Tip chose to wriggle you couldn't hold him in one arm as you might a terrier, you required both, and even then if the doggie made up his mind to wallop but once, he was out of your grasp and off like an eel.

"You're no goin' to the woods the day, I can tell you, Tippie," Bunko had told him. "We have gentry folks comin' to tea, so you maun come and help me."

Bunko was dressed in his best, in his Sunday clothes in fact, and a fearful and wonderful rig it was—a Scotch bonnet as broad as a griddle with an immense red top on it, a soldier's scarlet coat, and a pair of tartan trowsers rather frayed at the bottom.

If you had told Bunko that the bonnet was too big for him he would probably have replied: "If ye dinna like it, ye can look the ither road. Anything sets [becomes] a weel-faured face, if it were only the dish-clout."

In that great rugged wall of rocks that went stretching away out into the western sea there was just one break, and this occurred a little beyond the poet's cave. A kind of glen or small ravine it formed. At low-water you could approach it from the sea between two tall frowning rocks, but if the tide were up you must descend into it by a perilous little pathway leading from the cliff above. Only once, in the memory of the villagers then living, had this glen been invaded by a high-tide. This had occurred some years before the date of the commencement of our story, and, strange to say, when the sea receded it left behind it a stranded whale.

This whale was a Godsend to the poor fisher folks. One way or another, what with its whalebone, its oil, and its great jaws, it had been sold piecemeal. But there still remained leaning against the cliff the huge ribs of the leviathan, and here the children used to play till one day it occurred to Bunko to make these ribs the framework of a good house.

Eean, the bard, took up the idea at once, and what with the help of an idle hand or two, always easily to be had in a village, the ribs were roofed and covered in all round, and when a floor and door had been put in, not to mention a fire-place and a little window, why surely never on earth was there a better or more romantic children's play-house.

The bottom of the glen or gap in this wall of rocks was grass, so Bunko's "mother-wit" came in handy once again.

"What for no' have a bit garden round the house?" Bunko had said.

"Certainly," said Eean; "but the soil isn't deep."

"Bide a wee, sir."

And, spade in hand, up he clambered to the cliff top. It was well for the old fisherman that he had divined Bunko's intentions and stood clear from under, for presently the earth began to descend in avalanches. Bunko in his excitement had evidently quite forgotten that anyone stood beneath. In less than a quarter of an hour a heap of mould big enough for the purpose lay alongside the igloo.

Meanwhile Eean had wandered round the corner, deeply absorbed in the beauties of Ossian. When he returned, much to his astonishment he found that poor Bunko had descended, and was digging into that heap of earth with his coat off as if his future life depended on it. Eean walked quietly up behind him, for Bunko was talking aloud, a word or two to each spadeful that he threw aside.

It is said listeners never hear any good of themselves. This case, however was an exception.

"O, poor Eean—O, poor dear old man—the best—and the wisest—and the bonniest—auld man—'tween here and Perth—and I've—buried him alive."

Eean had to laugh aloud now, and the look of astonishment blended with joy on the half-witted lad's face, as he looked about, was comical in the extreme.

Down went the spade, and Bunko seized Eean's hand and burst into tears. Poor fellow, never a word could he think of to utter at that moment except his grace after meals:

"For these and a' Thy other mercies, Good Father, make us truly thankfu'."

Having so far relieved his feelings, he picked up his broad bonnet and threw it in the air, and as soon as it descended he leapt nimbly on top of it, and cracking his thumbs danced the tenth step of the Lonach Hielan' fling without ever getting off.

"D'ye feel better now?" said Eean, much amused.

"That I do; but, O, sir, if I'd killed ye, I'd——"

"What, Bunko?"

"Flung my body o'er the cliff for the partans [crabs] to pick."

But the garden was laid out with a rustic railing round it, and all the summer through lovely flowers always bloomed therein, with roses and honeysuckle, and wild convolvulus trailing over the fence.

On this autumn afternoon, the bright crimson Scotch tropæolum, that refuses to grow out well of its native land, encircled the igloo doorway with its masses of flame-like flowers.

"Tippie, Tippie, here's the gentry. Run and meet them, Tip."

Yes, there they come—Fred and Frank and Toddie, and the sturdy old weird-looking bard himself.

Bunko stood by the garden gate, pole in hand, as the party approached. "Shoulder arms," he shouted. "Present arms."

And in due military style he stood there at the present till they all filed past.

"Fancy taking tea in a whale!" cried Frank delightedly. "And such a tea! Crisp oat-cakes, scones, butter, and honey. Dear me, how mother would enjoy this!"

Eean took off his bonnet, and holding it before his face asked a humble blessing, and then the meal proceeded right merrily, Bunko waiting as sedately as a butler, and Tippetty sitting on a stool with a bib on him— Toddie's doings—as solemn as a judge.

Conversation never slackened all the time.

"What made you call it an igloo?" said Frank.

"Well, you know," Fred replied, "I wasn't sure what to call it at first. A wigwam puts you in mind of Red Indians, and there's no wild Indians here except Toddie there. A toldo is the tent that the Patagonian tribes dwell in."

"Big men the Patadonians," Toddie told Frank confidentially, "all diants, you know."

"Hush, Todd. Well, I didn't like kraal because ito puts you in mind of Hottentots, and Daddy Pop there said an igloo was the house the Eskimos lived in, and as this whale must have come from there I thought I——"

"Oh, I see now!" Frank interrupted. "Good idea too."

Toddie was looking very much absorbed. At last she turned to Eean.

"Daddy," she said, "oo don't think, does oo, that the whale will ever tome alive adain?"

Then her bright eyes sparkled with merriment as she clapped her wee pink hands.

"Oh, what fun," she cried, "if the whale would tome alive adain dust now, and do [go] away to sea wi' us all sittin' here!"

Frank laughed and Fred too. The idea was even too much for Bunko's gravity, so he gave vent to a loud guffaw; and Tip took the opportunity of barking for another piece of buttered scone, and got it too.

Then, tea being over, they all sat round the fire, and the bard took out his pipe.

"I'se dust wonderin'," said Toddie, looking wisely at the blazing peats, "wherever this poor whale tame from. Plaps," she added sadly, "he had no mammy Mop to look after him."

"Oh, yes!" said Daddy, "he had a mother, Toddie."

"Tell us; oh, tell us," cried Frank, "another story!"

"No, no, master Frank; I'll only just talk a bit."

"You've been to Greenland, sir?"

"Oh, yes, Frank! I've been blown about all over the world, and got stranded on the beach here at last, just like the whale in which we're now sitting so cosily."

"Yes," Eean continued, "with all due respect for Toddie's wisdom, I must differ from her; the probability is, that this whale had a mother.

"You know, children, that whales are not fish, but great beasts. They couldn't live long beneath the water without being drowned; half an hour at most. When they are chased by boats and harpooned they go through the water at a terrible speed, so quickly indeed that the sea rises up from each of the boats' bows like two sheets of green glass. But the whale soon gets so breathless that he can't go under water at all.

"The male or he-whale is called a bull, the she one a cow, and the young one a calf, and it takes milk from its mother just as any other calf does from its mother.

"Now the bulls are very kind to the cows. They are good-natured, kind husbands. So we may suppose that after this whale that we are now sitting in was born, and was strong enough to swim funnily round and round his big mammy, and knew enough to creep under her flipper if he saw a ship coming, the bull said to the cow — — "

"O Daddie," cried Toddie, "whales tan't talk."

"Yes, Toddie, they talk with their eyes, and their tails."

"Of tourse, of tourse," said Toddie, "dust like Tippetty does. Do [go] on, Daddy Pop."

"Says the bull to his wife —

"'What would you think of a little run to the south, my dear? You've been looking rather pale about the nose of late, and it would do you good, and little Johnnie too.'

"'Little Johnnie was the calf, you know.'

"'But I don't really care to leave you,' says the cow.

"'O, nonsense, dear, go by all means. Mind you, Johnnie isn't a strong child, I don't believe he weighs more than ten tons now, and he hasn't cut his whale-bone teeth quite yet.'

"'Well, my dear,' says the cow, 'I'll just go to please you.'

"So straight away down south comes the cow and her calf. It was a long, long journey for them. Sometimes Johnnie, her big baby, would fall sound asleep, and then his mother would spread one great loving flipper over him, and paddle along with the other so quietlike as if afraid of waking her darling.

"Then by-and-bye Johnnie would awake, and, like any other calf, begin sucking at once, and nudging his mother all the time with his bottle of a nose, raising her a little above the clear blue waves at every nudge. Yes, boys, I've often seen what I'm trying to describe to you.

"South and south went the mother and her calf, and aye and aye the weather and the water grew warmer. What gladsome times the two had together in these sunlit seas! but Johnnie always kept close beside his mother when sharks appeared, because the sharks would have killed and eaten Johnnie. But one stroke of the whale cow's tail would kill five of the biggest sharks that ever swam, and the sharks knew that and kept well away.

"When the holiday was over, back the two went to their own cold home in the north. The cow swam homewards as straight as an arrow. She had no compass to steer by, and the stars, if she went by those, were often obscured; but the wonderful instinct implanted in her by God, who makes and rules all creatures and things, never deserted her, but guided her on and on and on, till the tall icebergs once more loomed out of the dark sea, with stars and aurora shining and dancing above.

"Of course the husband was glad to see her.

"'How well you look, dear!' he said, as they rubbed noses.

"'Yes,' she answered; 'and hasn't Johnnie grown wonderfully!'

"'I hardly knew him, indeed,' said the bull.

"Well, now, when Johnnie was about a year old, a whales' ball took place in Baffin's Bay.

"Yes, Frank. Mind, this is not a fairy tale. I'm speaking from the great book of Nature.

"Well, it isn't a real ball, you know, Toddie, only Greenland sailors call it so because the young whales all meet and dance about, and leap and jump, and whack the water with their awful tails, till the whole sea around is like a whirlpool, and covered with froth and foam. It is an interesting and a terrible sight. Ships may view it from afar off, but they know better than to go too close with boats, else these boats would be smashed into match-wood in less than a minute.

"Well, I suppose Johnnie danced too much at this ball, or ate too many gallons of the little shrimp things that whales feed on. Anyhow, next day he didn't feel at all well.

"'I tell you what it is, Johnnie,' said Johnnie's mother, 'you must take a run south, it will quite brace you up again.'

"'What, all by myself?' cried Johnnie, wagging his tail. 'Oh, that will be fun!'

"Johnnie's mother was very sorry to part with him, but she thought it would be all for the best. Ah! little did she think she would never see her boy any more.

"Johnnie started off in great glee at first; but when he was fairly clear of the ice, and the last white berg had disappeared behind the horizon; when as he rose on the great tumbling billows he could see nothing around him but an illimitable expanse of ocean, without a vestige of life in or over it, then he began to feel very lonely indeed, and half repented having come away at all. There was Providence, however, to guide and to guard him too, so he went steadily on and on, south, south, south, by night and by day. It was dreariest at night, when the stars were all shimmering above, and not a sound to be heard save now and then a sullen boom or plash, that told Johnnie plainly enough there were his enemies the sharks plunging about in the darkling sea not far off. Sometimes he slept and dreamt ugly dreams, and awoke with a start, to find terrible-looking ocean monsters with awful eyes staring up at him from the dark depths. He could see them because they were all covered over with a silvery, ghost-like light called phosphorescence, which is very common up in these wild northern latitudes. By day sharks often met him—the huge hammer-headed sort—and pretended to be friendly, and tried to lure him away into shallow water, where they could easily have devoured him.

"But Johnnie thanked them, and said, 'No.' He knew his way, and would stick to it.

"Johnnie had many other enemies to encounter, such as the sea unicorn, with its long spiral ivory horn—a bold beast that will scarcely go out of its way even for a ship. He tried to stab Johnnie to the heart, and if he had done so the sharks would have come to the banquet, and eaten the pair of them. But Johnnie avoided the deadly thrust, and with one blow of his tail pitched the unicorn nearly up to the moon. At least so the beast himself told the other unicorns he met soon after.

"But Johnnie escaped all his enemies, and arrived at last within sight of the Faröe Islands, where the water was delightfully mild and the sun very bright.

"Now, had Johnnie done what his mother told him, and not gone a mile further, all would have been well. But these sunny summer seas were so blue and pleasant that Johnnie went on and on. His life passed like a happy dream, the Shetland Islands hove in sight, bold black rocky isles crowned with green fields, with millions of sea birds all around them, then the lonesome Orkney, and then Scotland itself. There were strange birds in the air that cried to Johnnie, 'Go away, go away, away, away, away!' but Johnnie would not be warned and wouldn't obey his mother, and so——"

Eean was not allowed to complete his story.

"Oh!" cried Toddie gleefully, "I know what is toming, Daddy Pop."

"Well, then," said Frank, "can you complete the story?"

"I don't know, you know," said Toddie, "if I tan 'plete the stoly, but I tan feenis' it. The Dood God rosed a dleat stolm, and poor Johnnie was dliven on shore, and touldn't get back again to see his mammy."

"That's it, Toddie," said Eean.

And with that up jumped Frank.

"It is getting near gloaming," he said. "I'm sorry I must go; but, Toddie, I must do as my mother told me."

"Of tourse oo must, or plaps oo be deaded too, like the poor Johnnie whale."

Half an hour afterwards Frank Fielding had said adieu to his kindly though humble fisher friends, and was rattling along through the moonlit woods towards his home at Benshee.

# CHAPTER VII
## "FIVE YEARS AGO THIS VERY NIGHT"

The bay of Methlin was a very beautiful one, wildly so in fact, although that black beetling wall of rocks that went darkly stretching seaward had at times a weird and uncanny look about it, especially when half buried in mist, with the mournful boom of the seas under it, and far away, coming landwards from the grey gloom, the plaintive but eerie cry of sea-birds.

In summer days, when the sun shone clearly over the water, it was cheerful indeed to stroll along that cliff top. Whichever way one looked there was something to cheer the sight—the far-off ships on the ocean horizon, or a little island here and there that appeared to float in the drowsy haze; the deep, deep green waves below the rocks, rising and swelling as they rushed inland, as if measuring their height against the slippery blackness, the glorious hills themselves, changing ever in beauty of shade as cloud-shadows raced across their majestic brows; and the wee white-housed village itself asleep in a wildery of trees.

Even when storms lashed over the rocks and rose in snowy fountains to the green turf above, when the hills were half-hidden in mixing masses of inky clouds, and the sea's horizon lowered close in shore, there was a beauty about both seascape and landscape that probably only such a mind as that of Eean's could fully appreciate. His had a melancholy tinge imparted to it from the bitter memories of a life that had been nearly all disappointment. His too was the soul of the bard of Ossian or Homeric type, only deeply imbued with religion. No dark mythology was called upon to account for the fierce war of storms that often raged o'er sky and sea and land on this wild coast. No; there was method even in the madness of the tempest, there was golden light and beauty behind the blackness; no thunder could roll, no lightning's flash could rend the mountain rocks, no waves could swell and break without the will of his Father—and his Father was mercy and goodness personified—despite the fact that He

> "——moves in a mysterious way,
> His wonders to perform,

And plants His footsteps on the sea,
    And rides upon the storm."

Far away then, on that wild cliff top, the tall figure of the bard, with his broad bonnet and his wind-tossed plaid, might have been seen at gloaming-tide of the stormiest days. His face at such times had a sterner, more thoughtful aspect; his usually mild blue eyes seemed to retreat beneath his lowering eye-brows; yet ever and anon that face would soften, and a smile irradiate its every feature, as some happy thought crossed his mind. Such flashes were like the blinks of sunshine that sometimes fall from rifts of blue in winter storms.

Or, tired of his walk, he would seek the entrance of his cave, disappearing suddenly as if it were off the face of the earth—as he really did, but a stranger noticing that tall figure one moment by the cliff's side, and missing it the very next, would have made sure the old man had been blown over the rocks.

It was one evening, about a fortnight after Frank Fielding had gone home to Benshee, that Eean had retired from the green cliff above to his cave below. Though quite light above, the cave was every now and then plunged in total darkness by the dashing waves.

The bard stirred up his fire till the red light gleamed fitfully on the rugged grey walls, then he sat down in his chair leaning his chin on his hand to think.

He had a habit of talking aloud, a habit that is very easily acquired by those who delight in being much by themselves in very lonely places.

"Yes," he was saying, "just this very night five years ago that my wee pet came on shore."

Pit—pit—pit—pit. It was the sound of softly-padded feet coming trotting towards him, and next minute Tippetty with immense effort had sprang on his knees.

"Why Tip," said Eean, "what are you doing here? and gasping too, with a quarter of a yard at least of a pink ribbon of a tongue hanging out over your snow-white teeth?"

Tip looked up with those speaking brown eyes of his.

"Oh! Daddy Pop," he seemed to say, "it blows so high on the cliff top, and I've been running hard."

"Where is your mistress, you scamp? You didn't come all by yourself."

Tip's ears went away back on his neck in quite an apologetic sort of way, and he glanced uneasily towards the door.

"Dad—*dee!*" It was Toddie's voice on the stone stair staircase.

Tip sprang down to meet her, and next moment she came in with a rush, her hair all a-toozle, her bare, naked feet and baton legs as red as red could be, for never would Toddie wear shoe or stocking except on high days and holidays.

Next moment she was seated on one of Eean's knees, and Tip on the other.

Toddie put one arm round Eean's neck, and entwined her fingers in his hair, then looking up—

"Isn't oo dlad I'se tomed?" she said.

"Very glad you've got here safe, dear."

"Well, tiss me. Now, this is nice. Nice file bulning there, and all. Plaps I'll make oo sing to me bye'm-bye."

Toddie was a very despotic little queen in her own wee way. Queen she was of that old man's heart, and she seemed to know it.

He was looking at her very fondly just then with a curious kind of smile on his face.

"Wouldn't you rather I'd tell you a story, Toddie?"

Toddie put her thumb in her mouth and gazed into the fire.

"I fink," she said, "Plank likes stolies best."

"My own little Treasure-trove," said the bard.

"Daddy, don't oo make up such silly words."

"You *are* my Treasure-trove. Do you know where you came from, darling?"

"The Dood God sent me, of tourse."

"Yes, pet, the Good God sent you to cheer this old man's heart, and brighten his life. But do you know you came from the sea? That, years and years ago, five this very night, you were stranded on the beach down here?"

"Stlanded! What does that mean, daddy?"

"Thrown up by the waves, my wee one."

Toddie was looking at him now with eyes that were very wide indeed.

"What, daddy, dust the same as the Johnnie whale, daddy?"

"Just the same as the Johnnie whale, dear."

"Oh!"

She nestled towards him now, and gazed thoughtfully at the fire, and the old bard talked to her and to the fire at the same time apparently.

"Yes, Toddie, it was a fearful night that. There was a moon, but she hadn't a chance of shining; for the grey-black clouds dashed over her like the race of a mill-stream. Early in the afternoon a brig had been seen trying to round the point. But the wind blew high, and, alas! she tried in vain. We had all been on the beach for hours and hours watching her. Oh, what an evening it was! There had been sea-gulls in our garden that day, darling, as tame as chickens."

"Oh!"

"And we knew, Toddie, something terrible would soon happen. Mammy had hot water and blankets ready ever so long. Then the brig struck. Long before then Bunko had been sent off on horseback to warn a lifeboat. But the lifeboat never came. And small matter that she didn't. Hours after a spar floated up. We saw something white lashed to it, and all rushed to pick it up. I was first, and found you, Toddie."

"Oh!" thoughtfully.

"Mammy Mop took hours to bring you back to life. We have the old spar yet in the sail-house; it was loaded with iron—old axe heads—to make a keel; so, Toddie, you floated face upwards. That is the way you came, Toddie."

"Oh!"

"Dear little Treasure-trove. I hope you will not be taken from me."

He gathered her closer up to him.

"Sing now," she murmured, "sing soft and low, like mammy does."

He sat rocking her there, and singing low, sweet Scotch hits, till her regular breathing and closed eyes told him she was fast asleep.

Then he gently laid her on the bench, while he put on his plaid.

Every moment now the waves dashed high over the ports of the cave, and the wind shrieked like the voices of creatures in pain or despair.

Quietly he takes the sleeping Toddie up, and wraps her in the plaid folds close to his breast. "Come, Tip," he says, and crook in hand goes up the steps and struggles out into the storm and darkness.

On nights like this Eppie always had a light burning in her gable window to guide belated boats, and this was the star old Eean steered by.

"Praise be to Providence you've come," said Eppie. "D'ye mind what nicht this is?"

"Right well I do," said Eean. "Look at the innocent lamb. Take her gently, Eppie. Take her gently."

When Fred went in with a rush next morning to the room where Toddie slept in a tiny cot, wondering why she had not come down to breakfast, he found the little maiden standing half-dressed before her little mirror, with a thumb in her mouth.

I dare say she had little womanly ways about her, else she would not have been in front of that morsel of mirror. But the thumb in the mouth showed how deep in thought she was.

"Thinking again, Toddie."

"Yes, I'se finking, Fred. Cause, you know, last night I was in Daddy's cave, or was I dleaming?"

"You must have been dreaming, Todd."

"Yes, I must have been dleaming, Fred. And I dleamt that Daddy told me a stoly, that Daddy said I came ashole on the beach, dust the same as the Johnnie whale."

# CHAPTER VIII
## PLEASANT SURPRISES—FRANK'S YACHT—
## THE LAUNCH OF THE WATER-BABY

Winter had come and gone again, and a very hard one it had been. Of the ten boats that belonged to the bay, and were laid up when not in use in a rock-girt harbour, about half a mile from the village, few had gone out very often. But seldom a day passed that Eean's boat, the *Treasure-trove* was not seen scudding about somewhere, if wind and weather permitted; and always when Daddy went to sea—and this was no means seldom—the two children went with him, so that Fred had generally one complete holiday every week.

It must not be supposed that Eean was careless with regard to the boy's education on this account. No, indeed. Fred's day at sea was one of real utility, and, young though he was, he knew already how to handle the great boat, and how to steer as well. Toddie too was a capital young sailor lass. She was warmly clad; but though her brave little face might be red, or even almost blue, she never feared to look a storm in the teeth.

Frank had gone away south with his mother to attend a purely English school, for sake of *bon ton* and the pure English accent. But the children corresponded regularly.

Toddie's letters to Frank were marvels in their way. She could not write very distinctly, so every alphabetical letter was pen-printed.

Frank had not much to tell. His life he was sorry to say was a very humdrum one. He was at a very humdrum school, where the pupils, all "sons of gentlemen," were allowed to do pretty much as they pleased. When they fell behind or lazed it was put down to delicate health. The bold forcing system of the Scottish Church parish schools was unknown at the so-called college at which Frank was engaged in his so-called studies.

His dear mamma spent the winter in the south, that she might be near to her dear boy and only son. She even told the head-teacher, or rather proprietor, of the school that her boy was not in robust health, and that he must on no account be thwarted. The fact is, Frank was as hardy and manly a lad as there was at the college.

He went home to his mother's house every Friday evening, and Fred's letter came punctually every Saturday afternoon, with wee Toddie's printed scrawl enclosed. Toddie's scrawls were really love letters of a sort, and not badly put together on the whole, as regards composition. Daddy spelt every word for her, which she herself could not manage. Here is a brief extract, which shows really that she could write better than she could speak:

"I thinks lots about you, Flank, in my bed and on the beach. I dont love the winter, I loves the summer, cause there is plenty flowers and no chilblains. I loves Daddy and Mammy Mop best, then Fred then Tippetty, then my dolly fishes, and then Flank last, but O Flank the last is a big big much.

"Your 'ffection' friend,
"Toddie Treasure-Trove."

Mrs. Fielding really was a good-hearted lady in the main, but purse-proud, and not over deep in mind.

She always spoke of Frank's little friends as "those poor children." This used to make Frank angry, though he loved his mother too much to show it. Well, Mrs. Fielding was also generous. She had proposed sending "those poor children" some clothes.

"Oh, mother, don't!" Frank had gasped, getting dreadfully red in the face.

Frank's father was reading the newspaper. He held it down for a minute to smile and say:

"Frank's right, mamma. It would be taken as a terrible insult. You forget that Eean Arundel is a gentleman though poor. My countrymen," he added, laughing, "are all gentlemen."

"Well," Mrs Fielding had replied, "I don't care much for pride in people who have nothing to keep it up with."

Young Frank was thoroughly roused now. He had to keep striding up and down across the floor to restrain his feelings.

"Mother," he said at last, "they have honesty."

"A king can mak' a belted knight,
    A marquis, duke, and a' that;
    An honest man's above his might."

Frank went and kissed his mother, and then ran straight out of the room.

Now Fred and Toddie, arrayed in their best, had several times visited at the house of Benshee. Frank had driven them over, and Fred at Frank's request had always brought his flute. For a boy of his years he was a charming performer. Frank played a little trick upon his lady mother. He went into her studio, which abutted on to the lawn, leaving Fred behind a bush near to the open window.

When Frank was fairly seated beside his mother, Fred began to play one of those sweet, sad Scottish melodies, that can draw tears to the eyes of even an English audience. Frank kept talking to his mother; but he was soon silenced.

"Hush! hush, boy!" she cried. "Have you no ear for the beautiful?"

She sighed when the air died in cadence away.

"Some poor tramp," said the lady. "Run, Frank, and give him sixpence."

But Fred now appeared at the window, laughing and holding out his hat.

"Oh, you dear lad," cried Mrs. Fielding, "come and kiss me!"

Fred did as told; but not quite so gracefully as an English boy would have done. Only this episode supplied Mrs. Fielding with an idea for being generous without offering insult.

One day, therefore, while Eppie was preparing a nice creel of fresh lobsters to be taken by Bunko to a neighbouring village, she was greatly surprised to find the carrier's cart from T—— draw up at her door. The cart contained a large and wonderful-looking box. If it had not been addressed in a clear hand to "Master Fred Arundel," Eppie would have thought there must be some mistake.

She did not dare to look into it until Fred came from school, and Daddy from his cave; and then, I do believe, half the village came to see the opening of that box.

It contained, to the amazement of all, a charming little piano. Toddie's face was a study at this disclosure; and Frank's was a picture of mingled pride and joy. As there was but little room in the house, the piano was taken to the cave; a damp-proof covering being made for it, lest it should be injured by the air of the sea.

All through the winter after school-hours, and after lessons at home, Fred had studied systematically on his new instrument. Playing was one of

Eean's accomplishments, and Fred proved so apt a pupil that it was soon evident he possessed the gift of music.

And now spring had come. The larch trees were already green, and tasselled over with crimson; primroses and violets peeped out in sheltered places, larks sang their glad lilts high in air; the pigeons croodled low in the spruce thickets; but the mavis seemed to have gone out of his mind, so madly and merrily did he sing. The sea was often calm now, and the sky very blue, though the heaving swell of the great Atlantic broke in thunders on the beach.

And one day Fred came rushing in from meeting the post-runner, waving a letter over his head, and Tip barking at his heels.

"Hurrah!" he cried; "Frank's coming."

There was real joy now in the fisherman's cottage.

But that night, after the children had gone to bed, Eean and Eppie sat beside the fire to consider solemnly a letter of another kind.

It was from Mrs. Fielding. It was like Mrs. Fielding. It was written in all sincerity; but was a very thunderbolt to poor Eean.

She had proposed to adopt Fred as a companion to her boy, and bring him up as her own son, giving him a good start in life.

They talked the matter out from every point of view. The Fieldings were rich. They could give the lad a good start in life. Though it would break their hearts to lose him, and Toddie's heart too, was it right of them to be selfish? Would it not be best for the boy if they accepted?

Perhaps; but then perhaps not. Riches do not always bring success in life, and mixing in society that he was but little used to might alter all the lad's character, and spoil him for life.

For two long hours they talked and talked. Then Eean rose.

"Let us simply pray for God's guidance, Eppie."

And side by side they knelt, while Eean lifted up his open eyes and prayed.

Next morning Eean seemed to receive an inspiration; all that was doubtful the evening before seemed clear as day now.

"We'll leave it to the boy," he said.

"You like Frank very much, don't you?" Eean said to Fred after breakfast.

"Oh, very much!"

"He is very happy, isn't he?"

"Happy, daddy? I don't know. O yes, I suppose so."

"Wouldn't you like to be rich just as he is?"

"I'm so very happy you know, daddy, and I've so much to do, I never thought of that. And I have so much to learn too.

"O daddy," continued the boy after a pause, "poor Frank's letters almost make me cry sometimes."

"Now you surprise me. But I'm going to the cave, so come along and tell me all about it."

When seated by the open port—"You see, daddy," said Fred, "Frank really wants to learn things all the time; and at the school he is at there are so many holidays, and they get so much of their own way, and so much time is spent at football and cricket, that they have no leisure to learn much. But, you see, he won't require to be well educated, because he is rich. Will he, daddy?"

Eean laughed at this idea.

"And," continued Fred, "he would hardly believe me when I showed him my Latin and Greek exercises, and my books on algebra and history. And he bit his lip and grew red, and the tears came rushing into his eyes, daddy. And, O Daddy Pop, though he writes in English, *he can't spell.*"

Fred was almost breaking down here in boyish grief for his friend.

Now was Eean's time. He took Mrs. Fielding's letter from his pocket and placed it in the boy's hand.

"It is very good of her," was all the poet said as he did so.

Eean watched him as he read. Sometimes Fred's colour heightened, and sometimes his pupils dilated, as if he saw not the letter before him.

"What, daddy, leave you and Mammy Mop and Toddie and Tippetty— and my books? Oh, Daddy Pop!"

"And what have you done about it, Pop?" he added.

"Mop and I talked hours about it; then we prayed to the Good God, Fred."

"What did the Good God say, Daddy Pop?"

"He bade me leave it all to you, dear lad."

"Ha! ha!" laughed the boy. "I'm so glad."

Then a funny notion came into his mind, which he proceeded at once to put into execution.

"Daddy," he said, "you left it to me. I'll leave it to the Corsican Brothers."

As he spoke he deftly tied a bit of meat to the string, and lowered it into the sea with a plash; about a minute after up over the ledge straddled the Corsican Brothers—Eean's pet crabs. They knew Fred, and at once advanced. Fred gave them a morsel or two of food to whet their appetite, and not to deceive them; then the boy assumed a semi-theatrical attitude, and addressed them.

"We have a very knotty point to solve, my dear twins," he said; "and Pop says I may leave it to you. Read that letter."

Both crabs seized it at once. They thought it the biggest piece of white meat ever they had turned their stalky eyes upon. But finding it flavourless and unprofitable they lost their tempers, and tore it into shreds. So indignant did they appear, they even clawed up the pieces and tore them over again.

Then Fred brushed away the paper and gave the Corsican Brothers a bigger feed than ever they had enjoyed in their lives before.

So that was an end to Mrs. Fielding's kind, but somewhat thoughtless proposal.


When Frank called in his pony-trap he found Fred in his shirt sleeves, with a plane in his hand, and hard at work. He was making a table for the igloo, for carpentering was one of his chief hobbies. On the table near him lay a Greek grammar. He was conjugating the irregular verbs, while he sent the curling shavings flying all over Toddie and Tippetty, who were having fine fun on the floor.

That meeting was a very joyful one. There was much to say and much to be told on both sides.

Instead of going to the woods to-day the children got the cobble, and went off round the point fishing.

Frank's most interesting bit of news was embodied in the following words:

"I've been reading *Robinson Crusoe*," he said, "and I'd like to be a sailor. And what do you think?"

"I couldn't guess," said Fred. "Toddie, put the helm down a bit, the wind is shifting."

They had a sail on the cobble, and Toddie was bravely steering.

"Well, my mother has bought me a nice boat, and we are to keep it here in a boat-house. The boat is higher in the sides than this."

"Higher free-board," said Fred.

"And not quite so wide."

"Bloader in the beam oo means to say," said Toddie with a slight curl on her lip.

"How do you know all that, Toddie?" said Frank.

"Hush!" cried Toddie. "Tan't oo see I'se steeling [steering]. Oo must not talk to the man at the wheel."

Fred's eyes began to beam, as they always did when he caught up some new idea.

"O Frank," he cried, "I know what we can do. But what size is she?"

"Let me see. She must be yards and yards long."

Toddie began to laugh, and so did Fred. Poor Frank was no sailor.

"Never mind, Frank. I daresay she is big enough to deck over and step a mast in, and make a yacht of. Bunko and I can do it. You have no idea how clever Bunko is. And I have tools and wood and all."

In less than a week the boat came round, and was stabled, as Frank called it, in a boat-house on the beach. The boys could do what they liked with the boat, was Mrs. Fielding's request; but they must always have a man with a lifebuoy close beside them in another boat at sea.

Bunko took the village cows to the hill; but all day long the faithful collie Keelie watched them. The dog made a rapid run homeward every day, ate his dinner, which was always ready, then back to the hills he would scud again. So until eventide, when he went to take home his charge, Bunko's time was very much his own.

The decking and fitting out of the yacht, therefore, proceeded merrily enough. A fresh keel was put on her, and a good one too. Eean himself had seen to this. The mainsail was only a storm one, there was no topsail, and just a single jib. The rudder was very safely shipped, and so, though the boys did most of the work, Eean was the real ship-builder, and safety was consulted in every detail.

When all was complete, and the craft painted and furnished, a more complete little boys' yacht it would have been difficult to conceive.

The fishermen all said she was a perfect picture, and lay like a duck on the water, with a good many other complimentary allusions, all of which were Greek to Frank, but not to Toddie and Fred.

No expense was spared in the upholstering of the little cabin, and they even had a small galley, with a tiny spirit range, enough to make tea and boil eggs.

It was indeed a proud day for the boys, and Toddie and Tippetty, when they went for their first sail.

Their consort was a big cobble with a fisherman to row, and a silly sort of a sailor-fellow with a lifebuoy.

The villagers gathered down by the beach and natural harbour, to give them a cheer when they started away on their trial trip, with their saucy little red flag floating at the peak.

Her name was the *Water Baby*, and with great pomp and ceremony she had been duly christened by Toddie, a tiny bottle of eau de Cologne, brought by Frank, having been duly broken on her bows before she left the slip.

One day Mrs. Fielding herself went for a sail, and found it so perfectly safe that at Frank's earnest request she allowed them in future to dispense with the consort cobble, and the sailor-fellow also.

But they had to carry a lifebuoy nevertheless, and this was only right.

Boy though he was, Fred knew something about the signs of the weather, and always got into harbour in time to avoid a storm, or anything like one.


So spring merged into summer; the days grew warmer and longer, and the sea more calm and bright. Then Fred's summer holidays came round; and happier children than those three, Frank, Fred, and Toddie, were surely not to be found in all broad Scotland.

# CHAPTER IX
## PLAYING AT BEING PIRATES—A STORM AT SEA—THE WRECK

Frank Fielding's life was not quite like his friend Fred's in one particular; for Frank could always have a holiday when he wanted one. His father was an easy-going, non-ambitious man; he possessed all the comforts of this world, and very much enjoyed them. If you had asked him about his son's prospects in life, he would have told you that he was pleased enough to let the boy enjoy himself; that very likely there was a career of some kind before him when he developed; but that meanwhile he left all his educational affairs to his—the boy's—mother.

Poor Frank! The mother might have been doing her best, but to keep constantly sending a lad from school to school was not advancing his interests.

Fred had only the regular holiday given at Scottish schools, the summer one being the chief, and indeed the only one worthy of the name, because it lasted for six weeks.

Well, anyhow, Frank had found a companion after his own heart, and Fred had found a real friend. It was almost strange, a psychologist would have thought, how very much those two lads had come to love each other in so short a time. It was in a good many ways a case of extremes meeting, but they had a deal in common nevertheless.

Both loved Nature most ardently, although Fred knew ten times more about the habits of the wanderers in wood and field than did Frank. Every wild flower he met was an old acquaintance of Fred's, and so was every bird that sang or did not sing.

Fred was a great bird-nester. But, mark this, he never took a single egg, far, far less a helpless fledgling. But he knew where they all built their nests or laid their eggs without ever bothering about building a nest, in forest, in mountain, on moorland, or by stream. There was no pine tree or larch high enough to prevent Fred from getting to the top thereof, and in Scotland these trees are at home, and grow their very tallest. He and Toddie had other friends in the wilds as well as birds, so numerous indeed that I begrudge space in which to name them. But there were bees of all kinds, and beetles of every hue and shape; there were frogs and toads, charming lizards and lovely great snakes. Not adders. Even in the heather Toddie was as often barefooted as not, because she preferred "feelin' around with her foots as Tippetty did." So she said, and Eean would not thwart her.

Well, during the holidays they had many a long day in the woods and wilds; other days were spent at sea in the yacht, where they played at being pirates, and ran down and pretended to capture fishing-boats, and once they even overhauled a Royal Navy cutter that was dodging off the point. Fred lowered sail and boarded her, and when asked what he wanted, he boldly pointed to a black flag with skull and cross bones that Frank had hoisted; told the bos'n he was "The Pirate of the Western Wilds," and he must submit to give up his craft and walk the plank. There was no little laughing at this; but finally the *Water Baby* was taken in tow, and the children spent a downright madcap afternoon with the sailors on board the cutter.

When it was getting near sunset farewells were said, and over the side went the pirates bold, the men giving them three cheers as their fairy-like yacht bore away for Methlin Bay.

Once it was caught in a puff of wind, and had to run for harbour; but the way Frank and Fred took in sail was a pretty sight indeed, while Toddie sat at the tiller with Tippie at her side.

Oh, I can assure you this playing pirate was fine fun! But I think, on the whole, Frank had more sense of the humorous than had Fred. He took a less serious view of life in general, and was always up to some lark or another. Once, for instance, he met Bunko in a neighbouring village with a creel of lovely lobsters, and, right or wrong, Frank must have that creel, and did have it, and, with Fred and Toddie following up in the rear, he marched boldly through the little country town, crying, "Lobsters, all alive O!" They were all dead and boiled, but that didn't matter. Frank—a laird's son—selling lobsters! Every woman and child ran out to see him, and in half an hour he had sold the lot.

How proud he was of his success! and how Bunko did laugh to be sure!

Now Frank did not wear the ordinary Highland garb such as gentlemen wear while shooting or fishing. It pleased his mother to put him into a real tartan kilt, with black jacket of velvet, skean dhu and sporran, so you may fancy what sort of a figure he cut with a creel on his back. But it wasn't all over yet; for, another day he actually bought a creel for himself, and having made some private arrangement with Bunko, the two set off together to see who would sell out the sooner.

Fred and Toddie were there as usual; but, lo and behold! just in the midst of the fun, who should drive up the street but his father and mother in the landau.

Not a bit taken aback, Frank walked right up to the carriage.

"Buy any beautiful lobsters to-day, madam?" he said, with true fisher "twang."

The lobsters were red, but Mrs. Fielding's face grew redder.

"Oh, Frank! Frank!" she cried, "how could you— —"

"Quite fresh, madam, I assure you. Only boiled this morning. Feel the weight of this one, my lady."

His father could hardly speak for laughing, and the coachman's fat sides shook till he nearly fell off the dickey.

Mr. Fielding himself bought that lobster, and the carriage drove on.

Frank looked after it with a very comical expression on his face.

Then he laughed as he turned to Fred.

"I shall have that lobster to-night for supper," ha said, "and such a wigging with it from mother, you know. Father is fond of fun. Come on, Bunko. 'A man's a man for a' that.' Lobsters, all alive O!"


"I fink," said Toddie one morning as she stood looking at the sea with her thumb in her mouth, "I fink, Fled, it will blow a ten-knot bleeze to-day."

"Yes," said Fred, with a glance at the sky as if he had been a hundred-years-old fisherman, "it may blow a ten-knot breeze, but bless you, Tod, we haven't got the press of canvas to carry us anything like ten knots."

"No, oo's twite light [right], Fled, we tan't do it. We tould tally more tanvas too."

"Now, Tod, don't put on airs. Skip. Frank'll be here in a minute."

Toddie and Tip did skip, and after running stark staring mad on the sands for a quarter of an hour they went to say "Dood-bye to the tsilden dolly fishes" in the aquarium.

The blennies were waiting to be stroked, and all waiting to be fed.

"Dood-bye, dolly-fishes;" cried Toddie, waving her hand as she stood in the cave mouth. "Be dood tsilden till oo mammy tomes back, and oo'll all have something nice."

Frank was careering over the sands on the Shetland pony looking for Toddie, and he gave her just one wild gallop before they embarked.

"Don't go far out to-day, bairns," cried Eean. "I'm not sure it isn't going to blow, bright and all as it is. And the breeze is off the land too."

After they had made a good offing, Fred said, "Let us stand right away to the west for a few miles, then tack back. That'll make a nice long sail of it."

The breeze was very light, and they were about five miles from the coast in an hour, a long way decidedly for children to be out on an uncertain day, albeit two of them were children of the sea.

Fred now had the mainsail lowered, and they just kept moving while Frank made coffee, and undid a package containing a splendid veal-pie.

What a delightful feast that was! And the sea and sky and shore looked somehow even more lovely after their hearty meal than they had done before. Even Tip must have thought so too; for he stood with his two fat feet on the gunwale, and barked in a daft kind of way at the sea-gulls.

What glorious tints of blue and opal and purple and green overspread seascape and landscape!

They were looking at all this in a dreamy happy way, when Fred suddenly pointed towards the mountains. "Look! look!" he cried, "at those great white clouds rising like giant's heads, looking over the hills."

"Dust like diants," said Toddie.

"Let her come round, Todd. Thank you."

The mainsail was hoisted, and she came round like a swan.

Tippetty was sent below, and Toddie too, and Fred took the tiller himself.

In less than half-an-hour the storm was over them. Fred saw it coming, and knew he couldn't face it, and so got round to scud all in good time.

The wind had gone round points and points, and the wee yacht fairly flew before it, lying over till the gunwale nearly touched the water—aye, and did at times.

"Don't be afraid, Todd," shouted Fred, laughing. "It will soon be over. Cheer up, Frank!"

Honest Fred! he knew the danger they were in, but kept the secret to himself.

Well, the *Water Baby* proved a grand little sailer. Fred really felt proud of her as she rose so nimbly to each green sea, and dashed the spray from her bows.

He would have been happy but for thinking of the anxiety of those at home. However, he managed to keep Toddie in the dry; and Frank and he got their oilskins and sou'-westers, and perfect little tars they looked now.

In about an hour they were far away at sea and no land in sight; but the wind had settled down to a steady blow, the seas raced up behind them, the sails were as stiff as pasteboard, and all danger seemed past.

"Aren't we going from home rather?" said Frank. Fred laughed, though he felt it was rude.

"We can't beat," said Fred, "we must run; but we've no cloth to speak of."

"Oh!" said Frank, "it is well to know that."

"I mean, you know, it is impossible to get back till this bit of a summer puff blows over. All right down there, Toddie?"

No answer. Toddie and Tip were fast asleep on the cushions.

Frank began to nod next, and finally collapsed, half in half out, of the little cabin. Fred pulled a tarpaulin over him, and then felt very lonely indeed.

It must be remembered Fred was only a youngster, though strong for his age. One thing anyhow I am quite sure of, he was not afraid; a better sailor he might have been, but fear—no.

Westward and westward with a bit of south in it went the *Water Baby* all day long.

Just as it was getting near to gloaming a haze spread over the ocean, obscuring everything except the green seas close aboard. Fred did not like this new turn of events. He liked it less when suddenly dark rocks loomed like gigantic black castles over him—over him—on both sides—around him. Swish! Crack! Dash! The yacht had run on shore, and the mast went by the board.

The seas hissed around the wreck—if wreck she was—like snakes, but a big kindly wave at last came sweeping on, and lifted the *Water Baby* high and dry on the sands.

Fred knew it was high-water just then, so there was no more danger to be apprehended.

Somehow or other the *Water Baby* lay on an even keel, with the wreck of the mast and the tattered sail astern of her. Frank was certainly frightened. It was a terrible awaking for anyone; but it might have been worse.

"I fell asleep sayin' my players," said Toddie, emerging from the cabin. "And poor Tippetty are both so hungly."

"Do you know where you are, Toddie?" said Fred, taking the child on his knee. There was little else to be done, he thought, but nurse Toddie, and he was so very, very tired.

"Oh yes, of course I do! We is all shipwlecked maliners now."

"Well, Toddie, don't sleep again. Let us get on shore for a run. Perhaps there is a house somewhere near."

A reddish mist appeared seawards, between the giant rocks they had been so fortunate as to escape, and Fred knew the sun had set.

The wind appeared going down with it too, so his spirits rose.

It was only a small island after all. They searched about and called and shouted, but no sound or sight of human life could be discovered; so they returned together towards the little cove, and prepared to make the best of it.

"Get on board, Frank, and light the lamp, and boil some water for tea. Toddie and I will go and gather dulse."

"All right, Captain Fred," said Frank, who really appeared now to be enamoured of their romantic situation.

When Toddie and Tippie and Fred got back from the beach it was nearly dark; but the little cabin seemed quite cosy, and after some delicious tea, and the rest of the pie, they all felt as happy as happy could be.

They had books in the cabin, and so Fred volunteered to read a story, after talking for some hours. The story was one of their favourites—*Sinbad the Sailor*.

It must have been long past nine when Toddie began to nod; so Fred put her to sleep with Tip on the little sofa, and covered her over with a plaid.

By this time the wind had quite gone down; so after a turn on deck, as Fred phrased it, the boys went below and turned in all standing. More of Fred's phraseology, meaning that they lay down on the floor with their clothes on. And the sun had risen, and was shining yellow into the cabin before they ever moved again.

# CHAPTER X
## ON THE DESERT ISLAND—TODDIE'S ADVENTURE ON THE CLIFF—THE BONFIRE

What a gladsome, joyous morning! And how brimful of health and happiness were those two lads, Fred and Frank! Both seemed to wake at once; then they looked in each other's faces, blinked a little in that yellow ray of sunshine, then burst out laughing.

In about five and a half seconds, as nearly as I can judge, they were both on deck rubbing their eyes and looking about them.

"Isn't it famous?" cried Frank.

"Oh, it's grand!"

"But I say, you know, what about my mamma and your Mammy Mop?"

"Oh, that'll be alright! Daddy and mammy are so sensible, both of them."

"So are mine, but——"

"But what?"

"Well, they know I'm not. They haven't forgotten those lobsters yet."

"Well, I'm going to forget everything as much as I can. I have my wee sister to comfort and see after. Daddy will pray for us, and then he'll be content and happy."

"I say, are you hungry?"

"Yes; so now I'm Captain Fred, and you're my lieutenant."

"Oh, no, captain, you're Crusoe, and I'm your man Friday."

"Well, Friday, bustle about and get ready breakfast; cook down there by that rock, and I'll see to the Fairy Queen—Toddie, you know."

Now there was going to be no starvation for some days to come, if indeed they were not rescued before then. Fred had always an eye to eventualities, and he had had the little yacht stored with biscuits and preserved meats and milk in tins. Frank had insisted on paying for all his stores, as he was owner, though Fred was sailing master.

Down below went Fred. Toddie was still sound asleep, and as for Tip, who lay in her arms, he would have slept for two days if his little mistress but lay still. Fred did not wake her just yet.

It had just occurred to him that there was scarcely a drop of water in the ship. This was terrible, for perhaps there was none in the island.

But then they had seen sheep. Oh, there must be water!

So off the boys went with a can to explore. There were no savages on the island, and so Toddie would be safe. They found a patch of scraggy bushes near a rock. A great striped snake wriggled away, and then Fred felt sure there was water near by.

Yes, trickling out of a rock, a lovely wee crystal rill. How sweet and cool it was! Both drank and felt refreshed. They filled the can and hurried back to the ship.

Fred got a nice basin of the cool water, a towel and soap, and descended once more to the cabin.

To his dismay, Toddie was gone! and Tip was gone! For a moment he was bewildered; then he called Frank, and off they ran all round and up and down the island, which was certainly not a large one. They shouted again and again, but there was no answer. At long last though, they saw Tippetty at some distance, standing with his paws on the very edge of a dizzy cliff, looking over.

Fred's eyes felt starting from the sockets with fear. He did not even notice that poor Frank had fainted and fallen on the green turf.

On and on towards Tip went Fred—slowly, silently, his hands stretched in front of him—walking as one dreams of walking in a terrible nightmare.

At last—oh, joy!—Tip started away from the cliff with a joyful bark, and next moment, catching by a scraggy bush, Toddie pulled herself up, and quite laden with a curious kind of mauve stonecrop, came rushing to meet her foster-brother.

Fred clasped her in his arms, kissed her face, and burst into tears.

Toddie could not quite understand the terrible danger she had been in, nor the extent of the fright she had given them, till they found Frank. He was just reviving.

"So foolish to faint," he said sleepily.

"Oo is vely, vely white," Toddie said. "O Flank, I'se been a naughty dirl!"

"You are safe, Toddie. Come."

Toddie went and sat by him a short time, and made him laugh at last; then the boys made a "Queen's chair" by interlacing their hands. Toddie sat thereon, and thus, laughing and running, they returned to the cove, Tip barking round them all the time.

Toddie promised faithfully not to go near the terrible cliff again, so happiness was completely restored.

How they did enjoy that breakfast to be sure! But they could not sit there all day, so up they got at last. Toddie took off her stockings and shoes, and rolled up her sleeves, and commenced at once to wash up and clear away, while Crusoe and his man Friday went to examine the yacht. She was deeply imbedded in the soft sand, but her bottom was found to be sound, though doubtless she would leak when floated again. The sails were intact, but the mast had gone by the board.

So they unloosed the former and spread them out to dry, and hauled the mast out of reach of the water. Then down they sat to consider their position, while Toddie, having tidied herself and done up the cabin, went to paddle on the beach with Tip. Fred was full of resources.

Frank was more full of fun than anything else.

"Have you anything to propose, Friday?" said Fred seriously.

"Yes," said Frank, "I propose that I should listen and nod my head to all you say. I'm only a nigger you know, a black irreclaimable savage."

"Well, you know this island is only a solitary patch in the middle of the sea, and there are hardly any others visible; but I think, you know, we could float the *Water Baby* and rig the broken mast as a jury."

"You're the best *judge*," said Frank, "so it will be judge and jury."

"Be quiet, Friday; how dare you, sir!"

"All right, sah, I'se goin' to be quiet and circumspecful like."

"We haven't a spade, but we have an axe," said Fred; "and I saw some old spars up there, so we could soon make a spade, no, two spades. Then we could dig away the sand all round her at low-water, and at high-water she would float; then we could shove off, and if the wind would favour us, we could steer for the east, and get home all right. I really think it can be managed."

"Oh, look, look!" cried Friday. "Why it's a goat! Oh, if we could only learn him to dance, what fun it would be, massa Crusoe!"

Then up jumped Frank.

"Tip, Tip, Tip," he cried. "Toddie, Toddie, Toddie."

And the wild wee maiden with her daft wee doggie came bounding to the call.

"I'm going for an explore," said Frank.

"But our work?" said Fred.

"Oh, bother the work, that can wait!"

"Well, we can all go for a little while. Put on your stockings and shoes, Tod."

Toddie gladly did as she was told, and away the shipwrecked mariners went. There was a high bit of ground, almost a hill in fact, in the centre of the island, and they climbed this first. They found a goat and two kids up here, but they went bounding away like red deer.

"I don't think they can be taught to dance, massa Crusoe," remarked Frank.

"I fear not, Friday."

From the hill they could see all "wound the world," as Toddie phrased it. What a beautiful world it was too, a world of peaceful blue waters, a world of blue sky, fleecy cloudlets and sunshine, but apparently a world of lonesomeness! They could barely see the mainland, and they could just make out some islands lying far away to the west, with one steamboat, the smoke trailing like a dark snake far in the rear, but never a ship was there to be seen, and not even a boat.

As they were gazing westwards Toddie noticed a fountain of white spray rise up out of the blue water, and presently another. She clapped her hands with delight.

"Oh," she cried, "it is a Johnnie whale!"

And the Johnnie whale came nearer and nearer till they could see his huge bulk rising and falling in the sea.

Soon after a merry shoal of porpoises passed close to the island. They were leaping out of the water, and even cooing in their joy. But Toddie's thoughts and sympathies were with that Johnnie whale.

"Oh," she said, as if the whale could hear her, "don't tome near the shole, Johnnie. Swim home, oo silly whale, oo mammy will die if she never sees oo any more."

The children walked all round the cliff edge. They found one other bay or harbour, but with the exception of this and the cove into which the little yacht had been so providentially thrown, the shores of this island presented to the waves a dark and impenetrable barrier. They explored the little harbour. There were the ashes of a fire that had long, long been extinguished, but no mark of a single footprint in the sand to show that any boat had been recently here. So they went slowly back to their yacht. The sea-birds screaming in myriads about them, and the wild rabbits here and there on the stone-covered sides of grey hillocks standing up on their hind legs and wonderingly looking at the little strangers. Indeed, the wildness of the sheep, and the few goats, and the exceeding tameness of the coneys and gulls, were proofs that the island was seldom visited.

For the time being our little heroes were undoubtedly monarchs of all they surveyed.

Dinner, however, was the first thing to be thought about. That discussed, the boys left Toddie and Tip to clear up while they started work.

"The first thing, Friday," said Crusoe, "is to build a fire on the hillock. There is a lot of brushwood, so come on."

They gathered plenty of stuff, and heaped it up, all ready to light after nightfall, or rather in the gloaming; for the nights were now short, and unless boats were actually sent out to look for them there would be small chance of the fire attracting much attention. And smoke seen during the day by any passing ship or vessel would only be considered the work of some shepherd or tourist.

There was more wood down in the little bay that they had explored, but a fire there would not be easily seen; besides, even if seen, sailors or fishermen would put it down to kelp-making.

There was quite a wealth of wild flowers here also, many that even Fred had never seen before, so they culled great bouquets and, brought them back with them to Toddie, who at once set about decorating the yacht. This work kept the child busy, and Tip too, who took intense interest in all his little mistress did.

"Suppose, Friday," said Crusoe, "we inspect stores?"

"Suppose, massa," said Friday, "we read a book instead?"

"No, no, Friday boy. No laziness. Get up the stores at once."

So Friday obeyed, and Crusoe carefully counted all the eatables.

"We have enough to last us for over a week," was Crusoe's summing up.

"Then we can fish."

"Oh, yes, Friday, I hadn't thought of that! Get the lines out, and we may catch some for supper."

There was one thing they were rather short of, namely, spirits for the stove; but they contrived a regular gipsy-fire of wood, with stones so arranged that they could place a saucepan over the glowing embers. Toddie brought her picture-books down to the rocks, and the boys began to fish.

Fishing is a dreamy kind of employment anyhow, so it is no wonder the time flew fast away.

"Oh, isn't all this jolly!" said Friday, as he pulled in his fifth grey mullet. "Now, massa, how nice it would be to stay here a month, if we could only catch a seagull and send it home with a message."

"That would be glorious. But see, Friday, the sun is nearly down. What lovely colours!"

"Now for supper," cried Frank

The fire was soon made, and the fish were roasted as Indians cook their fish, by attaching them to a sloping wood grating close to the dying embers.

"It is a supper worth being shipwrecked twenty times for," remarked Fred.

This sentiment was agreed to by his friend, and seconded by the little queen.

"Oh!" said her majesty, "Tip and I is twite full of joy and—and——"

"Grey mullet," said Fred, laughing. "Come, Tod, we're going to make this bonfire."

That was a blaze. Surely it could be seen a hundred miles away! What fun they had too, chasing or racing round the flames and through the smoke till Toddie looked like a gipsy's bairn, and Frank was black enough for any Friday.

Then they heaped more wood up with damp stuff to keep it alight.

They washed themselves at the rill, dried their faces with their handkerchiefs, then joined hands and went singing back to the boat.

Frank read aloud from Robinson Crusoe for quite an hour, then they said their prayers and turned in.

But on this night Fred and Frank slept under the sails on the sand, so that they might hear if any boat came, and Toddie and Tip had all the cabin.

"You won't feel lonely, will you, Tod?" said Fred last thing.

"No," said Toddie, "I've dot Tippetty you know, and I s'pose the Dood God isn't *vely* far away."

# CHAPTER XI
# "FRIENDS FOR LIFE"—
# ROUND THE CAMP FIRE

The next morning after breakfast Crusoe and Friday set to work in earnest. They very soon fashioned rude spades, and the tide being well back they commenced digging around the yacht. They dug and dug for hours. Then the Crusoe stood up to straighten out the "kinks from his backbone," as he himself phrased it. He scratched his head and smiled.

"Well, massa," said Friday, "you look very wise."

"We're a pair of fools though, Friday. Just listen, we're not doing a bit of good, we're only sinking the yacht lower, and as fast as we dig a canal down to the sea, as fast will the waves fill it up with sand."

Friday cried, "Hurrah! I am so glad!" Then he threw away his spade. Friday was not fond of work. You see, reader, theory is one thing, practice another.

They went away now to the hill again to rebuild the fire. It was quite out, and it was evident enough no one had seen it, or taken much notice of it at all events.

"I'm not sure, you know, that the fire will be of much use," said Fred, "but it is the correct thing to do, so we must do it for Toddie's sake. You and I, Frank, wouldn't mind this life for a month."

"Yes, for dear Toddie's sake, brother Fred."

There was something in the look that Frank gave his companion, more than in the words themselves, that went straight away to the heart of the fisher-boy, and on the impulse of the moment he stretched out his hand, and right heartily was it grasped.

"For life," said Frank.

"Yes," said Fred, "friends for life, Frank."

And so the strange compact was sealed.

A compact such as this men may smile at, but there is far more in the love that often exists 'twixt boy and boy, than many old heads could imagine or would be willing to believe.

As soon as dusk fell again the fire was once more lit, and once more the children danced and played in its rosy gleams, then, somewhat tired, though certainly not weary, they went home to read and talk around the camp fire, and then sleep again sealed the eyes of our shipwrecked mariners.

Another day and another went by just the same. The island seemed quite out of the course of steamboats, and fisher-boats never came near it.

But all through the glad sunlit hours they played at Crusoes, at pirates, and smugglers, and all sorts of children's heroes, and the day did not seem half long enough to contain all the jollity and joy that had to be crammed into it.

I'm not sure that the hour around the camp fire just before turning in was not the jolliest of all, for on board the little yacht they had all sorts of pleasant story books, and while Frank or Fred read aloud, the other two permitted their fancies to run riot in the pleasant land of imagination.

But why, they often wondered, did no boat answer their signal? It was kept up now even in the sunshine. It was as Fred reverently said, a pillar of cloud by day, and a pillar of fire by night.

Yet nevertheless they seemed forgotten of all the world.

But one evening, just at sunset, and before the night fire was lit, to their joy they saw a boat coming straight down under sail towards the island. It came near enough for them to see the fishermen's caps and faces.

They ran down to the cliff top, and the boys, took off their coats, shouting loudly.

Yes, they are heard; for look! there is a commotion in the boat, the sail shivers, the boat's way is all but stopped. Next minute, to the consternation of the children, and to their astonishment as well, round goes the mainsail boom, and away on another tack flies the boat.

The truth is, this little island was supposed to be haunted, and these superstitious fishermen, who had probably come from a far-off island, believed they had seen ghosts in daylight. The forms of Toddie, Fred, and Frank, on that dizzy cliff top, scaring the myriads of wild birds with their waving garments, appeared to their frightened imaginations as giants warning them away from the place.

When the children lit their fire that evening, they did not think of dancing round it, and hardly one of them spoke as they went slowly down to the beach again. Even Tippetty was dull, and lagged behind.

"Don't lead a stoly to-night, Flank," said Toddie. "I's so tired."

Then Fred took her on his knee and nursed her, and she soon fell fast asleep. Between the two of them they carried her on board, and put her to bed with Tip.

The boys turned in as usual under the sail on the sand; but about two o'clock, or half-past, just as the dawn was creeping gray over the sea, Fred awoke, and getting up went straight away to Toddie.

Tip looked up, and gave a little low coughing bark. He was afraid to bark aloud lest he should wake his charge. But poor Toddie never opened her eyes. Fred felt her hands and arms, which were tossing uneasily about. They were hot. He put his cheek to hers. It was burning.

Then the terrible truth flashed over his mind, Toddie was ill, and in a fever.

"Oh," he moaned, "what if no help comes, and she dies all alone on this island!"

He sat by her side now till seven o'clock. She only waked once and called for water.

She sat up in bed, but her eyes had a sparkle that Fred did not like.

"Are you ill, Toddie?"

"Oh, no; I'se not ill, oo know. Only dust feepy (sleepy); but, Fled, I didn't say my players. Will the Dood God be angry?"

There was a big lump in Fred's throat, and he did not dare to speak, only snuggled her up, and she slept once more.

All that day she lay like a wee dying bird, and it was indeed a long and a lonesome one to the boys. No more Crusoe now, no more Man Friday.

When sunset came again they went to the hill and lit the fire. Tip would not come. Like Toddie, he had eaten nothing all day; the spirit seemed clean gone out of him.

Neither Frank nor Fred could go to sleep to-night, so they brought the lamp down to the cabin and sat on the floor, whispering low when they talked at all, Fred holding Toddie's hot wee hand.

It almost broke the boys' hearts to hear the poor child raving in her delirium about her dolly-fish and the Johnnie whale, and calling for Daddy Pop.

"Oh, Frank!" said Fred at last, "Toddie's going to die to-night, I feel so sure, so sure!"

Then his head dropped on his friend's shoulder, and he fairly broke down and sobbed.

"Fred," said Frank, "you're generally the bravest of the two"—Frank took no note of his grammar to-night, poor lad—"but now I must take you in hand."

"Oh, Frank! but you don't know how much I love Toddie, no one can ever know; and if she dies, and I'm sure she will, I don't want ever to do anything again."

"I tell you, Fred, she won't die. Now don't be silly, Fred." Frank patted his friend, and soothed him as if he had been a baby. He really was a baby in heart at present, for the dear boy had had no sleep for so long a time, and sorrow weighs the eyelids down.

He was quiet at last, sobbed a little now and then, opened his hands once or twice very wide, clutched his right hand, and slept.

Then his friend lowered him gently to the deck, placed a jacket under his head, and gradually drew himself high enough up to watch Toddie.

Tip looked at him with his sad brown eyes. "Somebody has hurt my poor little mistress," he seemed to say; "can't you help her?"

It looked as if nothing could ever help Toddie again. Her breath came in gasps, and her eyes were only partially closed.

Suddenly it occurred to Frank that he had in the ship that little fever mixture his mother always made him take a teaspoonful of when ill. It was there in the cupboard, and he got it at once.

Tippetty watched him.

"I'm going to make your little mistress well, Tip."

Tip wagged his tail just once, as if he were not too sure about it.

Then Frank poured a little in a glass.

"Can you drink, dear?" he whispered, gently raising her head and shoulders.

The child opened her eyes, smiled faintly, and drank.

Then he lowered her back on the pillow.

"Oo is a dood daddy whale," she muttered, and closed her eyes in sleep once more.

A whole hour must have passed away—a long and weary one for the watcher. Frank had been holding Toddie's hand all the time.

"Flank! Flank!"

It was Toddie's voice, and she sat bolt upright on the sofa.

"Oh, Toddie, lie down, dear!"

"No, Flank, I's listenin'."

With her great glistening eyes, open to their widest extent, she quite terrified the boy.

"They is toming, Flank, they is toming! I's going home, Flank. Oh, I's going home!"

Frank was petrified with fear. He had never seen death, but something told him it must be like this. "listen, Flank; listen!"

Frank did listen now. Then he could distinctly hear a shout.

"Fred, Fred!" he cried, forgetting even Toddie in his excitement. "A boat, Fred! a boat! We're saved, and Toddie will live."

"Of tourse," said Toddie, "I's doin' to live. Listen adain."

They could now hear the sound of oars in rowlocks, and both the boys rushed overboard and down to the water's-edge, just as a cobble was beached.

Bunko jumped plash into the water and quickly drew the boat up, then Eean himself descended.

"My poor boys," he cried, "how you must have suffered! And Toddie, is she well?"

Fred would have spoken, but Frank grasped his arm. "She is just a little feverish, sir," he said.

"Look! look! she is coming," he cried now, and hurried back to the yacht.

Tippetty had jumped on to the sand, and Frank's sturdy young arms were just extended in time to save poor Toddie from falling after him.

Next minute she was at home in Daddy Pop's strong arms.

Bunko was standing on the beach in the morning dawn, leaning on his pole, and looking picturesque enough in his red coat against the dark gray of the rocks.

"It's no' very sodger-like to greet (cry)," he said, hiding his eyes with his raised arms; "but—forgive me, my friends, I canna really help it."

A great red ball of a sun was rising through the summer morning's haze, and throwing its crimson over the sea as Eean's boat, the *Treasure-trove*, stole silently away from the Crusoe isle, with both the cobble and the yacht in tow. Bunko was in the cobble with his pole, and it took him all his time to prevent the two crafts from colliding.

But a westerly wind sprang up, and by one o'clock all were safe in Methlin Bay.

The children and their little yacht had long, long been given up for lost; only somehow hope remained in Eean's breast. He had therefore cruised about for nearly a week, and at last chanced to fall in with the very boat our heroes had seen approaching the haunted island.

They told him a strange and garbled story about gigantic spirits having been seen dancing in smoke, and Eean had at once come to the conclusion that the giants might be the dear children he was in search for.

Immediately after the arrival of the *Treasure-trove* in the bay, poor wee Toddie was handed over to Eppie's tender care, and Bunko was dispatched for the doctor. But nevertheless I feel quite sure it was owing more to Mammy Mop's tender nursing than to this doctor's physic, that Toddie at the end of two weeks was enabled once again to join Fred and Frank in their rambles.

It is needless to say that Mrs. Fielding had been half wild about her boy. It is almost needless to add that she spoke of depriving the boys of their yacht. But Eean got her to listen to reason at last.

"It was all an accident," he argued. "The lads could not have behaved more heroically, or shown themselves better sailors, and she ought to be proud of her boy."

"Indeed, Mrs. Fielding," said Eean in conclusion, and talking almost bitterly, "Frank would be a man if you would only permit him to be so."

So, much to their joy, the boys were allowed to go yachting and fishing again, and playing at pirates too, and once more Tippetty took his old seat at the bows where he could best bark at the sea gulls, and once more Toddie bravely took the tiller.

# CHAPTER XII
# THAT AWFUL NIGHT AT SEA—A
# RIDE FOR PRECIOUS LIFE

During this long summer holiday Fred made quite a sailor of his friend Frank, that is as far as anyone could, for the lad was not entirely cut out for a seafarer.

In return for this instruction in seamanship Frank taught Fred to ride, and riding was really an accomplishment of Frank's. It takes a plucky boy too to acquire the art of horsemanship with a Shetland pony, especially when, as Frank insisted, the learner had first to practise bare-back.

"You'll never get the grip with your knees else," he told him rightly enough; but this daft wee horse was probably just as difficult to ride before you knew his tricks and his manners as any to be met with in all Scotland.

However, Fred was declared master after a time, and then the pony became far more serious and manageable.

But this delightful holiday came to an end at last, and once more Mrs. Fielding took her lad south to a fresh school she had heard such good accounts of.

"Poor Frank!" said Eean, when he heard of it.

Some people would have condemned the fisherman bard's plan of training Fred. I myself do not think it was wrong. He was certainly kept strictly to school, and his lessons were superintended by Eean himself at night; but then he had unbounded exercise, and he was also taught to work. Before he was fourteen years of age he was a fairly good carpenter, and could help to make a cask, while he knew all the mysteries of fish-curing.

Then he had his hobbies, namely, his music and his aquarium, and he had his amusements as well. The wild woods were his home, and on the sea he felt as safe as in his own bed in the fisherman's cottage.

Fisher folks are a very humble and unambitious people; but I really know no other class so innocent in their mode of life and manners. If

Christianity flourishes anywhere in Scotland, it is in the obscure villages of honest fisher people.

Very superstitious they are, however; but surely there is no harm in this.

Kindly they are too, and clannish, hardly caring to mix much, far less intermarry, with the peasantry that dwell around them, and when grief falls upon one house it seems to fall on all. A wedding causes happiness and merriment to the whole of a fisher community, and a death, especially by drowning, brings grief to every cot.

Although Eppie was not by any means very old, she was looked up to as the matron of the village—a veritable mother in Israel. She was supposed to know far more of medicine than the old doctor who used to put in an appearance about once a week riding on a wonderful old white pony. When I tell you what this pony did one day, you will, I think, admit he was entitled to be called "wonderful."

Frank, on his Shetland, overtook the old doctor in a wood, and touching his hat to his grey hairs, immediately commenced a conversation.

"That's been a nice pony of yours, sir, in its day."

"Humph!" said the medicine man, "I daresay you think both he and I are out of the hunt, eh?"

"Oh, no, sir! But I say, sir, this is a nice bit of road, isn't it?"

The doctor laughed.

"I do like a cheeky boy," he said; "but see if I don't accept your challenge. From the first milestone to the next, then.

"Now here's the milestone; are you all ready?"

"All ready, sir."

"Gee—ee—up, then!"

And away they went.

For the first half mile Frank was far ahead. So confident of victory was he that he took off his bonnet and waved it back at the doctor.

But before he was aware a streak of lightning seemed to be coming up behind, and Frank had to fly. Hand over hand the doctor came on; it was soon neck and neck; and after this poor Frank was nowhere in the running.

But Eppie was an herbalist; no witch, however. She did not gather her simples at midnight on the moor under the light of the moon, nor utter incantations over them. No; she used to walk out in broad daylight knitting her stocking, with Toddie and Tip coming up behind her, each carrying a basket.

As she passed through the village on her return she would call at many a little cot, and she had a welcome wherever she went. The old women would get up and dust a chair for her, and the toddling bairnies would run laughing to meet her. And honest Eppie never came away without getting a blessing, and leaving one too. She would leave something else as well for the sick; namely, a bunch of roots or fresh green leaves, with instructions how to brew a decoction therefrom.

"These reets [roots] are, may be, no vera bonnie," Eppie would say, "but they're the best things for the bluid you ever saw or heard tell o'."

Eppie was as good as an elder among some of the sick people, and she had a way with her of administering spiritual advice that never gave offence. How prettily she could tell a Bible story, or describe in, simple language the plan of salvation, those who heard her speak in her own broad East of Scotland Scotch—for she was not a native of this wild west village—may remember to this day.

Eean never visited; he was naturally shy but he conducted service in his cave every Sunday evening all the year round.

On calm summer evenings boats containing stranger tourists would sometimes stop beneath the cliffs, and greatly would these holiday-keepers marvel to hear the sweet sad strains of "Martyrdom" or "London New," coming whence they could not tell, for no one was visible on the cliff or about it, and the ports of the cave were not easy to distinguish.

The village of Methlin was a very small one from a fisherman's point of view; but though the boats were few, they were manned by hearts as brave as ever dared to face the stormy ocean. Nor were the fishermen idlers or laggards. They did not depend on the herring season for a living—they found fish all the year round if it were possible to go out; then there were always lobsters and crabs to be caught in the cage or creel. The haddocks were smoked, and cod were salted. There was a town about twenty miles from the village, and here there was a ready market for all the produce of this industrious people. Instead of loitering about the street corners on days when fishing was an impossibility, the men found plenty to do in their gardens, which were kept in great perfection, or on their little crofts of an acre or two each in extent.

If ever a stray tourist or strolling artist came to Methlin, he was at once struck by the beauty of the gardens and the quaintness of the cottages.

On the whole I am rather proud of my wee village, and do not hesitate to say it was unique, and of its kind quite idylic.

Next to Eean and Eppie, I'm not quite sure that honest Bunko did not rank as the greatest favourite after the adventure I am now going to describe.

I should state, to begin with, that Scottish fishing boats are not like those used, say, at Yarmouth and in England generally; these latter are decked over, and therefore fit to stop a week at sea; the Scotch are open all amidships, and, though very strong and high in the free-board, would quickly fill and perish in a sea-way with a strong gale blowing.

But the hardy Scot, like the Viking of old, takes his life in his hand, and boldly ventures far to sea in these boats; yet, woe is me! never a season passes that widows and children are not left to weep and mourn for dear husbands and fathers they ne'er will see again in this world beneath.

It was in the autumn time, when the corn in the fields was ripening yellow, when the leaves on the birchen trees were growing darker and darker, and when almost every bird save the robin and skite had ceased to sing, that there came a boat into Methlin Bay reporting fish to be found in immense shoals a goodly way to the nor'ard and west. On board this boat was a wealth of silvery herrings, amply proving the truth of the boat-owner's words. He had called here to give the villagers a friendly hint.

What hurry, commotion, and excitement there were now! The men, women, and even the tiniest children were busy for a time; but soon this passed away, and there fell over the village that strange hush that only the women of wigwams in the Indian districts of America west, when their braves have gone on the warpath, know, or the wives of Scottish fisher-folk, when their husbands are hurried away to sea.

Eean had gone with the rest, and with him both Fred and Toddie, for the latter would not be denied.

The weather was to all appearance most propitious for deep-sea fishing, and everyone was cheerful and merry. "Why, Toddie, you coming with us!" said Eean's best hand. "Why we'll have luck, my little lass!"

As Eean rolled his wee girl in a pea-jacket, and set her near him at the helm, he could not help crooning to himself some verses from Longfellow's "Wreck of the *Hesperus*."

> "It was the schooner *Hesperus*,
>   hat sailed the wintry sea;
> And the skipper had taken his little daughter,
>   To bear him company.

"Blue were her eyes as the fairy flax,
　　Her cheeks like the dawn of day,
And her bosom white as the hawthorn buds,
　　That ope in the month of May."

Away went the boats. The women and children watched them from the cliff-top till a gathering haze swallowed them up, then went somewhat sadly back to their homes. "I dinna like the looks of the weather," said a fisherman's wife that evening after sunset. "The moon has an unco' queer look about it, and there are clouds rising in the east that'll soon chase ilke starn [star] out o' the lift."

"Hush, Jemmie, hush!" said Eppie, heaping more peat and wood on the fire. "Our men have been mercifully preserved on mony a stormy nicht, and I've little fear of them noo, even should the wind blaw ower the hills in hurricanes."

About ten o'clock that night Eppie was dosing in her chair, for her day's work had been hard, when an anxious knocking was heard at the door, and she speedily got up and drew aside the bolt, admitting three neighbours.

"Oh, woman, woman!" they cried, "hear at the wind, and Johnnie Stevens' glass is doon, doon, doon! It'll be the wildest nicht at sea that ever a boat was oot in."

"Sit down by the fire," said Eppie. "I've been listenin' to the wind. It's no a cheery sound; but oh, women, do you no ken that the Lord can hold the sea in the hollow of his han'?"

But I fear Eppie was trying to impart to her neighbours a comfort she herself was very far indeed from possessing. No one thought of bed or rest that night. Nor could the wives who had gathered around Eppie's blazing hearth sit long in one place. They must keep pacing about, often going anxiously to peer out into the darkness, shuddering and shivering as they heard the wild howl of the tempest and the rattle of hail and sleet on the window panes. The kindly-hearted Eppie kept them talking as much as possible, and she herself seemed no whit affected, though in reality her heart was a heavy one indeed. But there were, in spite of all she could do, spells of silence, broken only by the wail and "howther" of the wind, and the sobs of those grief-stricken women.

It must have been well on towards morning when every eye was turned towards the door, for the "sneck was tirled"; and next moment the outer door was opened.

Who was coming?

Every heart beat quick with anxiety. Then the inner door was thrown wide, and in stalked Bunko, red coat on and pole in hand.

His bonnet was pulled down over his ears, and his face was rain-battered and red. He looked indeed an uncouth figure.

"He is a good man," said Bunko, "and bringeth good tidings."

"Oh, may the Lord love you for they words!" cried one of the women; "but speak, Bunko, speak!"

"It's like this," said the half-witted lad. "There is hope yet, ye mustna let down your hearts. I've just come back from the harbour, and ae [one] boat has just come in."

"Oh, bless you, Bunko! Who's boat is it?"

"None o' your men."

The women wrung their hands.

"It's Will Scroggie's boat. Will had a mis-shanter, and bore up afore the brunt o' the storm cam' on. But the boat is sadly tashed. And a' the rest are blown oot to sea."

"Oh, Bunko, Bunko! is that a' the comfort ye have to gie?"

"Wheesht, women. Hold your din till I tell ye."

"When I returned sair for-fochten" (sorely over-powered), "I found the public-hoose open, and in I gaed to taste a drap for my stomach's sake. And wha saw I sittin' there by the fire but Sandie Grigg just returned from the sea. He'd heard the awfu' news, and was condolin' wi' me about it, when up he sprang frae his stool. I have it, I have it," he cried.

"Hae ye ta'en leave o' your seven sinses?" said I.

"Na, na, Bunko," said Sandie, "and if you can ride you may save every boat."

"I can ride anywhaur, or do onything to save but ane o' those bonnie boats," I cried.

"Well," he said, "it's twenty miles and a bittock to the town of D— — whaur I came from the day. The gunboat *Sandpiper* is there. She sails at seven sharp. You may catch her. Rin, Bunko, rin, and tell the women folks, and I'll hae Jock Leggie's brown mare at Eppie's door in a hand clap."

Even as Bunko spoke there came the sound of hoofs on the stones outside.

"Quick, Eppie, quick!" cried Bunko, dashing his plaid and pole on the floor, "give me a drink o' milk. That's it. Noo tak care o' Keelie. Keelie, lie down, sir, till I come back."

Eppie thrust a bannock in his pocket. Bunko pulled his cap down still farther over his brow, and hardly waiting to hear the prayers and blessings the poor women hurled after him, though he fain would have waited, he pulled the door open and dashed out.

"You've three hours, but its deed against the storm you'll ride."

"I'll do it or die," cried Bunko.

And away towards the woods he flew, hardly visible in the hurricane mist that obscured the dawn of this awful day.

He hurried on, but aye as the gusts gathered extra force he waited for the lull, then once more struck his heels against the sides of his willing steed.

Poor honest Bunko, he was Scotch to the back bone; and as he tore along he kept up his courage with verses from the Bible, and snatches from the poems of Burns.

"Go on, good mare!" he cried. "It's life or death, my lassie! Clothe your neck wi' thunder, as Job says, and rejoice in your strength.

"'But sich a nicht he took the road in
As ne'er poor sinner was abroad in.
The wind blew as 'twould blawn its last,
The rattlin' hail roared on the blast.
Near and more near the thunders roll,
The lightnings flashed from pole to pole.'"

At long last he is near the town, in sight even of the harbour. He can even see the white steam and the smoke of the *Sandpiper*. Her commander was one of those daring men whom no wind off a shore would keep in harbour if he once made up his mind to sail.

Nearer and nearer comes Bunko; but, alas! the mare's strength gives out, she staggers and falls. Bunko is on his feet in a moment, and flying by himself now towards the harbour steps.

The last boat has just returned.

The gunboat is already in motion.

But these boatmen knew not Bunko; and his red-coated figure, bareheaded, and with face streaming with blood, was startling enough, no doubt.

They positively refused to take him off.

"But," cried Bunko wildly, "it's to save precious life, I tell you! I'll give you one hundred pounds to take me!"

"In you jump then, lad. Shove off, men. Give way with a will. We'll hardly catch her."

But Bunko tore off his red coat and waved it wildly in the air, and next minute the good ship stopped.

The commander heard all Bunko had to say, and loudly praised his gallantry. "I'll save your friends, boy, never fear, if they are still afloat."

So back to the shore Bunko was rowed.

The poor mare was on the top of the steps, but she would need a long rest before she could take the road again. And Bunko himself felt the need of rest; so, leading his mare, he betook himself to the nearest inn.

Meanwhile Captain Heydon, of the saucy *Sandpiper*, lost no time in steaming away in search of the missing boats.

He came up with the distressed fleet about four in the afternoon, and barely in time to save the lives of those poor struggling fellows. Not a boat had as yet sunk, but they were filling fast; while the crews were completely exhausted, and had given way entirely to despair.

The faint cheer they gave, when they noticed the brave little war-ship bearing down to their assistance, could scarce be heard amid the howling of the storm.

Boat after boat was emptied of its crew, old Eean, Toddie, and Fred being among the first to be hauled over the side.

Weak as she was, Toddie resolutely refused to be taken on board the gunboat, till she had seen her pet Tippetty in safety.

The half-drowned men were at once seen to by the kindly sailors, and were soon in warm hammocks or sitting around the galley fire.

The boats as well as their crews were taken in charge, but several were stove and sank; so that when at last the *Sandpiper* steamed into Methlin port only four remained afloat.

It was late when they got in, and the first intimation of the safety of husband, brother, or sweetheart received was from the men themselves.

But oh, what joy was there! Some might have been seen dancing, others laughing and weeping by turns, while others knelt by their humble firesides and prayed aloud. It was an affecting scene.

But scenes like these, and many far more sad, are to be witnessed only too often on the wild Scottish coasts.

Concerning this very adventure, Thorn, the sweet bard of Ury, writes in graphic language—

"Man dies but once? O, say it not!
　　He lives again to die,
When the surly surly sea has taught
　　The hope-dissolving sigh,
When the stubborn arm, that strains for life,
　　Falls feebly on the oar;
When the loved last look of child and wife
Swims wildly o'er the settling strife,
　　O Death, what canst thou more!"

Just a closing word or two about the chief hero of the episode, poor Bunko. He did not return till next morning, and it is needless to say the welcome he received was a warm one.

He had taken plenty of time to ride back; but just before mounting his mare, the boatmen who had rowed him off came up to demand their fare.

One of them was rather rude.

"You're the village fool, arena' ye?"

"You're no over civil to say so, man," returned Bunko.

"Weel never min', we want that hundred pounds ye promised us."

"Ha! ha! ha!" laughed Bunko, turning to the landlord. "They took a fool's word for a hunner poun's, ha! ha! ha! Wha's the fool now?"

Then he jumped into the saddle.

"Come ower to Methlin," he shouted as he cantered out of the yard, "and you'll have a rattling good dram, and be thankfu'. Ta! Ta!"

And with this promised hospitality in lieu of fare the discomfited boatmen were fain to be content.

# CHAPTER XIII
# "A STRANGE, STRANGE STORY," SAID FRANK. "I WONDER HOW IT WILL ALL END"

The loss of nets and boats had been a severe blow to the honest folks of Methlin.

Gladly would Eean have made good his neighbours' losses; but, alas! he was poor. Sitting in his cave one evening, however, composing a poem on the recent disaster for a well-known American magazine that knew the fisherman bard's worth, he was looking around him at his picture-hung walls.

"Why not," he thought, "dispose of a few of these, and head a subscription with the funds thus raised?"

It was an intention that did him infinite credit, for he dearly loved those strange scenes; they were in reality the painted history of his life.

"Well, go they must," he said. "It is in a good cause."

As he was placing five of them on his table he heard footsteps on the stone stairs, and immediately after the white-haired old doctor entered.

"Good morning, poet," he said. "Versifying, eh? Well, there is five yellow boys towards a subscription for boats and nets for your poor people. If I were rich I'd give you more. No, I won't have thanks. I'll run away if you begin. But what are you bundling up those quaint and curious pictures for? Ah! good Eean, I see it in those shy eyes of yours. Nay, nay, you cannot deceive a doctor. But I tell you what, you shan't make the sacrifice."

"I must, and will."

"You shan't. Look here, I know a trick worth two of that. Have an exhibition of all the lot in Edinburgh. There is a character about them, and when people know it is for a good cause they will flock to it.

"Do it, man, do it," added the doctor emphatically.

And Eean took his advice. The newspapers took the affair up, and in a month Eean had raised nearly £700.

Bonfires blazed on every hill on the night Eean, the bard, brought back his pictures, and a huge bonfire in the village square as well.

On the Sunday after, every man, woman, and child marched in a body to the parish church to return thanks to Heaven for all His mercies sent them, the old minister preaching a special sermon for the occasion.

Frank was there along with Fred, and so was little Toddie and Tip. Oh, yes, Tip went! He refused to stay at home.

But the most noticeable figure of all was Bunko in a bran-new scarlet coat and Highland bonnet with which the villagers had presented him. Keelie marched solemnly beside him, and lay at his feet in the kirk till the blessing was said. For remember Keelie was a Scottish collie, and therefore knew what was required of him on the Sabbath-day.

Nearly three years passed away.

This does not seem a long period of time to the grown-up or the aged, so at the end of it there was very little difference indeed in either Eppie or Eean; but Toddie had stretched up, as the good people of Methlin said. She was nearly ten—quite old she thought herself—and she had grown less round-faced, more delicate in features, very much longer in the hair, and had lost her pretty prattle, that is, she could talk better English. Oh, dear reader, I do assure you I would rather have had her always the wee, droll, lisping Toddie! but my heroine and my heroes will shoot up and grow in spite of me. There is Fred and Frank for instance, fourteen or fifteen years of age respectively, quite men almost. Well, so they thought anyhow. And, without complimenting them in any way, two sturdier, brisker, or bolder-looking lads you would hardly meet in a long day's march.

"What do you think, Fred," said Frank one day, "mamma wants me to be?"

"Couldn't guess," said Fred. "Not a minister."

"Fred, don't be foolish. I'm not good enough for that."

"I know you're not. I was only joking. Well, a lawyer; but then you're hardly bad enough for that."

"Just what I told dear mamma. She is so foolish you know. But I'm to be a barrister; so I suppose I'll have to enter some old mildewed office in London, with a red-faced, white-haired solicitor as my slave-driver, and never see the sun shining except through the cobwebs. Then I'll have to work my way to the bar; but oh, Fred, just imagine me with a flappy old black gown and a stiff white wig on! But I'm going to another good school first, and then to Oxford, so a lot of things may happen before I'm called to the bar. Oh, I hate the very idea!"

Toddie was feeding her blennies in the aquarium while this conversation went on, and the boys were lying on the floor of the cave near by.

What a happy three years that had been though! How many delightful sails they had had in the yacht, musical evenings in the poet's cave, and tea with stories to follow in the inside of their dear old Johnnie whale.

On this particular day, as soon as Toddie had fed her dolly-fish, they all went together to spend the afternoon in the igloo.

The little garden never looked more gay nor lovely, the cosy wee room had never looked brighter or cosier, and yet both Toddie and Fred were sad; for on the morrow Fred was going far away to Glasgow, to spend five months at a school previous to passing his examinations as a midshipman in the merchant service.

He might have gone as an apprentice, but Eean greatly loved the lad. He had given him the education of a gentleman, and wished to hurry him on; for after all, in the race of life at sea, the middie has fewer hurdles to leap than the apprentice. And Eean well knew what a sailor's life really meant, and how wild and rough it was in the forecastle. Tippetty wouldn't keep out of his mistress's lap to-night. He seemed to know there was grief of some kind afloat in the air.

"You'll come often and see Toddie, won't you, Frank?"

"Oh, Frank," said Toddie innocently, "I can't live if you don't."

Frank patted her hand, and as he did so Tippetty took the opportunity of licking both their hands at one and the same time.

Then Bunko came in to lay the tea, and by-and-by Daddy Pop himself arrived, and Mammy Mop too, and there were story telling and singing, so that the night did not pass so sadly after all.

The tide was a long way back at nine o'clock, so they all went home to Eean's cottage across the sands, and there Frank stopped all the night.

Three months passed away and it was winter, a hard and frosty one too; for weeks and weeks the ground was like adamant, and the rocks were masses of crystal. Peat became scarce in the village, and much driftwood and logs of pine were burned.

The yuletide came round, and Fred came home for a few days' holiday.

"We maun keep good fires on while you're here," said Bunko one day in the wood shed. "Here's a log noo," he said, "that'll mak' a fine lowe (blaze)."

It was a piece of a spar or ship's mast. As he spoke Bunko pulled it down and commenced to saw it through the centre. When half-way through the tool struck on something hard, and Bunko took a big axe and finished the work the saw had begun.

To his utter astonishment and that of Fred there rolled out a handful of gold coins, and the head of a rusty axe.

"Oh!" cried Fred, "that is the log dear Toddie came ashore on. Daddy would never have it touched, but he couldn't have known of the coins. I'll run and fetch him."

"Leave me, lads, for a few minutes," were the first words old Eean spoke when he entered the shed. Then he sat down on the wood pile. Scarcely could he have stood just then had he tried. His feelings were not altogether those of excitement, though he was much moved. Something told him that the mystery of the little waif Toddie was to be revealed to him. The gold that had fallen from the log he felt sure was but a portion of the store therein, and he felt certain also that he would find papers of some kind relating to the child who had so woven herself round his heart, that to tear her away would be an affliction he could not survive. He tried to pray—this was ever his solace in life; but how hard it was just then to say from the heart those words, "Thy will be done."

Now he nerves himself to action.

Why, he wonders as he proceeds to examine the log, did he not think of doing so at the very first, when it was washed in from the wreck supporting its little burden, that but for his wife's skill in bringing back the apparently-drowned to life would now be slumbering in the quiet kirk-yard?

The axeheads in the old log had not only served as a keel, he soon found, but also to keep in position a piece of wood supporting a long belt of canvas. It was this latter Eean now hauled hastily forth, though with trembling hands. It was damp and decayed, and the gold coins—Portuguese they were, he could see at a glance—that rolled out lay unheeded on the ground, while he quickly unfolded a piece of paper that had lain among them.

It was written in Spanish, a language with which he was well acquainted. Before he began to read it a strong wave of temptation passed through his mind, but was bravely resisted. "Why," whispered the tempter, "not burn the letter before reading it? It could but tell the child's history, and he would have in conscience and honour to give his darling up."

Eean had need of a strong will at that moment, the will that in times of trial like this can boldly say, "Get thee behind me, Satan."

He muttered a word or two of prayer once more, then reseating himself on the wood proceeded to read the document.

It was very much frayed, and the writing in part obliterated. Evidently it had been written during the agony of the brief time between the striking of the ship against the rocks, and her heeling back and sinking.

All the portion that has connection with our story may be briefly told. The vessel was the *Santa Maria*, homeward bound from the West Indies. The mother of the child had died, and been buried at sea. The crew had mutinied, partially robbed the ship, and left in boats, all but a devoted few. Hence the mismanagement and the running on a lee-shore. The child's only living relative was or "would soon be"—so ran this strange epistle, written in the hour of death—"her uncle— —" only decipherable word.

"If— —" here was a blank, "is spared by the waves, may heaven be good to those who are good,— —" a blank again, and the letter went but little further, only a word here and there being readable, these were, "uncle— — villain— —malediction— —."

The signature itself was frayed out, no letters of it remaining except four, "*PINT*."

The gold in all, which for the time being Eean left lying where it was, hardly amounted, as far as he could judge, to £150 sterling.

"Gold!" he said, actually spurning it with his foot. "What is gold to the love and companionship of my little girl? My own now, it is evident."

Then he shuddered as he thought how nearly he had yielded to temptation, and done that which would have made him miserable for life.

His wife and he had a long talk that evening over the fire, and next day the fisherman bard started for Edinburgh. It was evident to all the villagers—from whom he kept nothing back—that he was going to consult his advocate, and the look of contentment on his face when he returned two days later showed plainly enough that his interview had been of the most successful character.

Nor had he returned alone, and Toddie and Tip were both wild with joy when, from the spring-cart that had brought them all the way from the nearest big town, not only the poet himself, but the two boys descended. Eean had met Frank by accident in Edinburgh. It was getting near Christmastime, so the lad was as usual on holiday. Both ran through to Glasgow to see Fred, and at Frank's intercession he was permitted to accompany daddy and his friend back to Methlin.

The group around the fisherman bard's fire that night was an interesting one. Just as on that summer's evening long ago when Frank had first entered this humble cot, Eean sat in his tall chair, Eppie was there at the everlasting wheel, Toddie, Fred, and Frank, and even Bunko, were here too, while side by side on the earth lay Bunko's dog Keelie and honest little Tippetty.

Bunko replenished the fire with peats and wood, till the little oil-lamp that hung in the corner seemed sadly superfluous; the bright red gleams lit up the cosy old-world room, made every face seem doubly happy, and were reflected even from the dark, smoke-varnished rafters overhead.

To-night Eean told Toddie's story all over again, much to Frank's delight.

Toddie herself took an interest in it now, and that is what she had never, never done before.

"Weel," said Bunko, "you're a good man, Mr. Arundel, and I'll niver but believe it was an angel o' the Lord that put the saw in my hand, and made me cut up Toddie's log."

Frank had taken Toddie's hand as Bunko spoke, and he still retained it as he said, "But what a strange, mysterious story! It is just like what we read of in books. And, Toddie, there is no saying what you may turn out to be, you know, when the mystery gets all cleared up. Perhaps some Spanish princess, and a chariot and six white horses, all caparisoned with blue and gold, may come some day to take you off."

Toddie drew away her hand, and nestled her head against her Daddy Pop.

"I would not leave you, daddy," she said, "if they did come."

"What would you do, then?" said Frank, laughing.

"Oh, send Bunko away instead!"

"Well, anyhow," said Frank, after gazing thoughtfully at the fire a few moments, "it is a strange strange story. I wonder how it will all end."

# CHAPTER XIV
## "DUTY, LAD, DUTY. STICK TO IT THROUGH THICK AND THIN"

This is a world of changes. There is nothing certain in it save death itself. Yes, it is a world of changes, and the sooner in youth one finds this out the better. The richest and the greatest men on earth would be fools were they to say to themselves, "Here we stand, and we shall never be moved." For all things pass away, and very often those we value the most are the first to vanish.

No one could have wished to see a happier, more hopeful face than that of Frank Fielding, as he turned about for the seventh or eighth time to wave an adieu to Fred and Toddie, standing yonder at the door of the old-fashioned whitewashed cottage.

Frank was going home to spend his Christmas at Benshee House; and a right happy and merry Christmas everyone connected with the house had determined it should be. Mr. Fielding himself, who had gone to London on most important business, would be down in time to partake of the festivities, so he had written. Nor was he coming alone. At least a dozen of his own and Mrs. Fielding's friends would come with him to spend the holy week, in a not over-holy way perhaps. So extra servants had been hired, and even an extra cook, "a *chef*," he called himself; and all throughout the parish, for a fortnight before this, nothing had been talked about except the great doings that were to take place at Benshee House.

The one and only drawback to Frank's happiness was, that his friends Fred and Toddie would not, or could not, be there.

This was no fault of Frank's, it may easily be believed. He had mentioned his wish to have them with him to his mother.

For once in a way she was haughtily obstinate.

"I can't help saying, Frank, I am just a little surprised at what you ask. There are very many and very weighty reasons why those poor children——"

Frank stuck his fingers resolutely in his ears till his mother ceased talking.

It was a rude thing to do; perhaps it was even unkind; but—well, he really could not help it.

He solaced himself, however, with the thought that nothing should prevent him riding over on his pony and spending an evening with them, as soon as he could leave his aristocratic friends at Benshee House.

Now, except in large towns, Christmas is not a day of great rejoicing in Scotland. But at the fisherman's cottage it was always kept, though in a very quiet way. So while mistletoe and evergreen hung in the halls of Benshee, and mirth and music were the order of the evening, Eean, with his family and a few humble guests, surrounded a table in the best room of the little cot, spread with such a variety of good things, and such a weight of good things as well, that in the brief intervals of conversation it was positively heard to creak and groan.

Nor were evergreens wanting as decorations; and it had taken Fred and Toddie a whole day to put these up after Bunko had brought them home with him from the snowy woods.

Such a splendid fire burned in the grate too as quite set cold at defiance, and crackled and roared so pleasantly, that neither the wind which howled around the chimney, nor the boom of breakers on the beach, could be heard.

There was mirth in the kitchen as well as in the best room. Bunko was there in fine form, and many of the humbler among the fisher folks, both old and young. And if Tippetty occupied a proud position to-night on the parlour hearth-rug—one-half of him on the footstool, the other half off—Keelie the collie was not a whit less snug at the other end of the house, and had quite as many bones and tit-bits placed at his disposal.

But by ten o'clock quiet once more reigned in Eean's cottage home, for guests had gone, and prayers were being said.

Seldom a night passed throughout the year, that the fisherman bard did not go out to have a look at the weather and the sea just before turning in. It must have been fully half-past eleven on this Christmas night when he opened the door and walked out into the darkness.

Darkness did I say? Well, dark enough it ought to have been, for there were neither stars nor moon, and while a wild east wind came roaring through the woods, the clouds hung close above them. But darkness, no. He noticed as soon as he shut the door a strange glitter on the white walls of the cottages, and on rounding the corner of his own house perceived, to his astonishment and consternation, that the whole of the eastern sky was illuminated by gleams of flames, and that banks of white rolling smoke obscured the sky.

His first thought was that the forest must be all on fire, and that the conflagration was rolling towards them. But this was unlikely, for the trees were green, snow-laden pines.

He was presently joined by Bunko, who was coming towards the cottage.

"Oh, sir!" cried the half-witted lad, "it's on our bended knees we should a' be this awfu' nicht. The day o' judgment's fast approachin', sir."

"Nonsense, Bunko. But we must find out where the fire is at once; for if it be in the woods we must cut down trees to make a gap, else it will sweep our village off the earth, Bunko."

Running in hurriedly for his plaid and crook, and to tell Eppie what he intended to do, he presently rejoined Bunko.

"Now, Bunko," he said, "you can guide us to the top of Ben Maroo; a mile will take us there, and we will then find out where the conflagration is."

The two were joined by at least half a dozen of the neighbours, to say nothing of Keelie.

Keelie and Bunko went first, straight away into the darkling forest, and straight away through it too, for no better woodsman lived than Bunko, assisted by his dog.

It was rough walking here; but when the little party once more emerged from the shadow of the trees, and commenced to ascend the mountain, it was rougher still.

They struggled up the west side, and after a climb of fully half an hour they found themselves nearly at the top, then they crossed right round above a yawning precipice to the east side.

All in a moment, as it were, they were confronted with the full glare of the terrible conflagration.

Benshee House was sheeted in flames!

This ancient seat was one of those fine old mansions still to be found in the less wild portions of the Scottish Highlands. Though I call it mansion, it really was more of a castle than anything else. It had been the seat of many a lord and laird in by-gone feudal times, and had more than once probably even stood a siege, or at least red-handed war must have raged on its ramparts and around its moats.

The largest portion, however, was unoccupied, a modern-looking wing or two alone being retained as the residence of the Fieldings.

The fire had doubtless broken out here, but by the time Eean and his party reached the mountain brow, this portion was already roofless and gutted, and the flames had full possession of the main block itself.

Flames were issuing from every port and window thereof, and the turrets and towers were but shapes in the centre of gleaming tongues of fire and clouds of rolling smoke. Far over the woods to the westward flew the sparks as thick as the flakes in a snow shower.

The burning of Benshee House will be remembered by many who read these lines, as one of the grandest but most awful sights ever witnessed in the western Highlands.

Eean and his neighbours stood for hours on that bleak hill-top, regardless of the bitter wind that raged around them. Indeed they seemed spell-bound.

Then slowly home through the heather and the forest they returned to their peaceful village by the sea.

But news of even sadder import spread through the country within the next two or three days.

At the very last moment Mr. Fielding's friends had to start from London without him. He hoped, he said, to return next day.

Alas! next day saw poor Fielding lying dead in his town house.

On that very Christmas night, while his Scottish home was being consumed by fire, he was closeted with his solicitors.

A very great city commercial failure had taken place the day before, and Fielding was a ruined man; nay, it was even more than ordinary ruin, he was poorer that dread night than some of the beggars who shivered on the Thames embankment.

When his servant went to call him in the morning he found that master had never been to bed.

Yonder he sat in the arm-chair near the fire, apparently asleep.

There was nothing in the grate but cold white ashes, and — — master would soon be ashes too. He was dead and stiff.

It is well to pass over the events that occurred immediately after the burning of Benshee, and the death of Fielding. Some things are best not told. But even did I desire to describe the grief of poor Frank, and that of his proud—all too proud—mother, words would fail me.

Suffice it to say that both she and he must now depend, for a time at all events, on the charity of friends and relations. And oh, charity is a cold, cold thing at best, but doled out begrudgingly by the hands of uncles, aunts, or cousins, it is colder and more bitter than poison itself.

Financial ruin, death and fire, and all to happen within forty-eight hours! Am I not right in saying it is a world of change and a world of grief?

One day in spring a sturdy boy, in dusty garments and stick in hand, knocked at the door of the fisherman's cottage.

It was Toddie herself who opened it.

The stranger was Frank, but so changed she hardly knew him.

But she dragged him in, and seated him by the fire, as in the dear old days, and sat down on a stool beside him.

Tip, the dachshund, was rejoiced to see the boy again, and made frantic efforts to jump on his knee. But, alas! he was far too long for that, so he had to content himself with licking Frank's hand, then resting his brown-tan cheek lovingly against it.

When Toddie saw this, something seemed to come over her all at once, and she burst into tears.

Frank was doing his best to console her when Eppie herself entered, and Frank rose to greet her.

She took both his hands in hers, and the tears rose even to her honest eyes.

"My poor, dear laddie," she said, "sae wan and sae woebegone. But cheer up, cheer up! Believe me, Frank, it may be all for the best."

By-and-by Eean himself came in, and even Bunko, and nobody that night had a thought for himself or herself. Every effort was made towards making Frank feel happy and at home. These efforts were not unsuccessful. Some natures are wonderfully resilient, and Frank's was one of these. He was a brave, open-hearted boy; and although no one could have felt much more keenly than he did his altered position in life, and the amount of unhappiness his fate had brought on him, still he was by no means inclined to let down his heart, as anyone might have gathered from a remark he made that evening. Tip had knocked down the boy's stick.

"Ah! Tippie," said Frank, "be careful of that; it is really all I have left me in the world."

Eean took occasion to add to this, "Nay, boy, you have hope, and you have youth, and you have health. Glorious possessions all; and if you trust to our Father, lad, He'll be a stronger rod and staff to you than that stick, sturdy and all though it be."

"Oh, well," said Frank, "I shan't need a stick long, for I've made up my mind to go to sea."

"What!" cried Toddie, "and be a midshipman like Fred? How nice!"

"Yes, that would be nice, Toddie; but, heigho! if I go at all it must be before the mast, or as an apprentice. Oh, Mr. Arundel," he added, colouring slightly, "even if I could afford the outfit of a midshipman I couldn't pass the examinations! I'm very stupid; but then — —"

Frank paused.

"What were you going to say?" said Eean quietly

"Well, I was going to say what I have no business to say, because my dear mother always tried to do the best she could for me; but, sir, the constant changing of schools, and being allowed to do as I liked, and to have as many holidays as I pleased, have—have made a dunce of me. I wish I'd gone to a Scotch school like Fred."

"You're not a dunce, lad. You haven't had opportunities of learning, that is all."

"Heigho! I fear I'm spoiled and idle; but I'm going to try my very best to learn and to do well."

"Bravo, boy!" cried Eean, "give me your hand on that. Work hard, lad. I've heard you talk before of the dignity of labour. Do your duty ever. It is because Britons—brave Scottish, English, and Irish Britons—have done their duty all the world over, and looked for a blessing from on high, that Great Britain ranks this day as a first power, if not the first power, among the nations. Duty, lad, duty. It is a sacred thing. Stick to it through thick and thin, and every good will follow; and even if death should come in the doing of it, your last thoughts will be thoughts of peace."

# CHAPTER XV
# THE GOOD SHIP "SAN SALVADOR."—A MYSTERY OF THE SOUTHERN SEAS

It was just such a night as a sailor loves—bright and starry, with a ten-knot breeze blowing, and enough sea on to heel the ship over to leeward, and make one feel one really is afloat on the ocean wave; a night to make one feel rather proud of his ship too than otherwise, if there really is any go and independence about her; a night on which the seaman is apt to pause in his walk fore and aft the decks, and gaze over the bulwarks at the lapping, leaping, bubbling waters, that lisp to him, whisper to him, sing to him, talk to him, and tell him of home.

If he is leaning over the lee side on a night like this with the wind abeam, the water seems ever so much darker and nearer, and the wavelets make pretence every minute to jump up and kiss the hand he extends towards them. If he is leaning over the weather side, the water appears brighter but far off, for it catches the glints of the starlight and the reflected shimmer from the long, clear line of wave-scoured copper, ever and anon showing up as the vessel swings to leeward.

The stars were as bright to-night as bright could be, and the southern cross was very high in the heavens, for the good ship *San Salvador* was well to the south'ard. She was ploughing her way across that wide and lonesome sea, that stretches from stormy Cape Horn far down in the fifties, to the Cape of Good Hope in warmer latitudes, but pointing to an ocean that is at times hardly less wild and tempest-vexed than that which laves the shores of Tierra del Fuego itself.

A single glance at a map, reader, will give you some idea of the width of this wondrous sea—five thousand miles if it be a league; but think of its loneliness. Almost entirely out of the track of ships was the course of the *San Salvador*, for here is no great ocean highway, so on, on, on over the deep and blue-black waters the good barque had been sailing for weeks, since the day she had rounded the Horn in a gale of wind, with ice on every hand. Sometimes the breeze had been favourable enough, at other times dead ahead, so that it was tack and tack all day long; but for days she had

lain becalmed—no, not lain, for she had come into a strong current, and been drifted far to the south out of her course.

They were trying hard now to make up that lee-way, and only this very forenoon they had sighted land, which, as nearly as they could make out, must have been the lonely isle of South Georgia. Never a ship had they seen, never a sail or even canoe. On an ocean like this, and under such circumstances, one cannot help feeling at times as if the world were all a world of waters, and that the ship on which one stands bears the only life afloat on it, and that it is doomed to sail for ever and for ever onwards, yet never reach a port or haven.

Seldom had they seen birds even, only now and then a solitary albatross—great eagle of the sea—that flew silently over them, nor deigned to turn an eye towards the ship, or the frigate-bird that flitted past like some dark spirit of the ocean wave.

No wonder that such a sea as this is supposed by old hands to be haunted. Not by phantom ships nor by Flying Dutchmen. Oh, no! Vanderdecken was never so low down in the world's great chart; but by strange creatures, dark and fearful, that raise their awful forms high out of the water to stare at you with wondering eyes as your ship sails slowly by.

There is always much that is mysterious about the ocean, much that we cannot understand, and creatures may exist therein that are more dreadful to behold than the wildest nightmares. It is on still, calm nights that these mysteries come up from the dark depths, so sailors will tell you. Even on the blackest nights they may give some indication of their presence. On this very cruise of the *San Salvador*, for instance, the men forward openly averred that the ship was followed, was "shadowed," they termed it, by some dread thing—they could not have told you what, for it had so many shapes. It was never twice seen alike. But they would have told you they always seemed to feel its presence, and knew that it was not far off even in daylight and in the sunshine.

In a fog, soon after they had got clear of the southern ice, men forward heard a fearful blowing, hissing sound on the lee bow, and soon after saw IT looming high above them almost like a black cloud. Then a plash in the water and IT was gone.

In the broad light of day once a flag had been dropped overboard. Now, it is unlucky to lose a flag, so the main-yard was hauled aback, and a whaler lowered, manned by five men. They could see the flag spread out on the water after they had rowed fully half a mile from the ship's position. They pulled fast and hard now, and soon reached it. Horror of horrors! the awful

IT was near the flag, and no oar was stretched out to recover the bunting. What it was like no man could rightly say; but all agreed as to its being all legs and claws, with a beak-armed head and terror-striking eyes.

Another day a boat went after a seal that was floating on a morsel of ice. When within about two hundred yards of the little berg a very strange thing occurred. A tall, black arm, higher and thicker than a fishing-boat's mast, was slowly raised above the water, and there remained, as if to warn them not to approach. It is needless to say the boat returned without the seal.

One dark night, a long, wriggling, snake-like line of bluish fire was seen rushing along the surface of the water. All hands were called when it was no larger than a ship's lantern far away on the lee bow. All hands watched it, getting bigger and bigger as it approached. All hands saw it cross the bows in the shape I have mentioned, the men being frightened almost to death, and clutching fearfully at each other, none daring to speak or move, till finally IT disappeared as it had come, far away on the weather horizon.

And every night, when becalmed, the men were sensible of some huge dark image rolling in the water at no very great distance.

Verily there are more things in heaven and in the earth and sea, than we have dreamt of in our philosophy.

But on this particular night the men of the good barque *San Salvador* were far more cheerful than usual, for IT had not not appeared in any shape or form for several days. Then the stars looked so comforting and seemed so near, while away in the west lay a long bank of rock-like clouds, the profile of which could be seen every few seconds in the glare of the lightning that flashed behind it.

There was not much light on deck, however, a glimmer from the skylight, a smoking lantern forward near the forecastle, and rays from the binnacle, but not sufficient to show even the faces of three individuals who were sitting on the grating abaft. You could have noticed that two were smoking cigars, the red tips would have told you that, and the aroma of Cuba confirmed it.

"Why, sir, if this wind holds, we'll go jumping across, and get into Cape Town harbour in a fortnight's time."

"And if," answered the captain, for it was he whom the mate had addressed, "*if* it doesn't blow more big guns, *if* you don't lose the sticks out of her by cracking on too much, and *if—if—*oh! there's lots of other *ifs*."

"If, for instance," said a younger voice to leeward of the captain, "IT doesn't appear again and scare the men to death."

"Why, Fred Arundel, are you there, lad? I didn't notice you, as you're not smoking. But no, I think we've left IT down to the south. Though you're not superstitious, are you, lad?"

"N——no; that is, not much, you know, only I had a queer dream last night."

"Ah! a dreamer of dreams are you? Well, tell us your dream. It's just a night for a song or a story."

"Well, you know, sir, I don't believe in dreams as a rule, they are generally so silly and upside-down-like. But this one was so vivid that I feel quite certain poor Frank is either dead and gone, or I shall soon see him again alive and well."

"It seems to me, Fred, that the dream reads in either direction. But who is Frank? You haven't told us that yet."

"Didn't I? I feel somehow as if everybody should know Frank. But Frank is—a—well, Frank is—Frank, you know."

"To be sure. I don't doubt you."

"Oh, excuse me, sir, for being so very stupid! Well, Frank Fielding *is*, or, heigho! *was*, my dearest friend on earth, we loved each other so; and when we were shipwrecked on a lonely island together we shook hands, and vowed we'd be brothers till death. And——"

"Wait a bit, Fred. I'm taken all aback like. Is this part of the dream?"

"No, sir, this is all reality."

"But you weren't at sea before to get shipwrecked?"

Fred was saucily laughing now.

"Oh, yes, sir, we were! Our craft was the good ship *Water Baby*, the owner, Frank Fielding, of Benshee House. I was captain, and the crew all told was my sister Toddie—who isn't my sister at all, however—and her little dog Tip."

"I begin to see through the milestone now," said Captain Cawdor. "Go on with your cruise of the *Water Baby* then."

"There's nothing much to tell, you know. We had put to sea well-provisioned, and all that, and were enjoying ourselves finely. We had just finished dinner, when a white squall came roaring over the mountains, and blew us far away to the west. I was the pirate of the wild west seas, anyhow."

"I say, mate, did you know we had a real live pirate on board?"

"No, sir, it's terrible!"

"Well, sir," continued Fred, "we were shipwrecked on a desert island, and played at Crusoes, till Toddie grew sick, and lay down to die. Then it was very awful; but somehow Daddy Pop found us, and we were saved."

"Go on, lad."

"Frank's people were very rich, you know; but as far as education went Frank, poor fellow, didn't know much. He was going to be a barrister, he told me, and confessed at the same time he hadn't cleverness enough to be a bar tender even, or a billiard marker. Then his father died on a Christmas night, and Benshee House was burned down—and my poor friend Frank was ruined. Daddy would have got him on as middie like myself, but he was too proud to accept a money favour, and he couldn't have passed the exams, either. But he went to sea, and I greatly fear he has gone before the mast. Oh, fancy, sir, a gentleman's son, and he himself a gentleman, working as a boy, scraping masts, and— —"

"Scraping fiddlesticks," cried honest old Cawdor. "Why, lad alive, I begun life just like that, and look at me now."

"Well," said Fred, "I am looking, but I can only see the point of your old cigar."

"You young rascal, you!" The captain gave Fred a kindly slap. "Do you feel me then? But heave round with that yarn of yours. Didn't your friend write?"

"Just once to Toddie from Demerara, but he gave no address, and didn't even tell her the name of his ship. Well now, sir, he and I have both been at sea for nearly four years," continued Fred.

"Yes, boy, it's going on that way."

"I've been twice home, and I've passed for mate, though Frank has made no sign. But now in my dream I saw him as plainly as I see you."

"What!"

"I don't mean that, because I can't see you, but I saw Frank Fielding coming smiling towards me and holding out his hand."

"How did he look?"

"He looked well-dressed, healthy and bonnie, and a sailor all over, sir."

"And you love this lad, Fred?"

"Ah! sir, he is the only friend I have about my own age. I love him *like a brother*."

Captain Cawdor smoked in silence for a time. Then he put his iron hand once more on Fred's shoulder, but this time he let it rest there for a time.

"Now, lad, I'll tell you what it is. Ever since you've come to me you've behaved like a brick, and a brave brick too. I've been watching all your doings, boy; I hope I've been a father to you."

Fred patted the big hand that lay on his shoulder.

"Indeed, indeed you have, Captain Cawdor."

"Well, you've done your duty, what man or boy can do more? Then, when in half a gale of wind our poor second mate Finch fell overboard, not a month ago, you stripped jacket and boots and dived after him, and you kept him afloat till we found you both. Had that mate of mine not been so fond of accursed rum he'd be living now. But his constitution was rotten to the core—rum-rotten. So his immersion killed him, and I've made you second mate of the *San Salvador*. And as sure as my name is James Cawdor, when we get back to old England you shall have the Albert medal for bravery in saving life at sea.

"Thanks, sir, thanks, but it was really nothing."

"Stop, let me finish. We are an officer short now, and if we do meet that friend Frank of yours, and he is worth an old ship biscuit, and up to the ropes, I'll give him a chance, just see if I don't. Don't thank me, I hate verbal thanks. Don't speak your thanks, *live* it."

"I'll *live* to please you, sir. Yes, I'll *live* my thanks."

"Well now, let us go below, and leave the mate to keep his watch. I want to hear you play a bit, I always think it cheers the men forward up to hear music aft. Down you go first."

Fred dived below and entered the well-lighted little saloon of the barque. Though not large, it was as snug and cosy as a lady's boudoir, and at the farther end of it stood an open piano.

And now that the light shines full in their faces, we can see both Fred himself and his kindly Captain Cawdor.

# CHAPTER XVI
# DEAKIN AND CO. AND THE
# LOST BRIG "RESOLUTE"

It had just gone one bell in the first watch, and so was nearly time for the frugal supper, partaken of every night in the saloon of the *San Salvador*. The fact is, breakfast was served sharp at eight o'clock, dinner at one, and a high tea at six. The tea was really a kind of a sea dinner in itself, for the meat and biscuits were always put down, with soft tack (bread) if there was any. Therefore supper after this was a mere snack, say a box of sardines with pickled onions and biscuits, washed down with coffee or cocoa.

To-night the steward spread the banquet as soon as the captain and Fred came down.

"Where is Cassia-bud?"

"I call him in one minute, sah."

What a mountain of a fellow this steward was! As black was he as the inside of an empty ink-jar when the cork is in. All black except two rows of white teeth and the conjunctiva of his eyes. These last, however, had a tinge of yellow in them. Quambo was really a giant, only a very good-natured one. But once or twice in a fight on shore the man had shown the kind of metal he was made of. He was very fond of Fred. One day the latter had interfered in Zanzibar to protect a poor little slave lass, that a fierce-looking Arab had been brutally using. The consequence was that the lad was mobbed. But from the window of the hotel Quambo had seen it all. Downstairs he rushed, and before he left the house with one terrible wrench he tore an iron bar from the window, then sallied forth. Fred was lying helpless and bleeding, and the Arabs and half-castes around him must have numbered fifty at least.

"Clear the way!" cried Quambo. "Sameela! Sameela!" (Make room! make room!)

Then the fiends turned fiercely on the negro. But Quambo's eyes were flashing fire, and his nostrils distended like those of a war-horse that scents the battle from afar. He mowed that ruffianly mob down right and left, drawn swords were shivered in pieces, and the thick turbans of the Arabs were no protection against the terrible weapon that Quambo wielded. He speedily rescued Fred, and bore him away in triumph. Fred and his friend the negro left the hotel half an hour after, but no one wanted to renew the combat.

Now Cassia-bud was also a negro, a poor, wee innocent mite of a fellow, and the ship's pet. Small enough was Cassia-bud to ride on the captain's great honest black Newfoundland dog, and small enough too for the men to make a ball of and play a kind of game with of a summer's evening.

"Kashie! Kashie!" shouted Quambo, and next minute Kashie appeared.

"Here, boy, pull my boots off!" The captain had flung himself into his easy chair and stuck out his legs.

What a good-natured, aye, and good-looking, man was this same skipper, as he liked to call himself! For well-nigh fifty years he had kicked about all over the world; but, barring his grey hairs and snow-white whiskers, you scarce could have told he was a day past forty. He was a thorough sailor every inch.

But is that our little Fred that used to be? That tall, handsome young fellow of seventeen, with dark blue eyes, a wealth of brown curly hair, and a budding black moustache. Verily, it is none other. Look at his rosy face and pearly teeth. Behold what the sea and a virtuous life has done for the young Scottish sailor!

Down he sat beside his captain, and the rapid disappearance of those sardines and onions, with the crisp toasted and buttered biscuit, would have made a cockney stare in wonder.

Fred swallowed his cocoa. Quambo mixed the captain's last cup. Cassia-bud put his master's slippers on, and then lay down beside Hurricane Bob, the Newfoundland, and took his fore-paws round his neck; then Fred began to play and sing.

Fred had a sweet voice, and so modulated his accompaniment that there was nothing but fascinating unison from beginning to end of the song he sung.

The captain was right, the music really was infectious, and had you come on deck half an hour after Fred began to play, and strolled forward to the galley, a happier lot of sailors than that around the fire it would have been impossible to have imagined. Spinning yarns and singing songs to the music of the cook's old fiddle had become the order of the evening, and even

IT—the mysterious IT, which had followed the ship so far—was forgotten in the general gaiety that prevailed, and in the harmony that reigned universal.

Like Fred himself, and a large proportion of the crew, Captain Cawdor was Scotch, and, like many Scottish skippers, he was part owner of the barque he commanded. This was good for himself, but it was also good for the other owners, none of whom were sailors. But they knew the ship was in excellent hands, and that while they were sleeping quietly in their comfortable beds, Captain Cawdor was sailing the seas here and there throughout the world, taking "a voyage," as he termed employment, wherever he got it, and thus oftentimes managing to pay himself and brother shipowners cent. per cent. Then the vessel was heavily insured, and were she even to leave her bones on some foreign strand, the insurance office alone would have to mourn, and they could well afford to pay.

Cawdor had neither kith nor kin belonging to him, all were dead and gone.

"I'm getting up in years," he told Fred more than once; "but so long as I remain at sea I feel a young man, and, please the Lord, Fred, I'll die on the ocean, and be buried as a sailor should be."

On this voyage the *San Salvador* was on her way from Valparaiso with a mixed cargo for the Cape, and with much specie as well. The men knew there was gold and silver on board, and that the boxes lay in the captain's cabin, and yet neither he nor his mate had the slightest fear, so well chosen were the seamen.

There were, it is true, a few half-caste Spaniards on board; but however much mischief they might have liked to have worked, they were in too small a minority to count for anything.

And so, despite the evil-augured IT that had dodged around them, the ship sailed on and on over that lonesome waste of waters, and no evil befel her.

At long last—glorious sight to those sea-weary mariners—Cape pigeons came flying about, and pieces of dark drifting seaweed; and then gulls appeared to greet them; and then the mountains of Cape Colony appeared, like a cloud in the nor'-eastern horizon. The men hailed them with three cheers.

The ship would lie for a whole fortnight at Cape Town, and they all expected letters from home; besides, Captain Cawdor was by no means niggardly in the matter of leave; so the hands expected a good spell on shore, and plenty of fun and dancing.

It was Fred's second visit to the Cape, but it had been winter when he was here before; that is, it was in the middle of June. This is really a pleasant time, for no snow lies in these regions, and indeed I have never seen it fall. The air, however, is cool and bracing, and there are clouds to temper the sunshine, while morning and evening sunrises are lovely in the extreme.

Now it was summer in these latitudes, and the sun, though tempered by ocean breezes, was almost fiercely hot; the sea was blue, and the sky was almost cloudless; while the great and glorious mountains seemed to simmer in the quivering naze.

All the first day of the ship's arrival Fred had to stick fast on board, for both the mate and Captain Cawdor were busy on shore, and cargo and specie both were being landed.

In the evening when he returned the captain brought letters from home for the ship's crew, and there were several for Fred. As soon as possible he hurried below and lit his cabin swing-candle, and, sitting down prepared to devour them. There was a very long letter from Daddy Pop, and one from Mammy Mop as well. Both contained much kindly and good advice. Then there was a long, delightful letter from Toddie. Poor Toddie was in grief, for not only was poor old Tip dead, but Bunko's Keelie too; for though dogs love us much, they cannot live for ever.

These letters were all loving and homely. As he read them the tears came welling into the lad's eyes, as the humble little fisher cottage rose up before him, the little whitewashed village among the green, drooping silver birch trees. He seemed to sit once more, as he used to do, in that charmed circle by the low hearth, with Eean in his arm-chair, Toddie on her low stool, and Eppie at the spinning-wheel. He thought he could hear the crackle of the blazing logs and the birr—rr—rr of the wheel, and see the firelight flicker on the old bard's face and glance upon the dark rafters, from which the brown hams hung, and the homely strings of onions.

He sighed, and I'm not sure a tear did not fall. He would have given a good deal just then to be able to visit but for one half hour the little cottage by the sea. He put the letters away in his desk, and walked on deck. Strange as it may appear, he believed so thoroughly in his vivid dream that he had really expected a letter from his friend Frank Fielding.

The captain took him on shore with him next day, and as they walked along the principal streets, Fred would not have been a bit surprised to have met Frank, just as he had met him in his dream.

The captain and he dined together well and heartily at one of the best hotels, and were sitting talking together over the dessert, when a tall, white-haired gentleman drew near to the table.

"I beg pardon, stranger," he said, "but are you Captain Chowder?"

"I'm Skipper *Cawdor*, of the barque *San Salvador*."

"The very individual. I thought it was Chowder. Well, Captain Chaw—Chow—I mean Cawdor, are you open to take a commission?"

"Sit down, sir. Have a glass of port. Your name?"

"Deakin, of Deakin and Co. We're shipowners, oil-merchants, anything."

"Well, I'm open to load up and go anywhere."

"When can you start?"

"In half an hour after the last bale's on board."

"But it ain't bales, captain. Fact is, a whaler of ours, the brig *Resolute*, that touched here eight months ago, and ought to have returned long since, is lost, and we've just got word from a vessel that has come from Kerguelen that in all likelihood the crew are saved, and living or existing on an island a long distance to the east and south of that black starvation rock."

"Yes, I see. Well, sir?"

"Well, it's like this. The brig's well insured, we don't care a dime about her, and we don't care a dime about any man Jack on board the *Resolute*, except one, and he's one of the firm, Señor Sarpinto. We would pay handsomely to have him; but, of course, you could bring the others."

"I understand. Couldn't well leave them, could we? And, Mr. Deakin, if I understand you, I'm to load up with extra provisions, and sail in search of this shipwrecked crew of whalers, and bring them here?"

"No, you needn't bring them here. We'll give you a light cargo for New Zealand, and orders to ship another there for San Francisco, where our principal house is, and where Señor Sarpinto will desire to be taken. Now, Captain Ch—a—Cawdor, have we met the right man in you?"

"You've met the identical individual."

"And you can start at once?"

"The morning after to-morrow."

"Well, captain, here's my card. Come to the office this evening before five, and we'll arrange terms. We wouldn't lose our partner for a good deal, I can assure you, sir. Good-day."

"Whew—ew—ew!" whistled Captain Cawdor, as soon as the door had closed on their strange visitor. "Well, Fred, here's a wind-up to a windy day. Worthy Mr. Deakin, of Deakin and Co., doesn't care a dime for either the ship or the crew of honest whalers, and owns up to it like a man, or rather like a Yankee; but they mustn't lose their Señor Sarpinto. Now, take my word for it, he is the sporting partner, fond of adventure and all that sort of thing; but he has also got the dollars, and the worthy firm of Deakin and Co. would go all to smash without him. They are willing to pay, and what is more, they'll have to. I'll wager a new sou'-wester a Scot knows how to make a bargain with a Yankee, see if he doesn't. Captain Chowder, indeed! I'll Chowder him! Ha! ha! But I say, Fred, write your letters home, and be brisk about it. There's a tidy cruise before us, but money in it mind for me, and a bit for you too, lad."

And Captain Cawdor drove a very excellent bargain indeed with Deakin and Co. That was the reason, and the only reason, why, just two days after this, the sturdy old barque was seen standing away from the Cape, steering south-south-east, with every inch of canvas set both 'low and aloft.

# CHAPTER XVII
# SOUTHWARD HO! TO THE SEA OF ICE

In a fortnight's time the *San Salvador* had placed at least one thousand miles betwixt her and the Cape of Good Hope. This was looked upon by Captain Cawdor as fair running, considering the wild weather the barque experienced. They had put out to sea on a glorious summer's day, on the wings of a gentle breeze, the hills behind them purple and green with vegetation and flowers; white-winged gulls sailing around them in the sky or floating on the hardly ruffled breast of ocean, the good old ship seeming to wish to linger near that lovely land. But hardly had the last seagull shrieked its wild farewell, and night and darkness begun to fall over the waves, than it could be seen, from the rising clouds, the moaning wind, and incessant sheets of lightning, that a tempest was brewing. So sail had been at once shortened, and everything done that could be done to secure safety and comfort for the night. Luckily the wind had come from the right quarter, so that although it blew big guns, and though green seas were shipped over the bows and came roaring aft, the good ship went tearing on, and daylight saw her staggering almost under bare poles, amidst such a chaos of mountain waves as probably is only to be seen in one part of the world, and that the ocean regions round the Cape.

And from that very day, all along, the wind had never entirely ceased to rage and roar, nor stormy seas to dash around the ship. She was always half battened down, especially forward, where in galley and mess-places lamps had to be burned all day long, and where, even down below, the decks were never dry. Little do boys who long to be sailors know of the hardships that men before the mast, aye, and apprentices also, have to endure in such latitudes as these, when the ship is far, far from land, and when no one knows or can guess what fate has in store for himself or his ship.

It was a trying time, but worse was to follow. I must say, however, that the men never grumbled, nor did they snarl and growl at each other like ill-conditioned curs, as sailors so frequently do under like circumstances, until verily the vessel they live in becomes a kind of hell afloat.

Fred Arundel was as much of a favourite forward as he was aft. His open, laughing, good-tempered face seemed to bring sunshine with it wherever he went. Nor was he ever too high and mighty to lend a helping hand wherever needed. Any day you might have seen Fred hauling away at tack or sheet, or even in a wild sea-way taking a dash aloft with the hands, and laying well out on a yard, helping to shorten sail. The men loved and respected him for all this, but they never took advantage of his good nature.

Many a dark night too, when it was not his watch, Fred would mingle with a group forward, and listen to their yarns, or even tell one himself.

As I have said, the crew was chiefly composed of Scotchmen. Well, Fred lent them books to read, just the kind he knew would please them.

Sometimes of an evening, when the captain was below with his boots off, Fred would promise the men a song, and they would slip aft and station themselves near the skylight. Then Fred would go below.

"D'ye mind having the skylight open a wee bit?" Fred would ask of his jolly skipper.

"You young rascal!" the latter might reply, "I'm up to your dodges. You want to play to the men, not to me."

"That's it," Fred would say, laughing, and next moment big Quambo would have the skylight open; that is, of course, if the weather wasn't altogether too rough.

Then Fred would play and sing. It might be the melting melody of "Auld Robin Gray," or "Afton Water;" or something more martial and bold, such as the "March of the Cameron Men;" or "Cam' ye by Athole?" But while he sang he never failed to hold the men entranced.

"Land ahead, sir!"

It was a shout from the look-out on the fore-top.

"Hard up with her!" cried the mate, and presently the land was brought well on the bow.

Only just in time, however; for what had seemed like a mass of cloud on the eastern horizon had suddenly resolved itself into black, beetling rocks, with a fringe of green on top, and waves foaming like cataracts at the foot thereof. So near to some of the outlying rocks or "whales' backs" had they come that they only just missed grazing them. As far as they could make out, the land now visible belonged to the Grozet group of islands. Soon afterwards they sighted land to the north.

Luckily the wind was fair and the day fairly clear; but it was an anxious time with Captain Cawdor until he got fairly clear of these lonely isles of the southern ocean.

These unknown seas of the far south are much more fraught with danger, than even the shifting sands and coral reefs of African shores. On the latter, so long as a man is kept in the chains, and soundings carried on, the vessel is comparatively safe, for the water shoals gradually; but in such latitudes as those in which the *San Salvador* was now sailing the lead was of little use. On dark nights heaven alone knows what dangers were not narrowly escaped, for by day oftentimes the first indication they had of the vicinity of a semi-submerged rock was the appearance of breaking water at that particular spot.

> "There is a sweet little cherub sits up aloft
> To look after the life of poor Jack."

Perhaps, and really this cherub was all the captain of the *San Salvador* had to trust to in the inky darkness of the night; but two very substantial cherubs were always in the foretop and cross-trees by day, and often one of these bore the blue eyes of Fred Arundel.

Kerguelen Isles at last. Blackness and desolation. Only the wild birds, that flocked and flew in myriads about the cliffs and rocks; only an occasional seal, or the head of a monster sea-elephant raised above the black water, to gaze wonderingly at the ship under sail, which, if the beast thought at all, he must have taken for some gigantic bird.

The captain landed in a bay. Yes, people had been here, and lately too. Whalers perhaps, or shipwrecked mariners; but no signs or sounds of human life were seen or heard now, so he came away and the voyage was resumed.

South still. South and east; and after five days of rough and tumble sailing, sometimes with showers of snow driving across the deck and almost choking the men as they kept watch, on a bright, clear morning the man at the mast-head once more raised the cry of "Land, ho!"

An island, undoubtedly.

Perhaps one of the outlying rocks of Donell's Group. They would have passed it, and sailed on their course to resume the search for the missing whalers; but young Fred's eagle eye noticed smoke, and instantly reported it.

"Haul the foreyard aback. Away, whaler!"

These were the orders, and speedily executed they were. Out swang the boat, and down, taking the water on an even keel, and in five minutes' time Captain Cawdor himself, accompanied by Fred, was steering away over the blue-black waters for a little bay in the desolate island.

Here, to their surprise, they found two men, and the joy the poor fellows evinced as the boat's keel rasped on the shingle was almost hysterical. They had been living in a cave near by, and from the way it was lined with sealskins it was evident enough that they had not gone short of provisions during their sojourn here, and that, moreover, despairing of being rescued for long months to come, they had commenced preparations for spending the winter in comparative comfort.

They had a large boat too, and the first thing that the captain noticed was the name painted on her bows — *Resolute*.

"Why," cried Captain Cawdor, "you are the very men we have come to seek for. But where are the rest of you?"

Then the faces of the two men fell, and they looked at each other confusedly and guiltily.

"Bill," said one at last, "better let us make a clean breast of it."

"Right, Nat. Guess it'll be the same in the end."

"We're about the guiltiest men out then," said the man called Nat.

"Mutiny and murder?"

"No, sirree; not so bad as that. Our hands are clean. But, sir, we are willing to own up to robbery. Yes, as base as base could be. But heaven knows, sir, we've suffered for it. Our ship, the *Resolute*, got in a gale of wind in the south-eastern ice down here, and we lost all our boats except this one here. Then we took the ice, or rather we were squeezed into a starvation creek or bay, 'nipped up' and thrown on our beam-ends on top of a floe. That's months ago, sir."

"I see," said Captain Cawdor, "and you and your mate here stole the only boat, provisioned her, and escaped in the dark."

"May the Lord love you, sir, that's it entirely."

"Well, you deserve to be marooned. If it wasn't for one thing more than another I'd take your arms and tools, smash your boat, and leave you here to perish. As it is, we'll leave the boat and take you. Is it far from here where your ship lies wrecked?"

"A good thousand miles, sir."

"A thousand miles! And how on earth did you reach here?"

"We kept hugging the ice all the way till abreast of the islands. Whenever it came on to blow we drew up the boat and lived on small bergs. Ah! sir, I assure you we're real penitent."

"You will have to prove your penitence then by guiding us to the wreck of the *Resolute*. If I find you false, I shall hang you both to the yard-arm as sure as my name is Jamie Cawdor."

"We'll be true as a needle to the Pole, sir. Won't we, Bill? We swear it."

"I swear it," said Nat solemnly.

They were then taken on board, and the voyage was renewed.

No time was to be lost now if the men of the *Resolute* were to be rescued this year; for the ice-floes in these regions are constantly shifting, and streams of bergs in another month would encompass every island in the southern sea, rendering relief to the castaway crew an utter impossibility.

For two more weeks and over the cruise was continued, the weather being on the whole crisp and clear and the wind favourable.

Being now about the longitude indicated by the men picked up from Donell's rocks, the course was changed and the ship steered south away, till at last the ice was made. Although there were many floating bergs or huge pieces, with green glittering sides and caps of snow, the main flow was in itself a wondrous sight. Imagine, if you can, a huge irregular perpendicular wall of ice of nearly one thousand feet in height, level on its upper crust of snow, and indented with many a bay, with the waves dashing in foam high over the water-line, and forming a ridge of the strangest and most fantastic stalactites that it is possible to imagine. Here were caves of ice and grottoes of ice and coral apparently, with pillars of every shape and size, from which, when the sun shone, the most radiant and lovely colours were reflected, rendering the whole scene dazzling in the extreme. As the ship sailed slowly along this scene of enchantment, it was impossible not to believe you actually saw strange figures moving to and fro in those fairy caves, figures in trailing garments, some all white, others green, or blue or crimson, but all emitting light, and all seeming to mingle and glide as ghosts are said to do. Several times, indeed, Fred could have swore he saw hands and arms waved towards him, and the more he gazed the more life-like the ice spirits grew, till at last he was fain to cover his face with his hands, as a strange momentary fear came over him that he was losing his senses.

The effect of the scene on the men was remarkable. They stared in silent wonder, not unmixed with a kind of superstitious awe.

At long last clouds banked up and hid the sun, then, as if the enchanter had ceased to wave his wand, the spectres fled, and only blue-grey shadows remained to mark the places where the caves of beauty erst had spangled and shone.

On sailed the ship, on and on.

At last, one night, the mate on watch noticed a bright glare of light far away to the southward and east, and reported it to the captain.

Though it was long past midnight, the two men of the *Resolute* were roused and brought on deck.

The light, they said, had often been seen. It was that from a burning mountain, and was nothing now to what it sometimes appeared. Just here, too, they averred the wreck would be found.

So the *San Salvador* lay to till daybreak.

Both Fred and Captain Cawdor were on deck long before the first faint flush of dawn. But neither then nor when the sun crimsoned the waters to the east were any signs of human life to be seen.

Just two hours afterwards, however, as Fred and his captain sat at breakfast, the mate's watch being on deck, they heard that officer's footsteps rapidly advancing along the quarter-deck. Immediately after the skylight was opened, and the mate sang out:

"Something large and dark lying on top of the snow in the bay down here, sir."

Captain Cawdor and Fred sprang up and rushed on deck, and presently, while the ship was kept away in towards the bay, every glass on board was levelled at that dark spot on the snow.

# CHAPTER XVIII
# SEÑOR SARPINTO

Nearer and nearer sailed the *San Salvador*, closer and closer into the bay; and soon the dark spot resolved itself into something with a definable shape. Presently all doubt was dispelled; it was a ship lying on the ice on her beam ends, and a few minutes after several men were seen clustering near her.

The captain took the glass from his eye,

"There is no doubt about it," he said aloud. "Yonder lies the wreck of the *Resolute*."

Then the crew manned the bulwarks, the capstan, and winch, and cheer after cheer rose on the icy air of the morning, such cheers as only can be heard from true British sailors.

Was it an echo from the cold and snowy mountain cliffs, or was it really a cheer in response to theirs, that now came feebly back over the dark waters? None could tell. But in a very short time the *San Salvador* was near enough to see figures running excitedly about on the ice.

They are soon near enough for safety, the anchor chains rattle out, and the sails are clued; and soon a boat is speeding shorewards, both Captain Cawdor and his young friend Fred being seated in the stern sheets.

And now I have a strange fact to record; and mind you, reader, facts are stranger far than fiction, and I must leave the elucidation thereof to the psychologist.

As the boat entered the bay then, and the mountains and cliffs grew taller and taller, and cast great shadows across the water, Fred was noticed by his captain to become strangely excited, and to look more and more surprised every moment. He kept gazing around him.

"Captain Cawdor," he said at last, clutching his friend's arm, "am I really and truly awake? Oh, sir, everything around me is familiar—every rock and cliff and gloomy hill! Oh, captain, I've been here before!"

He looked so wild as he spoke that Captain Cawdor really began to think he was taking leave of his senses. But he had more reason to think so immediately afterwards.

Fred started to his feet, his cap falling off as he did so, his eyes staring shorewards, in which direction also his right arm was stretched.

"I knew it! I knew it!" he cried. "It is my dream coming true—my thrice-dreamt dream! Look, sir, look! Yonder stands Frank himself!"

He waved both arms madly above his head,

"Frank! Frank! Frank!" he shouted, "it is I, Fred Arundel, your friend, your brother!"

He sank down almost exhausted.

Captain Cawdor noticed a young man in the garb of a sailor come staggering along the snow to the very edge of the black water, where he swayed about, so that those in the boat were in momentary expectation of seeing him fall into the sea.

No sooner had the boat touched the snow edge than Fred sprang up and leapt on shore, and next moment the two long-lost friends stood hand in hand gazing into each other's faces, though neither could speak a single word.

Frank was the first to regain his voice.

"God bless you, Fred; I knew you'd come."

"You *knew*, Frank?"

"I did."

"But how?"

"I dreamt you would. That is all. And night after night I dreamt that dream again. It is all God's merciful providence, Fred. Heigho! I feel so happy now."

"But how weak you are! Come into the boat and seat yourself. Captain Cawdor, we'll stick to the boat a bit; the men can go with you."

"Take a pull of this flask, my lad," said the captain in kind tones to Frank.

"Oh, thank you; no, sir!" he answered. "I have sworn never to touch *that*."

"As you please, boy; but go and sit down."

"I'll tell you in a word why I refused the captain's flask," said Frank, when the two were seated in the stern sheets. "My dearest friend on earth—he's not on earth now—whom I loved as much as you, because I hadn't you to care for, fell a victim to accursed rum, and one night he threw himself into the sea, Fred, and before my eyes I saw him torn in pieces by the sharks."

What a long story that was that each had to tell the other of their travels and adventures, since last saying farewell on the Broomielaw at Glasgow!

But it was not all told on the ice here.

Fred and Señor Sarpinto, with the skipper of the *Resolute*, and some of the ailing ones among the crew, were taken at once aboard the *San Salvador*.

The others remained in camp beside their ship.

The skipper, a little dark-skinned Yankee, told Cawdor at once that he believed it possible to repair and float the *Resolute*, and so that very day a picked crew was sent on shore to work at her. All the damage that could be found out about the brig had been done to her starboard quarter. Here was a big hole, but as the vessel lay on the port side, two days hard work sufficed to make good repairs.

Then came the tug of war. How was she to be got up?

The skipper's plan at once proved the boldness of Yankee device.

He would, he said, blast the ice from under her.*

> * A plan I have seen resorted to in Greenland more than once.

"Would this not damage the ship?" said Cawdor.

"Oh, no, sirree," was the reply. "We'll sink the keg of powder well under, and it will be the easiest work in the world."

"Well, we'll try," said Cawdor.

So preparations were immediately commenced. Luckily the weather continued fine.

A stout hawser was fastened to the *Resolute's* main mast head, and carried towards that of the *San Salvador*, which had been brought near the ice floe and anchored there. This was done with the view of causing the *Resolute* to take the water keel down, else she might actually turn turtle as it is called.

All being ready the keg of powder was lowered, and lighted by means of a long fuse.

Then ensued a long time of anxious waiting. Minutes on minutes seemed to elapse before the explosion actually took place.

When it did so, instead of being anything very startling, it resolved itself simply into the raising of a vast balloon-shaped fountain of salt water and spray which blinded everyone it fell upon. Pieces of ice also fell with rattling thuds upon the deck of the barque, but no one was hurt. The *San Salvador* shook and shivered and swayed about for a few moments; huge lumps of the *débris* of the blasted iceberg thundered against her sides; then it could be seen that the *Resolute* was slowly righting herself on an even keel, and sinking down to her water-line.

All speed was now made to cut the hawser, but there was no further danger. The rescued brig lay there like a duck upon the water; sail was soon after made, and both vessels moved slowly out to the open waters of the bay.

Much to everyone's surprise the *Resolute* made scarcely any water; so the Yankee skipper's daring had been well rewarded.

Next day a strong breeze sprang up from the south-west; and, taking advantage of it, away went the consorts under all sail *en route* for New Zealand.

Nothing, I think, affords such convincing proof of the limitedness of the human mind as the futility of the attempts we sometimes make to grasp or understand the infinitely great or the infinitely small. We are willing enough, for instance, to take it for granted that the milky way on which we gaze on some still starry night is in reality a mist of myriads on myriads of worlds and suns, millions of which are as large in comparison to our mite of an earth as a crownpiece is to a pin's head; but if we attempt to form any just conception of so great a marvel we feel our own littleness at once. Again, we may be told that every drop of stagnant water under the microscope resolves itself at once into a world in which creatures live, and move, and have their being, and act out their own little life-stories on their particular stage just as we do in ours. We can grasp this truth; but take it in the aggregate, and where are we? How many drops of stagnant water are in yonder pond? And how many microscopic worlds are there? We are best to leave all such calculations alone. They do but stagger and stun us. Besides there is the golden hope given us in the Bible, that though here below we see darkly in a glass, our hereafter will be more bright and intellectual.

I am led to make these remarks from a glance I have just taken at a map or chart of the world, and that portion of it in particular we call the

Pacific Ocean. On this map of mine the islands that dot its vast surface are fairly well marked to the extent of our present knowledge. But probably not a thousandth part of them are down here, nor have ever been visited even. And when we consider that most of them are teeming with life—with animal, human life even—and are the homes of creatures and peoples utterly foreign to us, as are also their fauna and flora, the thought is indeed somewhat startling. Then to think of the ages and ages that have elapsed during the formation of this mist of islands, whether by the breaking into pieces of vast continents, or the raising from the ocean's bed of isle upon isle by volcanic or coral agency! Is it not weirdly strange?

It is in the very centre of this wondrous mist of islands that the next scene of our story opens.

The vessels *San Salvador* and *Resolute* had reached New Zealand, and both had loaded up and were on their way home to San Francisco. Frank was strong and well again now, and had been transferred from his own brig to the *Salvador*, and proving to be really a fairly good sailor, Captain Cawdor had kept his promise to Fred, and duly installed him in the position of third mate. So all had gone well, and the two young men now felt as happy as the day was long, and just as bright as the days were.

Señor Sarpinto had also preferred to leave the brig and sail with Captain Cawdor. Frank was very fond of this Spanish grandee, as he called him. To all appearance there was not much of the grandee about him. He was a man of about forty years of age, small in stature, but as strong and lithe as a puma; his dark eyes at times used to glare and glitter when he talked, as if fires really raged within him that could not be concealed. His love of adventure and sight-seeing was remarkable. This it was that had determined him to go with the skipper of the brig *Resolute* to the southern seas, where whales and seals were said to swarm. This same love of adventure had made a rover of him all his life. He was wealthy, extremely so. He did not tell anyone this boastingly; he simply admitted it, and added that he could not help being rich. He believed, he said, if he were stripped naked, and put down in the midst of an unknown island, he would become a wealthy man in less than ten years. He was born to sprout and flourish like a green bay-tree, and every new speculation he turned his thoughts to was successful.

Yet he would have been deeply offended at anyone who ever hinted that he cared for money. No wonder Deakin and Co. would have been sorry to lose so fortunate a partner as this Señor Sarpinto.

Not a part of the world, even the most remote, he had not visited, or if such regions did exist, they existed but to be visited some day or other by this same adventurous Spaniard.

Being therefore a citizen of the world it will surprise no one to be told that the English he spoke was faultless.

During the long voyage to New Zealand from the southern ice he had made quite a favourable and friendly impression on Fred, and never did he seem more happy than when sitting between the two lads on the quarter-deck of an evening, smoking and drinking sherbet. He would not sit in the dark, however.

"I must see the faces of those I talk to," he said.

So wherever at night the señor sat on deck a lantern was swung.

The lads were never tired listening to stories of his strange life and adventures; they were thrilling in the extreme. At the same time they were natural and naturally told.

Yet with all his nonchalance and his gaiety our heroes often noticed that at times there came into his face a look of weariness, nay, at times, even of utter woe, that used to sadden while it surprised them.

They were old enough and wise enough to know from this that Señor Sarpinto had a life-story he never told; that deep down at the bottom of his heart was a well-spring of sentiment, no drop from which ever in their presence found its way to the surface.

There was no need to hurry, this voyage, the señor told Captain Cawdor over and over again. Life among the beautiful islands of the southern Pacific was far too delightful, far too idyllic to be hurried over. But a ten-knot breeze had the same effect upon both Cawdor and his mate that a red rag had on a bull. It excited them, and clap on sail they would.

So the only way Señor Sarpinto could think of for delaying the voyage, was to ask for a boat to visit every island they came any way near. The voyage was all that could be desired for a fortnight and over. Then contrary winds blew. This state of affairs was succeeded by a hurricane or tornado that blew both vessels very much out of their course.

It was a night of fearful darkness and storm; but next morning, though the waves were still houses' high, the wind had fallen to a dead calm. But where was the *Resolute*?

Her lights had been seen at eight bells in the middle watch; but when the sun shot up at half-past six, and apparently changed the round, rolling waves into blood and fire, the brig was nowhere visible.

Here was Señor Sarpinto's chance come at last then, to delay the voyage for a short time.

He could never think of leaving his good brig and his faithful skipper, so he told Cawdor; but the captain really could not help perceiving that it mattered very little to the señor where the *Resolute* was. So he told him.

"Ah! then," was the reply, "for courtesy and politeness' sake we will lie to for some days till she comes up. Or we will creep around and look for her."

But the *Resolute* never appeared.

The waiting for her, however, led to events that were indeed but little looked for, as we shall presently see.

# CHAPTER XIX
## A FAIRY ISLE—THE LOST BOAT

Not a breath of wind, not a sigh came over the sea. Never a cloud as big even as a man's hand in all the bright steel-blue of heaven's great dome, only the slightest pearly haze lying low on the horizon wherever one might look, and all between the glittering sun-kissed ocean.

It was no dead ocean this, however, on which our heroes, leaning over the bulwarks and talking almost in whispers, were gazing. No, the great sea was not dead, but sleeping. Note the gentle heaving of its placid bosom, rising and falling as if 'twere imbued with the breath of life. The white-winged sea-gulls that float on the water seem to have been lulled to sleep, too, by that swelling motion. Even the ship herself nods drowsily to and fro, and the useless sails half fill and flap to every dip of the masts.

Yes, the surface of the sea is all a-glitter in the sun's rays; but it is not the sheen that sailors love, the reflection is like that from polished pewter, and forebodes either a long dead calm, or a sudden storm coming in a direction no man can even guess at.

There is languor in the tropical air to-day. Even some frigate birds appear to feel it, for they have alighted with their long, drooping wings on the top-most yards, and hardly care to fly again. The gulls sail slowly but silently round the ship, as if too indolent even to scream; yonder nautilus, or Portuguese man-o'-war, that looks as if it had borrowed its cerulean colours from the azure of the sky itself, can scarcely move along. There is not wind enough to fill even its dainty sails, and see, what is that lying over yonder dark and curious? Fred Arundel lazily lifts the glass, and gazes in that direction.

"It is a shark," he says with half a shudder, "asleep, I think, in the morning sunshine, and with sea birds perching on its fins."

Frank answers not. His eyes are riveted on some far-off green-fringed mountains. It is an island, but it does not seem to lie in the sea. No, it is up in the sky, and floating there like a veritable fairyland.

Now Frank yawns and stretches himself, and next moment a hand is laid on his shoulder, and he looks up to see Señor Sarpinto standing smiling beside him. He is in dressing-gown and slippers, with the never-failing cigarette between his lips.

"My young friend is tired."

"Si, señor," says Frank, "I am tired—tired doing nothing. I'd fain be yonder."

He points to the distant island.

Señor takes the telescope, and looks long and earnestly at it.

"Ah!" he says, or rather sighs, "what a land of delight it is! And all the islands around here, how rich and varied! Young Frank, the day will come when each will bear its own happy population of prosperous white men. There are not even savages on yonder isle. It waits but for a Christian population. And there is wealth yonder too, wealth untold!"

Fred looks at the Spaniard in some little surprise. He had never heard the man talk thus enthusiastically before. Then a happy idea appears to strike Frank all at once.

"Señor," he says, "you have influence with the captain. Ask him for a boat, that we may visit yonder isle."

"I will not go there to-day," replies the señor, shrugging his shoulders.

Frank's face falls.

"There is not a banana nor a cocoanut in the ship," he says with a faint smile.

Señor looks at him quizzingly.

"Ha!" he answers, "it is not the banana, it is not the cocoanut my young friend wants, but the wild adventure. Well, he shall not be disappointed."

Away below hurries the Spaniard; but he soon returns laughing.

"You are to take the gig, your friend Fred, Quambo for your porter, little Cassia-bud for your coxswain and to climb the cocoanut-trees, the dog for companion, and one man besides.

"But I have promised you will return as soon as the flag is hoisted at the peak."

"Hurrah!" cry Frank and Fred both in one breath, and in five minutes more down rushes the boat, and all are in and off.

The young men wave their caps to the señor, who kisses his hand. Then they seize the oars, and off they push.

"Nay, but," cries Fred, "the occasion demands a song, and Quambo here is capable of a capital bass."

And for twenty minutes at least those on board the ship could hear the music from the distant boat come quavering over the waves, and for some time could even distinguish the words—

"Row, brothers, row, the stream runs fast;
The rapids are near, and the daylight is past."

At long last Señor Sarpinto sees the green of the distant island swallow them up, as the boat appears to have climbed the very sky itself into that floating fairyland.

Hours and hours went by, the sun had mounted higher and higher, and for a time blazed almost perpendicularly down on the broiling deck, then gradually begun to decline.

"I think," said Captain Cawdor, "the lads must have had enough of it now. Hoist the recall, Mr. Nelson." This to the mate.

The mate did as he was told, and the flag hung from the peak like a red rope, for there was no wind to lift its heavy folds.

Two minutes after the mate shouted, "Stand by there forward, lads; there is a puff of wind coming."

And sure enough patches of wrinkles began to appear here and there on the gloss of the sea's surface, as if handfuls of sand had been thrown on it. Soon these catspaws gather force and come together. The frigate-birds wake up and throw themselves from the yards, the seagulls are screaming now, the sails catch the breeze and bellow out.

Luckily the wind comes from the right direction, so she is kept away, and steered for the distant island.

Distant island? Yes, yonder green island that appears to float in the sky. The fairy-isle, as the lads called it, while they went singing and rowing towards it.

The señor had gone forward to the bow, where around the weather bulwarks was a group of men with a puzzled half-frightened expression on their faces. No one speaks; but a dozen hands are pointed in the direction of the green island.

It has strangely altered in appearance. The hills are lower. It has lengthened out along the horizon. It is receding as the ship advances.

Señor beckons to the captain, who comes hurrying forward, and speedily turns his glass towards the island. Just then some clouds that had come up out of the sea with the wind abaft obscure the sun, and lo! the fairy isle disappears, as if suddenly engulphed in the ocean.

Hardly knowing what he is doing, the captain keeps bewilderedly sweeping the sea for a time with the glass; but never a sign of land is to be seen, only the clearly defined line 'twixt ocean and sky, for the haze has lifted or melted away.

A strange wave of superstitious dread rushes over the hearts of the men standing there near the winch, and one or two of them are deadly pale.

A sailor, more bold than the rest, clutches the captain's arm.

"Tell us, sir," he gasps, "What does it all mean?"

"Alas! lads, it means a mirage."

"Pardon me, sir, but I take leave to doubt it."

"You do?"

"I do, sir. That island lasted too long and clearly for a mirage."

"And you think?"

"I think, sir, that the isle we saw was as solid as the ship we stand upon, and that it has sunk."

"Such things have happened," said the captain. "At least they tell me so; but——. No, no; the island was a mirage. Yet, none the less, the boat is lost."

The wind that had been blowing steadily from the east now began to fall, and in a very few minutes it was once more a dead and strangely impressive calm.

But clouds were now banking up in every direction. A curious blackness had overspread the sky to the nor'ard; a blackness that appeared to be steadily advancing, blotting out the sea as it came, and accompanied by dancing, quivering lightning, that appeared to run along the surface of the water. Ominous thunders too began to roll, and before sufficient sail was taken in the storm had burst all round them.

For a time there was only mist and blackness, but shortly the rain came down in sheets, the thunder-claps were deafening, and the sea looked like sheets of fire. Anon the wind came, and such a wind. Little sail had been left on her, but the squall appeared to lift the great barque almost out of the water. For a moment she plunged bows first into it, quivering all over from stem to stern like a stricken deer; then, as if fear lent her fleetness, she dashed forward and tore through the wind-chafed ocean, with a speed that the oldest sailor on board had never seen equalled.

All that day the wind blew with hurricane force, and all the next night, then once again the weather cleared. But a gloom that could not be dispelled had settled over the ship, and when four days afterwards, after searching fruitlessly for the lost boat, the *San Salvador* bore up once more on her course, all the life and soul seemed clean gone out of every man on board.

Perhaps the most unhappy man of all was Señor Sarpinto.

"Oh," he said over and over again to Captain Cawdor, "I'd rather have lost all my fortune than that this terrible affliction should have befallen us."

"My dear sir," said the captain, "we must not repine. We are all in the hands of a merciful Father, who knows what is best for His children here below."

"Oh," cried Sarpinto, "you are good, Captain Cawdor, you are good. But do not try to cheer me up, I must and shall repine. It is my comfort to repine, for, captain, was not the fault all mine, and now I have lost the only being I seem ever to have loved on earth—save one. All my good fortune appears to have deserted me, and my life is closing in darkness and gloom."

What words of consolation could Captain Cawdor find to assuage grief like this? He stretched out his hand and grasped that of the señor.

"I too am in grief," he said quietly.

"Oh, yes, yes!" cried Sarpinto. "I had forgotten. Forgive me, my poor friend. I am selfish. But now for your sake I will try to be brighter, happier."

# CHAPTER XX
## "WHAT THEIR FATE WAS TO BE THEY COULD NOT EVEN GUESS"

After the boat left the *San Salvador*, with little Cassia-bud steering, and the great Newfoundland, Hurricane Bob, lying at his feet by way of balancing her, and keeping her well down by the stern, "Steer right away for the island," cried Fred. "We are going to row and sing, and never look behind us."

But when they had rowed for fully half an hour, and the ship looked very far away indeed, Frank, who was stroke, lay on his oar, and the others followed suit.

"Why," he said, peeping round, "we ought to be there by now."

"Dear me!" cried Fred, "how deceiving! The island looks as far away as ever!"

"Yes, and it has altered in appearance somehow, hasn't it?"

"Well, of course; but then we are low down in the water, you know. Anyhow, I'm hungry and thirsty both. Happy thought, to have a rest and some lunch."

The good things were brought out accordingly, and everybody, even Hurricane Bob, shared and shared alike. Then Quambo lit a huge pipe, and Magilvray, the sailor—a stout young fellow with a merry-looking face of his own—bit a huge quid off a stick of niggerhead, and began to look very contented indeed.

After another half-hour's pulling catspaws began to creep over the water, and a sail was hoisted.

"We'll soon be there now," said Fred.

Immediately after there was a cry from the little black coxswain.

"Oh, massa Fred, I's so frightened!"

"Whatever is the matter, Kashie?"

"See, sah, see!" he cried, pointing away ahead. "De island done go clear away out ob de world, sah!"

It was difficult indeed for any one in the boat to believe his senses. Every one felt dazed, and looked dazed. The island was gone sure enough; yet how or whither seemed inexplicable.

But the wind kept increasing every minute, and to go back now in the teeth of it was utterly impossible. So on and on the little boat flew for a time. The sea had got up so high too, all at once, that they were afraid to venture on lying to, and to lower sail meant being pooped by the racing, threatening waves.

How long they ran before the wind they never could tell. They had given themselves up for lost, however, and sat there in the gathering gloom of the awful thunder-storm silent and despairing, like men without hope and energy.

Fred himself had taken the tiller, and Cassia-bud was crouched in the bottom of the boat, hugging his friend Bob in abject terror.

But if Fred and Frank were puzzled by the disappearance of the fairy-isle, as they had called it, their astonishment knew no bounds when the boat was suddenly caught up by a huge wave, and hurled forward into a chaos of broken water and roaring breakers. Hurled into it? Yes, and hurled over it, into water that was as smooth as a mill-pond stirred by a summer's breeze. Behind them and away in a circle all around breakers foamed and roared and thundered. There was the quick, incessant gleam of lightning from out the blackness of the weather clouds; but yonder, not a hundred yards away, was an island, low and almost level, but fringed with cocoa-nut trees, and with an undergrowth of waving palms and other tropical shrubs.

In five minutes' time the boat was drawn up on the snow-white coral beach, and the thunder-storm had burst over them in all its violence.

By-and-by the sky partially cleared, and though the wind still blew high they crept out from the shelter of a cave in which they had found refuge, and began seriously to consider their position.

It was some time, however, before the whole extent of their misfortune was fully realized by them.

But as the time went on, and the hurricane appeared to be again on the increase, causing them to seek for shelter once more in the cave, a hurricane such as no ship dare attempt to lie-to in, then indeed hope began to die out in their hearts, and they *felt* they were alone. They felt this still more when the sun went down, and pitch darkness almost immediately followed.

They dared even yet, however, to hope against hope; the ship would surely return and seek for and find them. It was gloomy enough in this cave certainly, with the wind tearing through the scrubby jungle and the cocoa-nut palms that covered the little island, and with the awful boom of the breakers on the circular reef of coral surrounding the lagoon, but then it was only for a night.

"*Only* for a night," said Frank.

"Yes, *only* for a night," reiterated Fred.

"If we had a light, though, it would be all the more cheerful."

"Yes, well I have matches, but there is nothing here to light."

"We'd better keep the matches," said Frank. "Are you sure you have them safe and dry?"

"But why so anxious, lad?"

"I don't know. I——I——"

"Oh, brother, don't think of it! I'm going out to feel for the boat and fetch the supper."

"And I'll go with you."

In the darkness this was no easy task, and the wind was so high they had to bend low, almost crawling in fact.

But they were lucky enough to find the food, and a portion being handed round to everybody, not forgetting Bob, all hands did justice to the good cheer, and then Quambo and Magilvray lit their pipes, and the cave was more home-like after that.

They sat talking there till it must have been far into the night, then, lying back on the soft, warm sand, one by one they dropped off to sleep.

They had not even thought of setting sentry. What was there here to be afraid of? Nothing, surely. Besides, the great, honest dog, Hurricane Bob, always made a point of sleeping with one eye a little open, so if anyone was sentry that night it was Bob.

The sun was high in the heavens when Fred awoke next morning, and shouted to his companions:

"What's for breakfast?" said Frank, sitting up and rubbing his eyes.

"Ah! what indeed?" said Fred, laughing. "Why we ate all our breakfast last night. But where is Cassia-bud?"

Cassia-bud was not to be seen, but presently he appeared out of the jungle laden with cocoanuts and pandany. This pandany or pandanus is the screw pine, which grows on nearly all the islands of these regions, and is one of the first to appear when coral reefs assume the shape and substance of islands, the seed being either floated thither on tree trunks or brought by birds.

Finding the cocoanuts had been a far too easy task, for every tree was levelled almost to the ground, one alone being left standing.

After breakfast Fred and Frank set out to explore the island, leaving the others on the beach with the boat. This exploration did not occupy much time, the whole island being only a few acres in extent, and scarcely anything growing on it except the few cocoanut trees, and the strange-looking scrubby pandanus. This tree, the leaves of which are like big vegetable corkscrews, grows from roots that are above ground, like the legs of a milking-stool, somewhat after the fashion of the mangrove trees of African shores.

The wind had almost died away, but the breakers still thundered on the reef that surrounded the lagoon. I trust I make the position of our heroes clear enough; the little island was nearly round, and entirely surrounded by a broad natural moat, let us call it, of water, which in its turn was encircled by the coral reef. The moat, however, was about seventy yards wide or more all round.

They now launched the boat, and embarking pulled right round the inside of the reef, with the view of finding out the lane therein that led to the sea. They did so at last, but it was so narrow that the presumption was, they had been carried right over the reef itself, on the previous day, by a high tidal wave.

Like nearly all Scotch boys who are brought up in the woods and wilds, Fred Arundel could climb trees well. It did not take him very long, therefore, to shin to the top of the solitary cocoanut tree, although it was fully forty feet in height. It afforded a splendid ocean view all around, and Fred managed to unsling his telescope, and scan the horizon on every side. As far as he could make out never a ship nor sail of any kind was visible, but his heart beat high with hope and joy when, away towards the south, his glass rested on what appeared to be the hills or mountains of some island in the midst of the sea.

His hopes fell again, however, when he thought of the fairy island that had lured them away from the ship the day before. This also might be a mirage. Well, if it were so it would dissolve away; they could but wait and see. So he came down again to report.

It was far on in the afternoon before they succeeded in getting enough dry stuff to light a fire withal.

Meantime Cassia-bud, who had constituted himself caterer and lions' provider, had found some huge crabs, and having killed them they were cooked in their shells, and a very delicious meal they made, washed down with a drink of cool milk from young cocoanuts.

When they had dined more bark was heaped upon the fire, and green stuff spread over that in order to raise as dense a smoke as possible. For trailing across the blue sea of the tropics smoke may be seen a very long distance off.

Before sunset Fred once more ascended the tree or look-out station, as he called it, and once more scanned the horizon. It was much clearer now, but no sail was visible.

But to his joy the island in the south was still there. So he concluded it must be real.

Cassia-bud had been paddling about in the lagoon all by himself, and just as the sun was dipping low towards the ocean he landed, and with a face that positively beamed with joy he threw down five beautiful fish at Fred's feet. They were beautiful in colour as well as in size and substance. "How lucky we were to have brought fishing-gear with us," cried Fred; "and really, Kashie, you're a perfect treasure."

Meanwhile Quambo had cleared the fire and erected a tripod of sticks over it with cross-pieces, and on this the fish were hung, and soon began to fizzle and steam.

Fred and Frank were lying on the smooth white sand, watching Quambo's preparations for supper. "I say, Fred," said Frank, "what does this remind you of?"

The tears rushed to Fred's eyes.

"Oh, Frank, I well remember! You are thinking of our Crusoe life on the desert island in Scotland. Ah! dear me, and now we are Crusoes in stern reality."

"Don't you wish that Toddie was here? Dear wee Toddie and the little dog Tip."

"I do and I don't. I wish we could only bring back old times, when you and I were young, though."

"Ah! well, we're not very particularly old yet, are we?"

"Supper is all ready, sah," said Quambo. And a glorious supper it was; for everyone was gloriously hungry.

The only part of yesterday's provisions that still held out was the salt. For in his hurry, when coming away, Quambo had rolled an immense piece in a table napkin.

There was enough fish left for breakfast, but they took the precaution to stow it away in the locker of the boat.

Next day and another and still another passed monotonously away, and it was now evident to all they might never expect to see their ship again. And do as they would, they now began to feel lonely and cheerless.

They were prisoners in this cockle-shell of a coral island, and the hope of being picked up seemed very remote indeed. Meanwhile what about food even? The fish might possibly fail them, the robber crabs might keep aloof, and they would soon eat up all the cocoanuts and pandanus fruit in the place.

To remain here, therefore, was but to wait for death, and to attempt to get away was—well, what was it?

"What do you think about it, Frank," said Fred one evening, as they all lay on the soft sand, with the cheerful light of the camp fire flickering in their faces.

"About what?" said Frank, whose thoughts had been far, far away indeed.

"Why about attempting to escape?"

"Oh, we are, very likely, a thousand miles and over from any civilized settlement!"

"Quite true, but the island yonder, for it is no mirage, affords us the chance of life that this island will very soon deny us."

"How far does it seem to be off, sir?" said Magilvray.

"As near as I can judge, about forty miles."

"A long pull, sir."

"True," said Fred; "but better, I think, to start early on a calm day and pull all the way, than trust to the treacherous winds of these regions, which in half an hour may increase to hurricane force."

"That is so, sah, for true," said Quambo.

"Then," said Frank, "supposing we manage to land there, what next?"

Quambo smiled grimly.

"What are you thinking about, Quambo?"

"I think, sah, dat if sabages lib on de island yonder, dey soon cook us all and gobble us up plenty quick. Dat all, sah."

"Yes, Quambo," said Frank, "that would be all."

There was silence for a time after this, a silence that Fred Arundel was the first to break.

"Boys," he said solemnly enough, "I believe I have thought the matter out in all its bearings. To me it is evident enough, that our only chance of life lies in an attempt to reach yonder island, and if death it is going to be, surely it is better to die at once, even at the hands of savages, then stay here to be slowly starved to death."

"That is just what I think too, sir," said Magilvray, "and what is more, the sooner we set about it the better."

So it was resolved that very night, that all preparations for the daring voyage should be gone into next day, and that on the day following, if the weather were favourable, they should leave the island.

Fred slept more calmly that night than he had done since they landed. Before lying down he had gone away by himself for a little distance into the jungle, and kneeling down beside a fallen tree, prayed long and earnestly that He who had hitherto protected and guided him through many a danger, seen and unseen, would condescend to bless their little enterprise, and grant them hope and safety.

He sat for some time on the tree stem, for the stars were shining very brightly and clearly, then slowly returned to the cave, and threw himself down on the warm white sand; and thinking of home and the dear ones in the fisherman's cottage, he was soon fast asleep. The preparations for the voyage were few but important; namely, the procuring and cooking of a good supply of food.

But fortune favoured them. They loaded their boat therefore the night before, and as soon as day broke over the ocean they rowed out through the narrow opening in the reef, and headed away for the distant island. What their fate was to be they could not even guess. They trusted all to God.

# CHAPTER XXI
## "A LAND FLOWING WITH COCOANUT-MILK AND HONEY"

A day of more anxiety or of greater fatigue it would have been difficult to conceive, than that which our heroes endured, in their perilous voyage towards the unknown island. The sun blazed almost perpendicularly down on them at mid-day. Both Fred and Frank had been red before, but now it seemed as though they would soon be burned as black as Quambo or Cassia-bud himself. So fierce was the sun's heat that neither of the lads could partake of the food they had taken with them. Their thirst became almost unbearable at last, and the cocoanut milk, or rather water from the young nuts, which they drank, appeared rather to increase than to assuage their thirst. What would they not have given for a draught of cool spring water from the little rill that trickled from the rock near the igloo at Methlin! Strange that they should have both been thinking about this at the same time, but so it soon turned out.

"I know where I should like to be, Fred, just for five minutes," said Frank, as they paused for a moment's rest.

"Oh, I know!" cried Fred; "at the igloo fountain!"

"Yes, lying under the rocks there, and watching the water trickling through the green grass and the rushes, and laving my brow with it, and filling my hands with the clear water, and drinking from my hands."

"Oh, I shouldn't! I should stick my mouth right into the well at the foot, and I don't think I would ever stop drinking."

It is not to be wondered at that in their dire extremity the boys talked thus; for I have found from experience that the next best thing to eating food or drinking water, when you are very hungry or thirsty, and cannot get any, is to think of it. This is natural, and seems to soothe one. When lying ill of a burning fever on African shores, I remember that in my dreams I used to fancy myself wandering by rippling burns in my far-off home in Scotland.

To-day Cassia-bud was coxswain as usual, but towards afternoon, when thoroughly faint and weary, many a look behind them did the rowers cast.

To make matters worse, they found that when still three miles at least away from the island the current was so strong it began to be a matter of doubt whether they should ever reach it.

The boat's head was kept well up therefore, and all hands redoubled their efforts to send her on. Fred even started a song, but for once in a way this was a failure. There was nothing for it but to struggle on in silence.

At long last they got clear out of the race of the tide, and now it remained to find a landing-place.

The island was a very lovely and romantic-looking one indeed, an island evidently formed at first by volcanic upheaval, but now green-clad, to the summit of its strangely-shaped hills, with a luxuriance of tropical vegetation such as no one in the boat had ever seen surpassed.

It was doubtless the reflected image of this beautiful isle of the sea, that had caused the mirage which lost our heroes their ship.

They now lay on their oars for a time, to rest and think. It seemed evident that the island was uninhabited. Never a canoe was seen anywhere near it, nor were there any signs of hut or habitation by the beach, and never a vestige of smoke.

However, it appeared to be a very large island, and as yet they had seen but a portion of it. They first made the northern end of it; but here all around was a wall of black beetling crags frowning over the sea, the waves dashing up the sides of it and breaking into snow-white foam with a booming noise, that, mingling with the cry of sea-birds, made a wild and weird-like chorus on the still evening air.

There was no time to be lost, for the sun was rapidly declining; so, noticing that the dip of the hills trended to the southward and west, they made haste to row in that direction. The crags got lower and lower, but jutted out to sea at last, forming a cape or rocky promontory. Once past this, they found a coral reef lying all along the tree-shaded shore, about three hundred yards distant from it. On this the breakers were dashing with great force, and tossing their white arms high in air.

They rowed along the edge of this terrible barrier; and just as they were about to despair of finding an opening, beheld in front of them a narrow, very narrow, creek of unbroken water.

"Hard a-port, Kashia! Round with her, boy!"

"Ha'd a-po't it is, sah!" cried Cassia-bud.

Round came the boat like a beauty, and next moment they were carried right into a splendid reef-locked harbour, large enough for the whole British navy to have lain snugly and comfortably in.

"Heaven be praised!" said Fred with a sigh, as he paused to wipe the perspiration from his brow.

In ten minutes more they had landed.

The sun was by this time nearly touching the water's edge; and almost before they had time to draw the boat well up, and find shelter from the dews of night under some friendly boughs, his last rays were tinging the foam of the breakers with crimson.

"Now, Quambo, open me a nice green cocoa-nut," cried Fred. "I can drink now, and presently I think I'll be able to eat as well."

Tired in the extreme though every one was, supper was eaten and thoroughly enjoyed. But soon after this Nature would not be denied; and although a daring attempt at conversation was made, it utterly failed, and one by one the Crusoes dropped soundly off to sleep.

The shadows of the mountains lay across the reef-locked harbour when Fred Arundel awoke next morning. The others were fast asleep, little Cassia-bud as usual with Hurricane Bob's paws drawn round his neck. So Fred got quietly up, and walked down to the beach. How clear and cool the water looked! How serene and beautiful the morning! The temptation to bathe was too great to be resisted, so he divested himself of his garments, and was soon splashing and swimming about to his heart's content. He had gone but a little way out, however, and was just thinking how delightful it would be to swim right away over to the reef and back, when his attention was attracted by the strange conduct of the Newfoundland. He was running along the edge of the beach, not only barking, but positively bellowing. A sudden and terrible fear at that moment got possession of Fred's senses. His very heart grew cold. He seemed to feel as powerless for the time being as a person under the spell of some hideous nightmare. It was gone in a second or two, and he was hastening towards the beach. He never looked behind him till safe on shore. It was well for him perhaps he did not, for a glance told him then that the water was teeming with monster sharks. The joy of the dog appeared to know no bounds, and if it had not been for this faithful fellow, poor Fred would undoubtedly have met a terrible fate.

As soon as breakfast was finished, it was determined to make an exploration of Good Hope Island, as they had named it. For aught they knew it might be inhabited by savages, in which case, instead of being "monarchs of all they surveyed," they would very soon be slaves, if indeed their lives should be spared.

It was arranged, therefore, that Magilvray and Hurricane Bob should be boatkeepers, and remain on the beach, while Fred and Frank went towards the hill-tops to make a general survey, and Quambo with little Kashie should "spy out the land" with reference to its food resources.

That the island was inhabited, Fred and his friend had not to advance far before finding out. The jungle was seemingly impenetrable at first, and while forcing their way through it they came upon some very ugly customers in the shape of snakes. Whether harmless or otherwise it was impossible to tell. When, however, they found one hanging to the branches of a tree they considered it best to give it a wide berth.

If there were no more dangerous beings in the island than snakes, they made up their minds that they would be content and thankful.

Presently as they got upon higher ground the trees got larger and more sparse. They soon found themselves on the ridge of what was evidently the highest mountain in the island. Owing to its being so well wooded it was seldom they could catch a glimpse of the world beyond; but soon it ended in a bare bluff covered with rough withered grass, and studded here and there with cactus bushes.

In less than half an hour they had reached the top, and sat down to rest. And lo! all the island, with its hills and dells and forests, and its wonderful flowering trees, was spread out at their feet, and all around was an unlimited expanse of ocean, asleep in the morning sunshine. For the most part the sea was blue, yet a blue so soft, so ethereal, as surely no artist in this world ever yet transferred to his canvas. Along the reefs that guarded the island were long lines of snow-white—the breaking water—and two sides were bounded by beaches of silvery sand. But as far as eye could reach not a dot nor particle of land was at first to be seen, with the exception of the little isle, with its rock-girt lagoon, which they had left yesterday morning.

They seemed to be right in the centre of a lonesome ocean, and in all probability on an island that was not even marked on the chart. Of this, however, they could have no certainty.

How very still it was up here on this high hill-top. The slightest sounds could be heard from below. Their camping ground, on the beach, must have been a good mile off, yet every now and then they could distinctly hear the deep mellow bark of the great Newfoundland dog. Somewhere in the woods, busy at work doubtless, were Quambo and Kashie, for occasionally their merry ringing laughter was audible enough. Nearer still were heard the joy-songs of thousands of happy birds; and, mingling with all, the drowsy monotone of the waves breaking on the coral reef.

Fred and Frank sat for quite a long time in silence, but by the look of calmness on the face of each, their thoughts could not have been unpleasant.

"Well, Frank," said Fred at last, "what do you think of the outlook?"

"What, the scenery or our prospects?"

"Well, both for instance."

"Why I never saw more charming scenery in my life. Its very lonesomeness, I think, is its chief charm. Just look at that immensity of sea stretching all round us, Fred. If it were not so blue and so bright it might be even a little eeriesome in its very lone beauty."

"Yes, Frank; but don't you see that very lonesomeness may prove our safety? With my glass now, just away out yonder, I seem able to raise the peak of a mountain, but it is very far away. I daresay it is an inhabited island, and very likely there is a group of them. Well, Captain Cawdor told me that all the islands for hundreds of miles around were filled with races of implacable savages and cannibals. But I think we are too far off to be visited by them. If they did come, heaven only knows what would happen, because we are not nearly numerous enough to fight them; so I am sure we are perfectly safe."

"So am I," said Frank, "and I feel very much inclined to enjoy the *dolce far niente* and just let things slide."

"So do I. Wouldn't you rather be a barrister though than a Crusoe?"

"Oh, Fred, just think of being stowed away in a stuffy cobwebby old office in smoky London, and thinking nothing about, or knowing nothing about, such a glorious free and easy life as this.

"True, Frank, and to think that it is not a long time since we were away down at the bottom of the map, as you might say, in the darkness and cold that reigns perpetually around the southern sea of ice! And to think, Frank, that I should have found you there!"

"That is the best of it. Oh, it just had to be, Fred!"

"Well," replied Fred, "I'm so glad. And do you remember the vow we made when little chaps, and while playing at Crusoes in Scotland?"

"What, to be brothers, Fred? Yes, lad, and here I do renew it."

Once more hands were clasped and eye met eye.

"Brothers yet," said Frank.

"Brothers ever," said Fred.

Then hand in hand down the hill they went towards the camp singing — singing quite as gaily as the bright-winged birds that hopped from bough to bough in those beautiful sunny woods.

They lingered here and there in glades and openings to gaze and wonder at the marvellous display of life everywhere spread out before them in jungle and forest. The air was filled with the hum of myriads of insects, the ground and ferns and bushes of every sort were instinct with life and joy, and happiness too, apparently. The beetles even were a sight to see, in their gorgeous metallic tints of blue and green and crimson, and the butterflies that floated from flower to flower, on shrub or tree, looked like splendidly-painted fans, while a rich and luscious perfume filled the air, that in some of the more sunny glades was almost overpowering.

Quambo and Cassia-bud were both back before our heroes. They came smiling to meet them.

"Well, boys," said Fred, "I see you're back, and I know you haven't come empty-handed."

"Oh no, massa!" said little Kashie, seizing Fred by the hand. "Run quick and see, massa."

He led Fred to the boat. Why the stern-sheets were laden with luscious fruit, even the names of many of which neither Frank nor Fred could tell. Nor had these faithful blacks forgotten to bring flowers. But this was not all, for Kashie pointed triumphantly to a dozen "sonsy" fish he had caught, and Quambo tapped the boat's breaker significantly — it was filled to the brim with pure, delicious water.

Nor had Magilvray been idle all the forenoon. He had not only a clear fire burning and ready to cook the dinner, but he had, by cutting down green boughs, succeeded in making a cool and delightful tent, that should be impervious to the heaviest shower that could fall.

Fred, as he looked around him at all these preparations for health and comfort, could not help laughing with very joy.

"Why, Frank," he cried, "and boys all, fortune has taken a turn for the better, and led us to a land that is literally flowing with milk and honey."

"Cocoanut milk and honey, yes," said Frank, laughing in his turn. "There are certainly busy bees about."

Then down the two brothers threw themselves in the cool, green shade to talk and build castles in the air till dinner was ready.

# CHAPTER XXII
# A TERRIBLE APPARITION

They spent the afternoon dreamily wandering about in the woods or on the beach; for Fred and Frank, not being used to real hard manual labour, had hardly yet got over the fatigues of the day before. But Quambo and Magilvray were not so idle. They were busy cutting down the dead branches in the jungle, and bearing them to the beach to serve as firewood. They soon had an immense pile handy.

So all the evening, from half-past six, when it fell dark, till everybody turned in for the night, the camp fire was kept alight. Not that heat was needed by any means, but simply because, as Fred phrased it, "it looked cosy."

And now, although these marooned mariners determined to take life easy, and make themselves as happy and comfortable as circumstances would permit, they took means, nevertheless, by which it was possible that the attention of some passing ship might be arrested, and so perchance their deliverance effected. This consisted in erecting a beacon on the hill-top, and on the very next morning they set about the work.

For once in a way little Cassia-bud was left, in company with Hurricane Bob, to mind the camp, while the others betook themselves to the mountain. Under the circumstances the task of preparing and hoisting the beacon was by no means a very simple one. It was easy to find a tree long and straight and tall enough, but having no other tools but their jackknives, it took a very long time indeed to cut it down, to trim, and hoist it.

At first it was proposed by Frank, and seconded by Magilvray, to turn the beacon into a kind of flagstaff, the flag itself being a large piece of spare canvas that happened to be in the boat.

"There is this objection to your plan," said Fred, laughing, "canvas doesn't make much of a show as a flag; it doesn't dry easy after a shower; and if it once gets wound round the pole it will cling like death to a dead nigger. No, I say let it be a beacon; and I've heard Daddy Pop remark, in days of old, Frank, that there is no beacon so effective as a broom."

"All right then," said Fred, "let us hoist the broom."

So the broom-beacon was hoisted accordingly; and if the reader wants to know what it looked like when up, let him imagine a tall and sturdy flagstaff with a huge bunch of branches attached to the very summit of it.

It looked splendid, I do assure you, and was not only visible from the camp, but capable of being seen from far at sea. After it was up, and the pole firmly fixed by means of stones rammed well home by hitting them hammer-fashion with other stones, Fred took off his cap, and waving it round his head timed his companions with a "Hip, hip, hip!" to three rattling good British cheers.

"Wowff—wowff—wowff!" that was the sound of Hurricane Bob's voice in response to the cheers, and it was afterwards discovered that little Cassia-bud, well knowing that his own feeble cheering would not be heard, had excited the dog to bark.

"Well," said Magilvray, looking up at the broom, "I must say, young gents, as how I'd 'ave preferred seeing a flag flyin'. The broom looks Dutch, don't it?"

"Oh, yes! by-the-by," said Frank, "Mac is right, Fred. There was a great Dutch admiral, you remember who once hoisted a broom at the mainmast head, and swore he wouldn't take it down again till he had swept the British from the seas. What was his name? Von Trump, or Von Dunk, or something, wasn't it?"

"Van der Decken!" said Fred seriously.

"You're laughing at me," said Frank. "But come on, men, I'm as hungry as a tiger, and nothing to eat but cold fish and fruit when we get home."

No wonder, indeed, that all hands were hungry; for hoisting the broom had taken them nearly the whole day.

They reached the beach about two hundred yards from the camp. Cassia-bud had heard them coming along through the bush, and had run along the white soft sands to meet them, Hurricane Bob bringing up the rear. Kashie was breathless, not with running, but with fear. It must be remembered he was little more than a child. The giant Quambo took him up in his arms, and clinging to his big friend's neck he cast frightened glances seawards, looking the very picture of abject terror.

"Oh, massa!" he gasped, looking piteously at Fred, "I'se seen de debbil, and I not want to stop any more all by myse'f near the sea."

"Seen the devil, Kashie! What do you mean, boy? When did you see him? What was he like, eh?"

"Oh, sah, he like one awful big fish, bigger than a boat, sah! He jump right up out ob de sea one, two, tree time. Jump right high up in de sky; and he all black, wid awful eyes, sah, and, oh! sah, *he had nuffin on but his head*. It was de debbil, sah, fob true."

Fred and Frank both burst out laughing, but the poor child seemed really and truly scared nearly out of his wits.

"Well," said Fred, "it is evident Cassia-bud has seen something. But surely the island is haunted! What a fearful apparition! The head of a fish as big as a boat, and awful eyes, or, as Kashie calls it, a fish with 'nuffin on but his head,' leaping black against the blue of the sky. Horrible!"

It took quite a long time to comfort Kashie; but when at last Fred said, "Well, come along, Kash, I'm hungry, bring out the cold fish," then Kashie wriggled out of Quambo's arms, and off he ran in front.

It would be hard to say whether our hungry heroes were more pleased or surprised to find that the boy had cooked them a capital dinner of roasted fish, crab, and plantains. The latter ate like mealy potatoes. Moreover, he had been up in the bush, and had found plates growing on the trees, big broad scented leaves of the lemon *Hibiscus*, and beside each plate stuck in the soft sand was a green cocoa-nut all ready to drink.*

> * The green cocoa-nut contains scarcely any kernel, but about a quart of most delightful, cool, and delicious water.

Poor little Kashie gradually grew happier now, and was soon his laughing white-toothed rolling-eyed little self again. And as for the others, they had not felt so cheerful and merry since they had been accidentally marooned.

I must say here at once, and be done with it, that one cause of the extra jollity exhibited by Quambo and Magilvray, was rooted in the fact that on this very day the giant negro had found a species of wild tobacco growing on the mountain side. I think it is called *krava* or *grava* by natives of Polynesia. I only judge by the sound. However Magilvray said to Fred more than once that evening that a load was lifted off his mind.

"I don't mind wanting rum or coffee," he said, "but better 'ang me at once, sir, than cut off my bit o' baccy. So here's good luck to 'Ope Island, says I."

And with that brief speech Magilvray took a large drink from his cocoa-nut, and stuck it in the sand again, with a look of satisfaction that was most refreshing to behold.

Long after the sun went down that night there was bright moonlight.

Only half a moon was shining it is true, but the air being so clear everything was almost as bright as day in England.

"What do you say to a row on the lake to-night?" said Fred.

"Yes, happy thought!" cried Frank, "a row and a song."

The sheet of smooth water betwixt the reef and the shore was called the lake by our Crusoes.

It was indeed a lovely night; a bank of coral-white clouds lay low on the horizon, otherwise the dark blue sky-depths were studded over with silvery stars of singular brilliancy, while the moon shed a broad band of clearest light across the rippling sea.

Shorewards the hills, and glens, and groves of cocoa palms were softened and spiritualized by the moon's mellow rays.

To-night Magilvray stayed at home with little Kashie, while Quambo and Frank rowed the boat, Fred took the tiller, and Hurricane Bob stood in the bows.

But Fred had another duty to perform, he had to lead the singing.

What a happy, hopeful time is youth! Here were our two heroes cast away on a lonely island in the midst of the sea, far removed from the tracks of commerce, with no means of communicating with the outer world—buried alive one might say—yet on this bright, beautiful night, rowing about on the placid bosom of the bay, as devoid of all thought and care as if sailing on Loch Lomond or Windermere. Some portion of the happiness they felt, and the hopefulness too, was undoubtedly due to the climate itself. The air here is so pure, the breath of the ocean, mingling with the spicy odours from off the island, so balmy, so life-giving, that only to exist is to live, only to have being is calmness and content combined.

For two whole hours they rowed up and down their lake, singing the songs of their far-off native land, only desisting now and then to lean on their oars and talk of home and dear old times—times that appeared to their young minds already long buried in the distant past.

They were slowly paddling along the inside of the reef, just beyond the range of the falling spray. But this last was but little to-night, for the tide was well out, and there was scarcely any swell on.

Yet the sound of the breaking waters was very soothing, and caused them to linger longer alongside the reef than they might otherwise have done.

Fred was just clearing his throat for another song, when he was attracted by the strange attitude of the Newfoundland. The dog was standing with his forepaws on the gunwale of the boat, his ears were forward, his hair on end from head to tail, and uttering a low, half-frightened, but ominous growl.

"Look at the dog," cried Fred. "He sees or hears something on the reef or over it."

The idea of savages in their canoes at once occurred to Frank, for nobody was even yet sure that the island was entirely uninhabited.

"Better pull a little way in, I think," said Frank.

"Give way then," said Fred.

The oars were silently dipped into the water, all three men listening intently at the time, with their faces turned towards the reef.

Suddenly on the other side of the surf they distinctly heard a hustling, rushing, fearful noise, accompanied by a low but startling cry, as of some creature in dire distress.

Nearer and nearer with almost the speed of a rocket it seemed to come, then ceased entirely, but at the same time, betwixt them and the moonlight, at least fifteen feet high in the air, they beheld an apparition that, in such a situation, was enough to frighten the boldest man that ever lived.

It was simply the great black head and two fins—no more apparently—of a monster fish with goggle eyes and open mouth. It took the water near the boat, raising a wave of breaking water that all but swamped it, and was seen no more.

When Fred looked up he saw both Quambo and Frank crouched down almost in the bottom of the boat, though it was half full of water.

Frank was the first to speak.

"Mercy on us!" he cried. "What was that?"

"Favaroo! favaroo!" said Quambo. "That is *favaroo*." His voice trembled as he spoke. "A devil fish; de evil spirit bite all away his body one day, and now he go everywhere trying to find he."

"Oh!" cried Fred, laughing now, "that is really the awful creature that little Kashie took for 'de debbil that hadn't got nuffin on but his head.' It is a sunfish as big as an elephant."

"Well," said Frank, "I've heard of such visitations, but I didn't know the beast could jump like that before. Let us bail out the boat. Why she is half swamped!"

"What a mercy the monster didn't fall on us. Where would we have been, Fred?"

"Look there," said Fred, pointing over the gunwale.

Frank gazed fearfully in the direction indicated. Two monster tiger sharks were floating quietly about near the boat.

Suddenly Fred sprang to his feet.

"Oh, men," he cried, "where is the dog? Where is poor Hurricane Bob?"

The question was by no means difficult to answer. Without doubt in the extremity of his terror he had sprung overboard, and been instantly devoured by the sharks. What a sad and sudden ending to a moonlight concert!

Bob was a favourite, not with Cassia-bud only, but with everybody, and to lose the noble fellow, and lose him thus. It was altogether too shocking to think about!

Straight away for the shore they rowed now, but in silence all. They had received a shock that it would take weeks to get over. Not from the terror of the apparition, but from the loss of the honest dog, who had really come to be considered one of themselves.

Their astonishment and delight therefore may be better conceived than described, when, as soon as the boat rasped upon the silvery sand, Hurricane Bob himself came joyfully bounding and barking to meet them.

Instead of attempting to get into the boat again he had simply headed away for the beach, and landed in safety. But, strange to say, the dog from that day forward could seldom be prevailed upon to go even a little way into the water, and when taken anywhere in the boat he invariably crouched down beneath the thwarts, lying there quietly until once more safe on shore.

But the adventure of this evening quite cleared up the mystery, of Cassia-bud's "debbil with nuffin but his head on."

# CHAPTER XXIII
# A SWIM FOR DEAR LIFE—
# PURSUED BY SHARKS

As long as the moonlight lasted the evenings were very pleasant indeed, and every night Fred, Frank, and Quambo went out for a row and a song. Hurricane Bob begged so earnestly to be excused that it was thought best to leave him on shore.

Magilvray and Cassia-bud also expressed themselves as perfectly content to take a back seat at the evening concert, or, in other words, to lie on the beach and listen there. Probably they thus had the best of it; for the sound of the singing floating over the water was weirdly tremulous and beautiful.

The singers, however, thought it safest to keep well away from the reef. There was something decidedly uncanny in the sight of that black and terrible apparition springing over the reef. Besides, as Frank said, if that was the brute's usual way of coming home of an evening, the wisest plan was to give him a wide berth. Explorations of the island, which was many miles in extent, took place every day. These little excursions formed a very pleasant way of spending the greater portion of the day, there was so much that were strangely foreign and beautiful to be beheld, and so many pretty peeps of scenery. The whole island, indeed, and everything in it, was as different from anything that Fred and Frank had seen before, as if it had been part and parcel of some other planet.

Sometimes it was Cassia-bud who came with them, at other times Quambo or Magilvray, and sometimes it was Hurricane Bob only. Whoever stayed at home had to cook the dinner, and just as often as not had to catch it also.

Cassia-bud was the fisher-boy *par excellence*. He was never better pleased than when out on the water all by himself, armed with rod and reel, or with hand-line only! His whole evenings used to be devoted to the study of bait, and when he went fishing he seemed to know the very spot at which to sink his line in order to procure some particular kind of fish.

He found several species of skates and rays, a huge kind of conger-eel—the first he caught frightened poor Cassia-bud, and almost as much as "de debbil fish" had—many other nameless and curious fishes, all good to eat, and mackerel. These last were not such as we in England are used to, but cooked as Quambo cooked them they were very delicious indeed. They were very numerous too in some parts of this reef-locked bay, and Quambo's plan was to start Cassia-bud out to catch two or three just half an hour before dinner, and pull on shore with them immediately. The fish were killed and cleaned, then cut up the back after the fashion of kippered salmon, and roasted before a clear fire. Served hot then with the acid juice of a species of lemon that grew on the Isle of Good Hope, they made a dish that might have graced the table of a king.

About every second day a visit was paid to the top of Beacon Hill, and the horizon eagerly scanned for sight of some passing vessel. Had any such appeared a huge pile of brushwood, both withered and green, would have been kindled in hopes of attracting attention. But days and weeks flew by and no sail was ever sighted.

When men are stranded on an island as our heroes were, it is always the first month or six weeks that seem the longest time. After this the Crusoe or Crusoes settle down more, and the time flies more quickly on.

As to reckoning the days, Fred and Frank were not reduced to the necessity of notching a tree, for one of them happened to possess a note-book with an almanack in it, and every noon one day was ticked off.

Of wild beasts the island possessed not a single specimen, but a curious kind of coney or cavy, they could not tell which, even after Cassia-bud one day succeeded in shooting one with a bow and arrow he had made. Cassia-bud roasted the beast and ate it for supper, for the lad had a wonderful appetite. Bob enjoyed the bones.

"Was it nice?" said Frank. "Did you enjoy it, Kashie?"

"Oh, sab, he just too awful jolly for anything!" replied the boy, licking his lips and rolling his eyes.

"Well, Kash, you must shoot some more you know, and then perhaps we'll all have a taste."

These creatures were to be found in very great abundance on one particularly rocky glen, where they had their burrows.

On the very next morning, after receiving his commission, Cassia-bud and Hurricane Bob both disappeared in the woods, and about noon emerged again, Bob carrying a coney that he himself had captured, and Cassia-bud carrying four.

"Bravo!" cried Fred, picking the lad up as soon as he had thrown down his burden; "now for a game of live-ball to make Kashie hungry."

"Play!" he shouted, pitching the little laughing black ball of a boy towards Quambo.

"Play!" cried Quambo, throwing him to Magilvray.

"Keep the pot a-boilin'," roared Magilvray, and next moment Frank had caught the lad and pitched him back to Fred.

They kept the game up for ten minutes. It was as good as dumb-bells, Fred said. The rule of the game was, that when anyone dropped the live-ball on the sand he was to stand out. At last there was nobody in except Quambo. He hoisted Cassia-bud right up on his shoulders, and there the boy stood erect while the giant went capering up and down the sands, with Hurricane Bob barking around them for joy.

Well, Cassia-bud's conies, or cavies, proved most delightful eating, and were quite a change from fish fish, fish morn, noon, and night.

But it must not be supposed that because there were no wild beasts in the island, there were no wild adventures to be had. No; for there was the sea, and adventure is inseparable from the briny ocean.

It would be difficult indeed to say how many different species of sharks there were in the bay. Quambo was rather an authority on the natural family *Squalidæ*, and both Fred and Frank had seen a shark or two in their time. Well, there were at all events the blue shark, the basking shark, the white shark, and the most dread monster of all, the tiger shark. This last was admitted by the other species to be *facile princeps*, for whenever one appeared the others modestly retired.

Strange as it may appear, Cassia-bud had not the slightest fear of these awful demons of the sea. But an adventure he had one day while fishing was surely enough to scare the senses out of any boy one whit less brave.

He was fishing as usual one afternoon when Fred and Frank had got home earlier than usual from their woodland rambles, and were lying on the sands watching his sport. The boy had caught about a dozen or more good-sized fish, stringing them one by one as he did so on a long, supple wand, that after he landed he could carry across his shoulder—so many fish behind, so many in front of him. Every now and then near Cassia-bud's boat the ominous-looking fins of a huge shark could be seen protruding from the water. The very sight made Frank's spine feel cold.

Suddenly, to their horror, they noticed that in leaning over the gunwale of the gig and hauling in his line, to which it appeared afterwards a huge conger was attached, the boat was capsized, and with a frightened scream Cassia-bud was precipitated into the water. Probably there is not an English boy who lives that would have done what this negro child did then. He seized his stick of fish, and commenced swimming rapidly shorewards. For a moment or two perhaps the sharks were frightened off, but they were speedily in pursuit of the boy. One, two, three, four great fins could be counted in his rear.

Both Fred and Frank started to their feet, and stood staring, speechless and aghast. They would have given a good deal could they have turned away their eyes from watching the threatened tragedy. On and on came the black, round head, with the frightened face and rolling eyes, and on and on came the sharks.

The onlookers marvelled, however, to notice that every now and again the pursuing sharks paused, and their heads seemed to be turned towards each other. But only for a moment or two; then they speedily took up the chase again, but only to pause as before.

Nearer and nearer comes Cassia-bud. Greater and greater becomes the suspense of Frank, Fred, and the others.

Will he be saved? Can he be saved? Is it possible he can elude his fiendish pursuers?

But now a new feature is added to the terrible interest of the scene. With a howl of rage and terror, Hurricane Bob comes dashing down the beach, and with a plash springs far into the sea.

Cassia-bud is not twenty yards away when the dog meets him, and tries to seize him by the shoulder. But the boy throws his arms around Bob's great neck, and in half a minute more both are safe and sound on the silvery sand.

And Hurricane Bob shakes gallons of water out of his hide, the spray of which makes a circular rainbow in the sunshine; and Cassia-bud stands there all white teeth, smiles, and dimples, holding up a solitary mackerel.

"On'y one po' fish," he says, "left out ob all dat lubley stickful! On'y one, sah, but I stick to he!"

"But how could you have escaped, my poor boy?" said Fred, who was trembling all over.

"Simply dis," said Cassia-bud coolly, "I feed de sharks all de time I keep swimming, one fish at a time, you see, massa. De shark say all de time day chasee me, 'Go on, little nigger-boy, gib us anoder fish, and we won't eat you.' Soon's all dey fish is done den de sharks gobble de poor boy up plenty quick."

"But weren't you dreadfully frightened, Kashie?"

"I dessay," said Kashie, "I'se looking radder pale, cause I 'llow I'se a kind o' sceered."

The idea of Cassia-bud turning pale with fear was so ridiculous, that both Fred and Frank burst into a fit of hearty laughing, and so happiness was restored once more.

After shaking another gallon of water out of his splendid coat, and making another rainbow, it seemed suddenly to occur to the noble dog that his little friend Cassia-bud really was saved, that the sharks had not eaten him up; and he was so overjoyed that, after taking his tongue across the nigger-boy's ear, he set off to allay his feelings in a mad circular gallop all around the silvery sands. Round and round he flew, and when he was too tired to run any longer, he sat down beside Cassia-bud and barked at the sea.

It really looked as though he was barking defiance at the sharks, for between every volley of "wowffs" he turned round and licked Cassia-bud's face, as much as to say, "Those awful fishes were going to eat my little Cassia-bud; but they haven't got him yet, nor won't."

It is needless to say that the negro lad was one of the heroes at dinner that day, and Hurricane Bob another. For it was evident that Cassia-bud had meant to hold on to the last fish; and it is just as evident that this resolve on his part would have cost him his life, had not Hurricane Bob dashed bellowing into the water at the moment he did.

However, all's well that ends well.

About an hour afterwards the boat and the oars also were picked up on the sands.

# CHAPTER XXIV
# STINGAREE

The love for adventure, which four years of a roving life in so many parts of the world had engendered in both Fred and Frank, was not to be bounded by the coral reef that shut in the bay near which they were encamped. So whenever there was a breeze with perhaps a bit of sea on, the Crusoes hoisted sail and, steering through the gap, went off on a long delightful cruise around the island or far beyond it.

On these occasions Magilvray and Cassia-bud were usually left to keep camp.

More than once, however, the boatmen found themselves benighted, and had to pass the long hours of darkness on some lonesome part of the coast, to the no small anxiety of those they had left behind them.

On one of these expeditions they had a strange and wonderful adventure with the dreaded stingaree, or huge sting ray of Pacific seas. While out boating Fred had several times come across these veritable "sea devils" floating on the surface of the water, and the desire to capture a specimen got possession of him. It would form a desirable change of diet at all events, for the red flesh of this fiend-fish is said to be exceedingly palatable.

These "terrible skate," as Frank termed them, grow to an immense size, some being as much as twelve feet long without the tail, and nearly ten feet in breadth of beam. The strength of a monster like this is truly astonishing. But the stingaree is armed with a dart and spines in his tail that make him the most dreaded of all fish that swim.

Some species have but a single barbed dart at the end of the tail. If a human being is struck with this in the body, there is no chance of life left; for the dart is poisonous, and a painful, nay even agonizing, death is the only result that can be looked for. If the dart has struck the arm or leg it breaks off, and if it be not cut out from the other side the flesh soon mortifies, and the unhappy man dies more lingeringly.

But this creature, at least one species, has also the power to shoot poisoned spines or darts at his foe, and these latter can pierce even a boat, so hard and strong are they. One would have thought that monsters like these were best left alone. Fred was of a different opinion quite.

So all preparations were made to go on the war-path after them.

Quambo was for many evenings busily engaged fashioning the harpoons from a species of very hard wood found in the island, rendered doubly hard by being half burned in the fire. He also made several long spears from the same tree. To one of these he attached a strong double-edged or dagger knife.

Assisted by Cassia-bud, Quambo also made a large number of fathoms of stout rope from fibrous stuff obtained from the cocoanut and pandanus trees.

All being ready the boat was watered and provisioned one evening, and next day at early dawn, and after a still more early breakfast, they put to sea in quest of adventure.

There was the slightest bit of a breeze on; just enough and no more to fill the mainsail, and keep the boat moving along at the rate of about five knots an hour. But there certainly was no occasion for hurry, and the wind was rather disadvantageous than otherwise, for it roughened or rippled the water, thus distorting the vision very much when they attempted to look at anything under it.

While sail was on her, Quambo stood in the bows on the outlook, Frank managed the sheet, and Fred had the tiller.

They had sailed half way round the island, on tack and half tack, and were preparing for a run the other way, and standing more out to sea, when suddenly Quambo's great bulk was seen to rise more erect and to quiver about, as he grasped his harpoon. He looked indeed like a tiger about to spring on his prey. Without turning round he motioned with his left hand to Fred which way he should steer, and next moment, with a whirring sound, the harpoon flew seaward from his right.

There was the sound of a dull thud; Frank grasped the gunwale of the boat, prepared, as he afterwards said, for anything.

In a few seconds Quambo drew in his line, and bursting into a loud laugh at his own expense, turned about and showed his shipmates the harpoon broken right across the centre.

"No good, then," said Frank, "after expecting such wild sport and such a capital dinner?"

"No, sah," answered Quambo, "not much good. I think I see one big stingaree, and let fly. All de same, sah; I strike the back ob one big turtle."

Fred and Frank both laughed.

"Better luck next," said the former.

"Perhaps," said Quambo; "but I not like de wind. He make too much bobbery on de water all de time, and I not can see."

But early in the afternoon the wind went down, and the water became as calm and still as a fish-pond. Sail was taken in and stowed, and Frank got out the oars.

Whole shoals of turtle were seen, but no rays, no stingarees, so they consoled themselves with dining, and after a drink of cocoanut water, Frank resumed the oars, and Quambo, smoking his huge pipe, once more took his station at the bows.

The afternoon wore on, the sun was declining in the west, and they were all beginning to show signs of weariness, for the day had been drowsily hot, when once more Quambo stood erect, grasping a fresh harpoon, and signing to Fred as before.

There was no mistake about the stingarees this time. The boat seemed to be in the midst of a huge shoal of them, and in a moment Quambo had hurled the harpoon into one of the very largest.

The commotion that ensued baffles description. The huge brute seemed for a time to be right under the boat, and almost lifting it up. Then he darted ahead, and the appearance of the creature now was terrible in the extreme. He had come right up to the surface of the sea, which was red with blood, while not only was the water lashed into foam by the dart-armed tail, but by the fins or wings at each side.

If ever any creature in the world merited the name of sea devil, it was that monster stingaree just then.

Meanwhile Quambo was making lunges at it with his dagger-pointed spear. This seemed to lash the monster to fury at last, and after a dreadful struggle or two to free itself from the galling harpoon it plunged forwards and stood straight away out to sea.

Now as the day wore on, after putting the dinner all ready for cooking—for our heroes were expected to return to the island before sun-down—Magilvray, with Cassia-bud and Bob, determined to walk to Beacon Hill. The road now was easily found, and in less than an hour they had stationed themselves beside the broomstick, as it was called, whence Magilvray could sweep the horizon with the spy-glass. They were just in time to see the striking of the stingaree, and witness the monster's fearful struggle for freedom. Then they saw it dash away seawards, pulling the boat behind it as a salmon might the float of a fishing-line.

They saw Quambo's efforts to round in the line in order to be able to ply his dagger-lance once more; then they noticed that the stingaree seemed suddenly to change its course. They saw Quambo cut the line, but almost at the same moment the boat turned turtle, and its occupants were thrown into the sea.

"Oh, oh, oh!" shrieked little Cassia-bud. In his agony he ran round and round the beacon, then threw himself on the dog, frantically weeping.

"Oh, golly, golly!" he sobbed. "Poor massa, for true, dey will all be drown. De big shark will gobble massa up plenty quick. Oh, I not can look no mo'! I not can look no mo'!"

Not heeding the boy's lamentations Magilvray sat there as if rooted to the spot. He saw the boat still afloat there, bottom upwards, with Fred and Frank clinging to its keel, after many ineffectual attempts to right it. He saw big Quambo swim after an oar, and picking it up come with it to the bows, and tie it with the others to the painter; and he could not help admiring the giant negro's wondrous coolness in what appeared to be the hour of death.

Then a long, *very* long time seemed to elapse without any change of scene or situation.

Was the boat drifting nearer to the island shore he wondered, or being carried further out to sea? At all events the poor fellows that clung to her keel must soon sink exhausted beneath the sea, or—and the thought made this sailor's blood run cold—they would be hauled under water, one by one, by the sharks, and torn in pieces.

Lower and lower sank the sun. It was already beginning to shimmer red across the sea.

But what was that moving slowly towards the upset boat and the clinging men? He brought the glass to bear on the spot.

Horror! it was the dark triangular fin of a huge blue shark, and it was moving in the direction of the boat—nearer and nearer. Not always in a direct line though, and often remaining for a time immoveable, as if picking up the scent.

Magilvray felt as if under the spell of some fearful nightmare. Then he sprang to his feet and closed the telescope with a snap.

"I shall go mad, *mad*," he cried, "if I gaze but a minute longer. Come, Kashie, come."

"Is it all ober, Mac?" cried the boy pitifully.

"Yes, Kashie, all over, boy, and we are alone. Come, boy, come."

The sun shot one blood-red glare across the world of waters, then sank, and all was gloom and night.

Neither Magilvray nor Cassia-bud could ever explain how they found their way back to camp that evening, through the rocky glens and the darkling forest. Perhaps they were beholden entirely to the dog.

But they did reach the beach at long last. The fire had gone very low, and hardly knowing what he did the sailor made it up and sat down near it, while Cassia-bud threw himself moaning on the sands. Hurricane Bob, satisfied in his own mind that the boy was ill or in pain, lay down beside him, and gently licked his face and hands.

Dinner was not even once thought of—grief was all-absorbing.

After a time Cassia-bud probably slept, for he lay there very still and quiet. But Magilvray still sat in the same position, dazedly gazing at the flickering fire.

A bright moon, that had been high in the heavens when the sun went down, sank lower and lower, and at last disappeared behind the western waves, and the clear stars had the sky all to themselves.

Not a sound now was to be heard, save the moan of the breaking water on the reef, and occasionally the eeriesome cry of some belated sea-bird.

Why, I have often wondered, are sea-birds sometimes to be heard at the dreary hour of midnight? What takes them away from their rocks at such a time? and in the darkness too. Sailors shudder when they hear them.

It is not the call of birds, they will tell you, but of disembodied spirits.

Magilvray half roused himself at last; but he sought not the shelter of the friendly boughs. He only crept a little closer to the fire, shuddering slightly as if cold, then exhausted nature claimed her due and the sailor slept.

# CHAPTER XXV
## "ROW, BROTHERS, ROW"—QUAMBO'S SHARK STORY—FAST TO A SWORD-FISH

The night wore on apace. It must have been well into the middle watch when there began to mingle with the toilsome dreams of the grief-stricken sailor the melody of song, and the sound of oars keeping time to the rhythm.

He woke up at last.

Cassia-bud was also awake, and both were sitting up, straining their ears to listen.

Yes, there it was again sure enough, very faint and far away certainly, beyond the reef, but, borne along towards them on the air of night, it was plainly audible.

> "Row, brothers, row, the stream runs fast,
> The rapids are near, and the daylight is past."

The song really appeared to come from the sky itself, and in the sky Cassia-bud evidently believed it was.

"O Mac," he said tremblingly; "I'se dreffully frightened. I'se as pale as def (death) with fear. Po massa! dat song he lub so much when he libin', and now, Mac, he am dead and is singin' same song in hebbin. Po massa!"

The music ceased at last, and there was a pause; then it once more rose on the air, but higher and nearer, and a song of a different sort. "Auld lang syne," to wit.

> "And surely ye'll be your pint-stoup,
>     As sure as I'll be mine;
> And we'll spend the evenin' thinking, boys,
>     Of auld lang syne."

"No Kash," cried Mac joyfully; "it aint in heaven they are. 'T aint blessed likely there'd be pint stoups in heaven. And I don't think they're ghosts at all."

He jumped to his feet.

"Speak, Bob, speak, boy;" he said to the great dog.

Hurricane Bob required no two tellings; he barked till reefs and hills re-echoed back the sound.

Then cheering was heard from seaward, which Magilvray and Cassia-bud gladly returned, and soon something dark appeared in the reef gap, and in about five minutes more our lost stingaree hunters were standing on the beach, receiving the congratulations of their friends, whom they had never expected to see again in life.

"Oh, Kashie is so glad now, massa!" cried the nigger boy. "I jes want to run and shout all de while. And you is sure you is alive, massa?"

"I believe so, Kashie."

"And de sharks not hab done gone gobble you up for true?"

"Not one of us. And now, lads, stir up the fire, and let us have supper, we're dying of hunger. That's what's the matter with us now."

"Shall we cook ye a slice o' stingaree, sir," said Magilvray slyly.

"Oh, bother the stingaree, Mac! Don't chaff us about the beast."

"No more stingaree for me," said Frank; "not even a little bit."

Mac was very busy now, and as he set about cooking the supper Fred told him how they had escaped.

They had heard the sharks splashing near them in the darkness; then, in an agony of fear, they made one more despairing effort to right the boat, and succeeded. Fred and Frank got in first, then Quambo.

"So you see, Mac, we've disappointed the sharks for once, and done them out of a good supper, and now we're going to make a good supper ourselves."

One evening, about three weeks after the adventure with the stingaree, as they all lay round the fire, and Quambo and Mac were blowing great curling clouds of the wild tobacco, the smoke from which, however, was not considered Rimmellian by either Fred or Frank, said the latter:

"D'ye know, lads, that I think flying fish is about the nicest fish in the sea—to eat I mean?"

"Well," said Fred, "I think Kashie here might catch some."

"Fly fish?" said Cassia-bud. "Oh, massa, you expects po' Kashie to catch the big debbil dat fly over de reef, with nuffin but his head on. Kashie not can do."

"No, no, Kashie. It is the little flying skip-jack business I mean."

"Oh, I see, sah! de flying herrings, sah?"

"A good name too. Well, Fred, do you know that a flying fish once saved my life?"

"Ah! a story? Eh? Out with it, Frank. 'Saved by a flying fish: a tale in two chapters; or, a romance of sea life!'"

"Well, lads, you'll admit there isn't much romance about it when you hear it. Scene first then opens with me lying sick and ill in a hammock on deck, on board the old *Resolute*. We were at sea you know, and a long way from land. I must say the skipper was just as kind to me as he knew how to be. He used to bring his bottle of rum on deck, and sit beside me and drink it for company's sake like; for you know I wouldn't have any. He was a very straightforward chap that skipper, I hope he is still alive and afloat, though I doubt it very much. 'If ye're so grand as not to drink the rum, young man,' he said to me sometimes, 'why I guess the next best thing you can do is to lie there, and see me drink it.' Well, until I gave up eating entirely the skipper had good hopes of me; but when I lay in my hammock as weak as a baby, and couldn't pick a morsel of salt junk or dried cod, then he told me plainly there wasn't a ghost of a chance for me.

"Then we got becalmed, and there was a blue shark, about twenty feet long, kept close to the ship all the time, waiting and watching.

"'He's waiting and watching for you, young man,' the skipper told me, consolingly. 'He's a fine big beast, and you'll fit in there nicely! Now if you've anything to say, or if there's anything you'd like done arter your de—mise, you had better speak now, for I calculate ye haven't got more'n a day to get ready.'"

"Oh!" I groaned, "if there was anything I could eat I think I'd get round even yet."

"'Well,' he said, 'we're having jest the nicest bit o corned horse and sauer-kraut for dinner ever ye smelt. It's just stale enough to be tender. If ye can't tackle that I guess ye ain't much good any more!'

"That is chapter first, Fred, and now for the romance. I was lying in my hammock, dozing I think, that same evening, only looking up at the clear bright stars now and then, and wondering how far heaven is beyond them, and if I shall know my dear father when I meet him there, when all of a sudden some cold splashy thing jumped right against my face, then commenced a very lively dance on top of the hammock. It was a flying-fish."

Frank paused.

"Well," said Fred, "but I don't see where the romance comes in, or how the creature saved your life."

"Why, man alive, I ate it!"

"You eatee he alive, sah?" cried Cassia-bud.

"No, Kash, I had it cooked; and it was the most delightfully tasty and toothsome morsel ever I put inside my lips. Another was caught next day, and lots more after; and I grew better from that very night, and so that also was a disappointed shark."

"Ah! yum! yum!" said Quambo, "dey is good food. I likee some now. Yum!"

"What, flying-fish, Quambo?"

"Oh, no, sah, de shark!"

"Well, Quambo," said Fred, "you can catch some for yourself, only you'll have to dine all alone when you have shark for dinner."

"When I a leetle boy," said Quambo thoughtfully, "I catchee plenty big shark—I and some oder nigger-boy, and two, tree, four nigger-men."

"Now for Quambo's story," cried Frank. "Heave round with your yarn, Quambo, lad."

"I lib along o' my ole mudder in Africa befo' I go to de States. On de Gold Coast dat were, gen'lem. Shark plenty value dere. Good fo' food and good for de skin, wot we cure and de white man buy.

"Plenty reef on dat coast, gen'lem. Well, we go close to de reef, all same's we were de night de big black head jump ober and swamp de boat. We go close to de reef. Den we hab one long strong rope wid a runnin' noose on de end o' he for to catchee de shark."

"Certainly, Quambo; but tell us the modus operandi."

"What ship's dat, sah?"

"I mean, how did you catch the beggars, Quambo?"

"Bery easy, sah, indeed. You see de sharks mos'ly goes to sleep in de middle ob de day. Dey creep into de coral caves. All de same, sah, de tail all lef stickin' out ob de holes, you see."

"And do you mean to tell us, Quambo, that you went and pulled their tails?"

"Not quite, sah Quambo not quite so big a fool as dat. But I myse'f and two more tiny boys go dive down, and plenty quick Quambo slip de noose ober a tail, den signal. De noose he tighten now, and de shark is pull right out and lift up all de way to de boat. How dat shark do squirm to be sure! When de man in de boat hab kill he propah, den down Quambo go again."*

"Well, Quambo, that is very awful, if true."

"Oh, he true, sah! I gib my word of honah on dat, sah."

"But, Quambo, did the sharks never retaliate?"

"Yes, sah, de shark 'taliate my leetle brudder, sah. I see my brudder try to make fast to one bery big tail. He not can do. Den de owner of dat big tail come out plenty quick. I dive up, sah."

"An' your brother, Quambo?"

"Oh, I guess, sah, he dive down. I hab no mo' leetle brudder after dat. I spose he 'taliated."

But flying fish were very plentiful round the island, and I think Cassia-bud must have lain awake a whole night trying to find out a plan to get some. He was completely successful. A kind of big butterfly neb was manufactured by Quambo and him. This was part of the flying-fish tackle, but not all. It is a well-known fact that flying fish will come towards a light held near the surface of the sea at night. Now it only remained to manufacture a torch, and Quambo came to the rescue.

In the South Sea islands one of the most lovely trees that grows in the forest is the Dooee-Dooee or Candle-mat tree. The broad silvery-green leaves, and the bunches of charmingly white and shapely flowers, render it an object of great beauty, especially if it stands near other trees of a darker green. The nuts that grow on this tree are heated, then cracked to get the kernel out. These kernels are strung together like beads, and the strings of kernels tied round with bark, and lo! the candle is complete.

So Quambo and Cassia-bud started out together one night, and splendid sport they had, and just as splendid a breakfast next day; for nothing could exceed in flavour the flesh of those flying fish.

But as often as not now Fred and Frank used to go after the flying fish together.

One night Quambo happened to be in the boat, and it was well he was, else an adventure that befel our heroes would, in all probability, have had a sad termination. On this particular evening flying fish were very numerous; and while rowing on a spurt after a shoal, suddenly the boat seemed to strike a rock, with such violence too as to throw both Fred and Frank over the thwarts. It was no rock, however; for immediately after the boat was shaken with terrible violence, and several times all but capsized.

Luckily, Quambo was equal to the occasion. He was forward in the bows, and lancing and lunging at the enemy—an immense sword-fish—almost before our heroes had time to gather themselves up. Suddenly the boat was pulled almost under water by the head; then there was a dull report, and she was free from the monster, and slowly righted herself once more.

She was now making water so fast that it was deemed prudent to get on shore with all speed. So her head was turned towards the gap in the reef. Quambo kept bailing all the time, and Fred and Frank rowed as they had never rowed before. They got her run up at last on the sandy beach; but it took all hands three whole days to make good repairs, for it must be remembered they had no tools worthy of mention to work with.

Little did they imagine, however, that they would soon be possessed of tools enough and to spare.

# CHAPTER XXVI
## "WHAT WAS THE MYSTERY SURROUNDING THAT STRANGE VESSEL?"

In the isle of Good Hope clumps of fine cocoa-nut-trees grew close to the sandy beach, and single, very large, pandanus, trees not far off. This pandanus or screw pine I have already mentioned; it is a truly marvellous tree, and bears truly marvellous fruit or drupes. This fruit is treated in various ways, and after a time a taste for it is acquired, so that it becomes quite an article of diet, and is relished even more than cocoanut; for this soon palls on one. But even the flowers of this tree are edible, at least Quambo and Cassia-bud found them palatable enough, though the others much preferred their perfume. Quite a quantity of the leaves of the pandanus were cut down to be used as thatch for the huts. They are long, strong, and tough, and being fastened on with string make very excellent thatch indeed.

It is in connection with this tree that I have now to relate an adventure, which it will be owned was of a very startling character indeed.

About two hundred yards from the camp, and about seventy from the beach, grew a clump or grove of pandanus. Some of the trees therein were very tall and spreading, and in addition to their aerial roots had let down props or stays from the upper branches to help them to sustain the weight of the branches. It was up these prop-roots that Quambo or Cassia-bud used to shin to cut down leaves or flowers.

It was the custom of Fred and Frank, of an evening after dinner, to take a walk back and fore on the sand, and they were usually accompanied by Cassia-bud and his friend Hurricane Bob.

One evening while strolling quietly in the clear starlight towards the pandanus grove they were surprised to see the great dog suddenly pause, and pointing towards the dark trees utter a low and ominous growl; but they were still more astonished, and not a little frightened, to note almost immediately after what appeared to be the form of a gigantic man stalk from out the shadow, and walk with a curious rolling shambling gait towards the sea. About half-way down he stopped, standing out clear against the snow-white sands, and fiercely waved his long arms in the air, but made no sound.

A more awful apparition it would be difficult even to imagine. Cassia-bud dropped half dead with fear on the sand, uttering only a sound that was half cry, half moan, as from one in a nightmare. Both Fred and Frank experienced a fearful kind of impulse to rush towards the terrible being, but next moment it dashed on towards the sea, into which it threw itself with a loud splash.

"In the name of heaven," cried Frank, "who or what was that?"

"Some dreadful mystery," replied Fred, "that I cannot solve. Come," he added, "you are superstitious, Frank."

"I am, for once in a way, Fred. If that wasn't an evil spirit, then no such being exists in the world, What did it seem to you like?"

"Well, you know the awful water fiend or kelpie, that is supposed to haunt deep, dark mountain lochs in the Scottish Highlands, and often, they say, carries away children and women to devour at the bottom of the lake. He is a hideous, tall figure, but with wings like a bat, that stretch 'twixt arms and legs. Frank, we have seen a water kelpie!"

"May the Lord be near us, Fred. I never felt so frightened in all my life."

They went slowly back to camp, giving many a furtive glance behind, for more than once they thought they could hear the sound of footsteps stealing softly up behind them.

They slept in their green tent that night, making a big fire up near the mouth of it, and more than once Cassia-bud started and screamed in his sleep.

But they were not molested, and the sun was shining very brightly indeed when they awoke, and Quambo proceeded to cook breakfast.

The first thing Fred and Frank did after their morning meal was to walk, somewhat fearfully it must be confessed, towards the pandanus grove.

They half expected to see human foot-prints in the sand. There was a trail across the beach, but no impression of feet of any kind, and this fact deepened the mystery that hung around the dread apparition.

That day Quambo ascended a pandanus tree to throw down leaves and flowers. These last are of a yellow or lemon colour, and look sweetly pretty against the dark-green of the long, screw-like leaves.

Quambo busied himself culling flowers for some time, then he hailed those below sailor-fashion.

"On deck dere, gen'lems!"

"Ay, ay, lad," cried Fred.

"Somebody else been heah las' night sah, gaddering flowers foh true."

"Who? what, Quambo?"

"Dunno, sah; surely de debil himse'f, sah."

That night all hands went along the beach and waited quite a long time, but the kelpie failed to put in an appearance.

Next evening it was suggested they should hide in the bush—not certainly in the grove itself. So here once again they waited and watched.

Nothing came out of the sea; but before they had been in hiding for half an hour they heard noises in the trees that convinced them the creature was there. Almost at the same time the dog barked loud and angrily, and something dropped with a dull, heavy thud to the ground.

As if by one impulse, but with Quambo firmly holding the dog by his collar, lest he might force the fighting with the awful unknown, they dashed forward. The creature could be distinctly seen against the background of sand, and strange to say it assumed various shapes, and moved but slowly away, as if in anger. At one moment it was the tall, dark kelpie-like monster waving its arms in the air, next it took the appearance of a huge frog, and immediately after rolled seaward in the form of a gigantic wheel. There was the same splashing noise when it took the water as before, and though they sat on the beach for a fall hour after this it made no further signs.

The kelpie, as Fred persisted in calling it, appeared many times after this, always coming from the pandanus grove, and it was not until one bright and radiant moonlight night that our heroes found out what it actually was.

They had been out after flying-fish, Quambo being in the boat, when it occurred to them to land near the grove. The boat was pulled cautiously near to the beach, and while Fred and Frank lay on their oars the giant negro stood forward in the bows with his terrible lance.

"Stand by," shouted Fred shortly after, "yonder is the kelpie. It is coming straight for us!"

So it did, and the boat was beached almost on the creature, which had come rolling like a wheel towards it.

A triple attack was made on it; Fred and Frank with oars, the huge negro with his lance, while armed with another spear Magilvray rushed along the beach and attacked it from the rear.

But the oars were seized and twisted in our heroes' hands, even the gunwale of the boat was grasped by those awful arms.

They knew now, however, what they were fighting with. It was no fiend or kelpie, but a huge specimen of the gigantic octopus, kraken, or devil-fish of southern seas.

It was literally hacked to pieces before it could be killed.

Lying on the beach there next day, with its mangled body, awful face, and snake-like arms, it had really a terrible appearance, and reminded Fred of some of the pictures of Doré's monsters in Dante's Inferno.

The castaways had now been over six months on this lonely island, and all that time had never seen a ship or sail of any kind.

How much longer they were to remain prisoners no one, of course, could even guess.

"Surely," they thought, "some day some ship must come."

Yes; and one day a ship did come,

Summer and autumn had ended. It was winter now, if the name can possibly be applied to such a climate as this. The time was June anyhow, which is midwinter in these regions, and it was the season of clouds and storms and dense fogs at times.

They had fully prepared for it, however, having greatly strengthened their hut, and thatched it round and round with pandanus leaves and cocoanut fibre.

The coneys or cavies had been very abundant of late, and the skins were stretched, salted, and dried. They might come in handy by-and-by to make articles of dress.

One day all hands had gone to the Beacon Hill for the purpose of repairing the broom, which had got nearly blown away.

They had been working very hard and earnestly, and had seldom looked about them, but having finished the work, they sat merrily down to eat their well-earned luncheon.

Quambo and Mac were lighting their pipes afterwards, and Fred was scanning the ocean with his glass.

"Oh, Frank!" he cried suddenly. "A ship! a ship!"

"A ship! Oh, you don't say so!"

Every eye was strained towards a little dark dot that appeared far away on the sea's deep blue. She must have been twenty miles to the south when first seen, and all that afternoon they watched her creeping ever so slowly nearer, and still more near, but at sunset she was at least ten miles off, as near as could be judged.

She was becalmed, and only moving with the ocean's current. But never a stitch of canvas could be descried on her when the great red sun went down, and night and darkness fell.

What was the mystery surrounding that strange vessel? It seemed inexplicable. However, they would have to wait for another day seemingly, before it could be revealed.

Slowly down the hill they went, and by many a devious path through forest and glen, till they stood once more beside their tent.

So anxious were they that hardly an eye was closed in sleep that night, and long before the stars had paled before the coming day they were *en route* for Beacon Hill.

# CHAPTER XXVII
# FRANK GAZED AGHAST

The sun had already risen when the party once more found themselves by the beacon. Frank gazed aghast almost; for almost close to the southern beach of the island, and evidently running ashore, was a strangely dismantled old brig. It was the *Resolute*.

Her sails hung in tatters from the yards, her jibboom and foretopgallant mast had been carried away as if she had been in collision, and there was not a sign of life to be seen anywhere about her decks. She was drifting almost broadside on towards the shore, on which, long before they could possibly reach her, it was evident enough she would dash like a heap of drift wood. There was, however, no sea on, and until it came on to blow she might lie quietly enough.

No time was now lost in getting back to camp and taking the boat out.

Hardly anyone spoke a word as they rowed out through the gap, round the point, and bore up towards the brig. They were willing to wait to find some solution of the seeming mystery of her arrival, rather than to hazard guesses concerning it.

Yes, she had grounded, but not broadside on to the beach, as they all thought she would. The send of the tide had caught her stern and brought her round, and she lay on the soft sandy bottom—bows on to the shore.

Evidently she was half full of water, else she would have drifted farther in.

It was by no means difficult to scramble on board, therefore, despite the fact that her iron works were a mass of rust, and her bulwarks green and slimy. So too were the decks. She lay with a slight list to port, and our heroes, who had boarded at that side, found it somewhat difficult to reach the companion, so slippery were her decks.

Before going below they stood for a few minutes to gaze about them.

Dilapidation everywhere! She looked as a ship that has been long sunk beneath the salt seas would appear, if suddenly raised again.

Frank and Fred exchanged glances.

"How do you feel, Fred?"

"I feel," was the reply, "like one who stands on the confines of another world. Oh, mercy on us, Frank! where has this ship been during these long six months and over, and where is her unhappy crew?"

"They must have left her, Fred. See, there isn't a single boat visible, and the iron davits are slued round towards the sea."

"Yes, it is evident, Frank, she is a derelict. And the probability is she had run on shore on some reef after being deserted, and has lain there ever since till floated by an extra high tide.

"Well, Fred, it's all a puzzle to me; but I'd give a good deal to know where the skipper and the crew are. Come below."

The ship had been partially battened down, making it evident that she had been deserted soon after, or even during, a gale of wind, the crew believing she was settling down.

Before going below they proceeded to open the hatches in order to let both light and air between decks. They had just passed the fore hatch, when their nostrils were assailed by a foul and awful odour proceeding from the galley.

"There's something wrong here, sir," said Magilvray.

"Mac," said Fred, "will you venture down?"

"That I will, sir."

Presently he re-appeared. He was looking scared and amazed.

"Oh, sir," he cried, "there be two skeletons yonder in irons, sir! I mean what I say," he added, in reply to the looks of astonishment depicted on Fred's face and Frank's. "And what is more, sir, they're the self-same chaps as we picked up afore we found the *Resolute* in the southern sea of ice."

"This is awful," said Fred. "Frank, will you come below?

"Yes, Fred."

Down the fore ladder they went.

It was a horrible sight their eyes alighted on. For a few moments the semi-darkness dazed them; but soon every detail became distinct enough. Both corpses lay on their backs, their skeleton legs still encompassed by the iron staples that bound them to a long strong bar of steel. Only by their clothes, and by a ring on the finger of one, could they have been distinguished. The old place was alive with gigantic cockroaches, and loathsome centipedes crept about the skulls of the skeletons, and disappeared to hide in their eye sockets, while rats, tame from starvation, crawled here and there on the deck. It was evident enough that the wretched men had been guilty of some crime that had necessitated their being put in irons, and that they had been entirely forgotten during the hurry and scurry of lowering the boats and leaving the ship. And so—awful fate!—they must have slowly starved and died. Probably been partly eaten alive by the rats, with which Frank said the ship had always abounded.

The young men were glad indeed when they found themselves once more on deck under the blue sky, and breathing the sweet pure air of heaven.

"I shan't be sorry," said Frank, "when we get on shore out of this awful charnel-house of a ship. I hope there is nothing dreadful to see in the saloon."

Thither they now bent their steps, and descended the slimy ladder.

There was everywhere below the same evidence of hurried desertion. The store-room door was open, boxes and small casks had been partially hauled out, and left where they stood. The compass that usually hangs under the skylight had been taken down, but left on the table beside the chronometer. In the captain's stateroom the bedclothes in the bunk were in disorder, and on a table near stood propped up a half-empty bottle of rum.

The ship's log lay on the saloon floor, and a glance at it showed that the last entry had been made on the very day our castaways had left the *San Salvador* for the mirage island.

"I'm glad," said Frank, "there are no more corpses here."

"So am I; but now, Frank, it is a duty we owe ourselves to save all we can out of this derelict vessel, that Providence has guided to the shores of our island."

"By the looks o' the horizon, sir," said Mac, "it won't be long afore we has a storm."

"In that case, Mac, we ought to begin work at once."

So a consultation was hurriedly held as to what should first be saved.

There were plenty of rifles on board and ammunition, and there were also carpenters' tools of all sorts. These to the castaways were by far and away the most valuable portions of the brig's cargo. So without any unnecessary delay these were got up and safely landed on the beach. None too soon, however, for already a heavy swell was rolling in from the south and lifting and bumping the after part of the vessel.

With the exception of some tinned meats and soup the provisions on board were found to be utterly worthless; but Quambo's eyes brightened, and so did Mac's, when they came across the tobacco cask. That was saved. There was rum in abundance, but no one evinced the slightest inclination to take a single bottle on shore. Books, the compass, and the chronometer were the last things to be taken away.

But the breakers were now roaring and thundering on the beach, and so it was deemed unsafe to go off to the derelict any more that day. Instead therefore of returning to their camp they built themselves a tent under the trees with spars and canvas taken from the vessel, and prepared to pass the night here, so as to be ready to begin work early next day again.

It was a very dark night, for the sky had become overcast with heavy clouds, and the wind was beginning to moan through the trees with a sound that betokened a coming storm. But dinner had put everyone in good temper, and luxuries to-night had been enjoyed that they had never expected to taste again. Besides, they had a lamp to burn and books to read. What more could any castaway desire?

They had saved also two chests of clothing, and would therefore be quite independent of cavies' skins for many a day to come, or, as Frank said, until the real living ship arrived with living beings on it instead of corpses, and took them away back to their far-off home beyond the seas.

I am afraid that long before dinner was discussed that evening, they had forgotten all about the terrible fate of the poor wretches who had been left chained up in the derelict to be eaten alive by rats. They were all very happy and very hopeful too to-night. A ship was sure to come some day, and a few months more or less on this island could not signify a great deal.

"Give us a song," cried Frank.

And it was not one song they sang, but half a dozen at least; and then they lay around the lamp and talked of home and old, old times.

It was just about this time, if they had only known it, that Captain Cawdor, after landing Señor Sarpinto at San Francisco, had left his ship, and crossing to New York, had taken the mail for Liverpool.

He went thence to Glasgow, and after meeting and reporting himself to his brother shipowners, and telling them of all his adventures and doings, he set out for Methlin, to break the sad news to Fred's people.

What a lovely summer's-day it was when Captain Cawdor, on board the cutter he had hired, sailed slowly into Methlin Bay.

How blue the hills looked, asleep under the cerulean sky; how sweetly green the birchen trees; how peaceful the village, with the wee, white, brown-thatched cottages. And he, this truly good and kind old sailor, had come to bring grief to all it contained.

"Oh," he thought, "if I could only give them even an atom of hope! But, alas! I cannot."

Eean was glad to see him. They had met before; but a glance told the old fisherman and his wife that the white-haired sailor was the bearer of bad tidings.

Long, long after Toddie—from whom the sad news was withheld— had gone to bed and was fast asleep, the old people sat beside the fire, and it is needless to say what the subject of their conversation was. But though Eppie's eyes were red with weeping, and she had even forgotten her spinning-wheel, neither she nor Eean were entirely hopeless.

"No, no," said Eean, "something tells me my boy still lives. He is somewhere in those seas; and though I am willing to submit to the will of our heavenly Father, I believe that he will yet return.

"And tell me now, Captain Cawdor, all about this Señor Sarpinto. Do you know, captain, I'm strangely interested in this man. And what is more, his very name seems familiar to me. But where I have met him, or how or when, is to me a mystery. I must dream over it, and—yes, and pray over it. Yet somehow I think Sarpinto is mixed up in our history."

Then Captain Cawdor told them all he knew.

"Why, Fred," said Frank, "the wind is rising! Listen!"

The wind was undoubtedly getting up. The canvas of the rude tent began to flap, and mingled with the boom of the breakers on the shore came the steadier roar of the breeze in the trees overhead.

In these regions storms come on at times with terrible suddenness, and rage with wondrous force. And this occasion proved no exception.

Half an hour after the wind had commenced to moan through the leaves of the pandanus forest, the storm was at its height, accompanied by such terrible thunder and such vivid lightning as none of our castaways had ever experienced before. Anon the rain came down in torrents, but the wind lost none of its force.

All that night the hurricane raged, and for the first time since they had come to the island our heroes knew what it was to feel cold. They were wet too, as well as cold, for the frail impromptu tent proved but a poor protection against the violence of so awful a storm.

Towards the earlier hours, despite the incessant noise, all must have slept, and it was broad daylight before they again awoke.

Fred sat up rubbing his eyes, and for a time wondering where he was. Then all the strange events of the previous day rushed back to his mind, and he got up and staggered out.

The wind still blew high, but it was evidently dying down.

But where was the brig *Resolute*? Was she gone again, or had it all been a dream?

# CHAPTER XXVIII
## COULD HE BE——DEAD?

Gone the *Resolute* most assuredly was. Hardly a timber of the old craft was left together, only a portion of the hull and some dark skeleton ribs pointing skywards through the white chaos of surf that boiled and swirled around them.

And the beach on both sides was strewed with wreckage.

"Frank," said Fred that same morning:

> "I had a dream, a happy dream,
>    I dreamt that I was free;
> That in a boat that we had built
>    We sailed across the sea."

"Bravo!" cried Frank, "I didn't know you were a born poet. Pass the sardines and the pickles, like a good boy. Fancy eating sardines in this world again. But, I say, you know, touching that dream, it is a real jolly one, and as soon as I've time I'll think it out Why shouldn't we, now that we have tools, commence to build a ship?"

"I don't see why we shouldn't really. But mind you it isn't quite such a simple business as you may imagine. She would require to be a biggish boat, you know, and there are two difficulties to be thought out at the very commencement.

"First and foremost, Fred, if we are going to build her close to the beach, we may reckon on getting our work all destroyed in the first gale of wind that blows; secondly, if we build her a safe distance from the sea, how are we to launch her?"

So no more was said about building a ship just then, but, nevertheless, the idea had taken root in the minds of all hands, and even Hurricane Bob pretended to look very wise when Cassia-bud broached the subject to him.

It took our castaways three whole days to get their stores round to the place where the camp was, as they were mostly all removed by sea. But the planks of the wreck that they thought might one day come in handy were dragged off the beach, and piled in a heap far beyond the reach of the water.

While engaged at this work they suddenly came face to face with those awful brothers in death, the ironed skeletons. They were sitting on the beach, having evidently been floated out of the wreck on a piece of the deck. Sitting there bolt upright, their sightless eye-sockets turned towards the sea, the arm of one of them slightly raised, the fleshless fingers pointing towards the distant horizon.

"Why this is awful!" said Frank.

"Yes," said Fred, "and it seems to me those spectres will haunt us unless we bury them out of sight."

It was determined to do so at once therefore, and Magilvray and Fred set about digging a grave high up on the beach.

"Poor wretches," said Frank. "Suppose, Fred, we read the English burial service over them. They had sinned, but oh, they have suffered! Shall we?"

"You're a right good fellow, Frank. Yes."

Among the books brought on shore was a church service, and Frank, being more English than Fred, in a solemn voice read the service. The bodies were then lowered into the grave and covered up.

Some weeks after this they raised a cross above the spot where they lay, and carved the names of the unfortunate sailors on it.

"Those wretches may have had friends and relations in America, who may be even now waiting and waiting, and hoping and hoping, for their return. Who knows?"

That is what Fred said, as in company with his friend he left the lonesome grave to return to camp.

For two months after the destruction of the derelict the weather continued unsettled and heavy. A deal of rain fell occasionally, and there were at times storms of wind that appeared to shake the island to its very foundations.

One evening, on their return from the woods, where they had been cavy shooting, Frank seemed quieter and duller than usual.

"What's the matter, old man? You don't appear to be your own saucy self to-night at all."

Fred laughed a kind of a ready-made laugh.

"No, strangely enough," he said, "I feel dull in spirits. I don't know if I am looking old, but I really feel to be about ninety-three or ninety-four."

"It's best to be exact, old man," said Fred, "but a good dinner will set you as straight as a plummet."

The good dinner was all ready, but it did not set Frank straight.

He lay down soon after, and Fred really for once felt sorry that his bed was one of green boughs. He sat till nearly morning beside his friend, who was now in a high and raging fever.

From the very first Frank's illness assumed a vigorous type. He was quite delirious. Sometimes, indeed, it took all Quambo's force to keep him still. He raved too, talking constantly of home and of his mother, and even of his dead and gone father. Or at one moment he seemed to be far away among the stormy seas of Antarctic regions, and the next sailing in the little yacht *Water Baby*, with Toddie and Fred, on the wild and beautiful coast around Methlin.

For a whole week he continued thus, being nursed and watched constantly by Fred and the others. Then he became quieter, and his friend feared weaker also. His ravings now were far less wild. It almost broke Fred's heart to hear him talking so constantly about his mother and Toddie. It was always mother now or Toddie.

He grew weaker and weaker, in spite of all they could do for him.

But he knew those around him now, and was very seldom delirious. When he did sink into a moment's raving lethargy, he would keep repeating over and over again the words, "I'm going home; oh, I want so much to go home!"

One evening, while seated beside him, Fred thought he could see the hand of death busy on his face; then he broke down entirely, and sat sobbing and weeping beside Frank's couch of boughs, as if surely his heart would break.

Frank awoke, and seeing Fred crying, stretched out his hand to him.

"Don't cry, poor Fred," he said, "We're brothers yet."

"Ay," said Fred, "brothers ever."

"Brothers till death," Frank muttered.

"Oh, Frank, Frank, do not talk thus! I will not, I cannot let you go!"

It did seem, nevertheless, that poor Frank was going home that night.

The scene in that tent of boughs was a strange but a solemn one; the sick lad—he was not yet twenty years of age—lying on the couch in the corner, with sad-faced Fred holding his hand as he squatted near him, little Cassia-bud sitting dolefully by the door, Quambo towering high above him, and the great dog, as sad as anyone, lying on the floor watching all. The lamp gave but a feeble light, for it was shaded by green branches; and this only added additional gloom to everything around.

"Are you there, Fred?"

It was Frank's voice, though it sounded very weak and very far away.

"I'm by you, dear Frank."

"Isn't it very dark?"

Fred's heart gave an uneasy thud. Had he attempted to speak now the tears would have choked him. Frank was dying, he thought.

"I'm going to sleep, Fred. Good night. Hold my hand."

There was not a hush now in the tent. Fred kept his friend's thin hand in his, his eyes on his face.

Fred was praying; and praying perhaps with greater earnestness than ever he had prayed before. Oh, if his heavenly Father, who had saved them from so many a danger, that loving tender Father, who heareth in secret, and to whom all the ends of the earth are well known, would but deign to hear him now, and spare his friend even at the eleventh hour!

How quietly Frank was breathing! How very still he lay! Could he be—*dead*?

Fred put his ear down to listen. Yes, he could hear his gentle breathing. This was not death, it was sleep—gentle sleep.

Never once did Fred move from his position all that livelong night; and when the sun rose and cast the shadows of the mountains across the placid bay, the lad was still at his post.

At length Frank opened his eyes, and seeing Fred, gently pressed his hand and smiled.

The sleep had done its kindest work.

Just a little cocoanut water, so cool and refreshing, then, like a baby, Frank dropped off again; and Fred went right away into the bush all by himself, and kneeling down beside a pandanus tree, returned thanks to Him who had heard his prayer.

Slow indeed, but steadfast, was Frank's recovery now from his terrible illness. For weeks he scarce could walk; but now in the matter of cookery Quambo quite excelled even himself. With the aid of herbs he concocted the most delicious cavy stews; he wrapped flying fish in fragrant leaves, and did them over a clear fire, and he even concocted strengthening broths, from birds they shot in the woods.

But Cassia-bud went wandering all by himself round the island one day, and, lo and behold! he found a bed of clams near the shore. The clams proved an unexpected delicacy to all, but more especially to Frank. Turtles' eggs, also discovered by Cassia-bud, completed the cure.

And so Frank grew strong again once more, and happiness and joy reigned again in the little camp by the sea. And now, not knowing how much longer they should have to live on this unknown island, Fred planned the building of a house and laying out of a garden; for though a tent of boughs is all very well in times of health, it is wanting in comfort when sickness comes.

For weeks the four men—note, I have come to call them men at last—the four men laboured hard in effecting a clearing, while the catering and cooking devolved entirely upon little Cassia-bud and Bob. Not that Bob did much, but he often caught a cavy, and besides he was such a companion to Cassia-bud, it is doubtful if the lad could have got on at all without him. For gardening tools our castaways were worst off, but they managed to manufacture spades of a rough sort from the wood of the pandanus tree.

So the work of clearing and digging went merrily on, and the exercise it evolved strengthened every muscle in their bodies, and caused them to feel as happy as the birds that sang in the boughs.

All round the garden they wove a snake fence, and hung gates; but the fence was more for show than utility, as there really was nothing to protect themselves from; all their enemies lived in the water, and, with the exception of robber-crabs, and an occasional octopus, never came on shore.

Trees were now sawn into planks, and exposed to dry, by being piled up so that the warm air could blow over them.

Twenty-four feet long by twelve wide, that was the size they measured out for their cottage; and it would be seven feet high at the eaves, and consist of two rooms. So they proceeded at once to plant or put down the uprights and strong cross-beams to support the roof. For these purposes many of the planks saved from the wreck of the *Resolute* came in very handy. The uprights were firmly fixed in the ground, and the cross-beams fastened with hard wooden pegs on top of these.

The plan they adopted for boring holes was certainly original and expeditious also. Quambo had proposed to burn holes in the planks.

"No," said Fred, "I know a quicker plan."

"You do, sah!"

"Now make a mark at the very place you want a hole drilled."

Quambo did as he was told. Fred picked up a loaded rifle, and in less than a second the hole was made.

Quambo laughed at this till the woods rang again, and Bob ran off to the woods expecting that there must be game of some kind to retrieve.

The making of doors and shutters for the openings that had to do duty as windows required considerable time, and an expenditure of skill also; but these were finished at last. Instead of being hinged on, they were made to slide backwards and forwards, and this also was Fred's idea.

There were no fire places, but ventilators; for it would be always best to do all the cooking out of doors.

At long last the cottage was finished, and when the slanting roof was thatched with leaves of the pandanus—some of these being six feet in length—very neat and wholly rustic it looked.

Table and seats were next made. These were rough enough in all conscience, but they suited very well indeed.

"I think," said Frank, "the front of the cottage looks rather plain and squatter-like."

"Well," said Fred, "let us build a porch, and plant wild climbing flowers from the forest around it."

So this was done.

The castaways now turned their attention to the garden. Walks were laid out and bordered with old plank, and covered thickly over with silver sand from the beach. Then flowers and flowering shrubs were planted, and when all was finished proud indeed were they of their charming cottage and grounds. Even the snake fence they had run up round the compound sprouted and grew rapidly, so it was partly hedge and partly railing.

There was no occasion to plant vegetables in the garden, for everything they wanted grew wild in the woods, including many kinds of spices and turmeric also, from which Quambo, after they settled down again, concocted many a fragrant and delicious curry.

Well now, on the whole, our castaways were not badly off. They owned a house and grounds, they owned a boat, they had rifles and ammunition, and no lack of food.

All they longed for was the sight of a ship.

But the climate in which they lived is not only healthful and balmy, but calmative as well, so they did not pine so much as might have been expected.

"I say," said Fred one evening, "to-morrow will complete our first year on this island.

"How the time has fled!" said Frank. "I couldn't have believed it."

So they celebrated their advent-day by having quite a banquet in their new-built cottage, and everyone admitted—including Hurricane Bob—that Quambo had never spread before them such a dinner as this, such fragrant curry, nor such delightfully cooked fish.

It was early summer in the woods now; early summer with the trees, with their gorgeous and glittering foliage, and their wealth of flowers—snow-white, yellow, lemon, and crimson; early summer with the forest birds, whose sweet low songs filled every grove and glen; early summer with the wild bees, the gorgeous beetles, and still more lovely butterflies; early summer with many species of seafaring birds as well, who built on the rocks and cliffs—gulls and noddies, and the swift-winged frigate bird; early summer on land and on sea, which shimmered in the sunshine like polished steel.

It was well that our castaways had saved tinned meats from the wreck; for among the cavies or coneys it was thought advisable now to institute a kind of close season. It was breeding time, and to slay the parents, leaving perhaps the young to starve to death, would have been cruel in the extreme.

# CHAPTER XXIX
# THE ARRIVAL OF SAVAGES

It soon became evident that the supply of petroleum oil saved from the brig would run short, but here again Quambo came to the rescue. He and Cassia-bud collected an immense heap of ripe cocoa-nuts, and every day for weeks were busy doing something or other to them. I think they wished them to decay. At all events at the end of that time they set to pounding them up by degrees, and gradually extracted from the mess quite a large quantity of clear and beautiful oil. This in a less warm country would have been solid. The lamps in which the oil was burned were simply cocoa-nut shells cut down. A little water was put in first, then the oil over this, and wicks of pith floated on top by inserting them in disks of wood. So the difficulty of light was got over. And this was certainly something to be thankful for, because the sun set every night soon after six o'clock, and to have had to sit for long hours in the dark before turning in, would have been anything but pleasant.

Besides they had books now, and Fred and Frank took it in turns to read to the others every night.

Sunday was kept as a complete Sabbath, or day of rest, and prayers were said and the Bible read, and long walks taken in the woods or along the rocks.

Fred and Frank could not help marvelling at the wonderful tameness of the sea-birds as they sat on their nests. Even the frigate-bird, for example, on its one big white egg, looked like Patience on a monument, and was not averse to being handled.

I must tell you something about Cassia-bud's pets. First and foremost he one day found a strange wee bird, that had in some way or other tumbled out of its nest. He brought it home, nursed it and fed it regularly day and night, but allowed it as much freedom as it cared for.

It grew so tame that it followed the boy wherever he went, and was as often perched on his shoulder or head as anywhere else. It had a low, long, plaintive cry too, but this was reserved for Cassia-bud's especial delectation, or for Bob's. The bird, if not on the top of Cassia-bud, or not eating its food, one would be sure to find on Hurricane Bob's back. Perhaps his long hair kept its toes comfortable, then the dog's coat glittered so that the bird often pretended it was water, and went through all the motions of bathing in it.

This pet of Cassia-bud's was pure white, with two long trailing tail feathers of charming crimson. A robber-crab was another strange pet the boy had. How he had managed to tame this droll and uncouth-looking monster I cannot say. He fed him regularly with cocoa-nut, perhaps that was the secret. The crab was at least two feet in length, and lived in the hollow root of a tree, always coming out, however, when the boy called him.

Now in early spring, that is, between September and October, the turtles used to come on shore at some parts of the coast to lay their eggs. It was very curious to watch them. They were exceedingly shy, and usually chose a moonlight night for their work. So having now no fear of kelpies or other apparitions, our heroes, accompanied by Cassia-bud, used to go to a distant part of the beach and lie in wait for the turtles. By-and-by a great beast would be seen waddling slowly and cautiously towards the scrub.

After listening, apparently to make sure no one is looking, she quietly digs a deep hole about a yard in width. Then presently the eggs are laid, probably a hundred or two, and one by one taken by the flipper, as if it were a hand, and gently placed side by side in the hole. In about an hour's time the business is finished, Then the eggs are covered with sand, and carefully patted down. Her wonderful wisdom is shown by the tact that she even tries to conceal the place by snapping down twigs and leaves and covering it up. She then waddles off towards the sea again. Now would have been the time for Fred and Frank to have rushed out and tried their hands at turtle-turning. But it seemed the height of cruelty at such a time. Besides, it would have taken them a long time indeed to have eaten a turtle.

But the eggs were very delicious. Pure white they are and round. They have no shell, only a skin, and in size are about four inches to five inches round.

Our castaways soon discovered a plan for supplying themselves with plenty of young turtle. They simply took the very wee ones, after they were hatched, and kept them in a natural sea-water reservoir near the reef, feeding them on different kinds of weeds. They could in this way have stewed turtle for dinner any day, just as in our country we have fowls.

Well, one day among the rocks, while gathering algae to feed the juvenile turtles, Cassia-bud noticed Bob coming wading out of the water with some huge brown thing. It was a turtle of small size, and probably not very old. Bob held it by the flipper. When he attempted, however, to put it down he found that this was impossible. The turtle had seized him by the collar, and held fast on to it.

Bob looked very serious over it. His catching the turtle was all very well and very clever he thought, but to be caught by the turtle in turn was turning the table with a vengeance. He had caught a Tartar. He shook himself again and again, but all in vain. Then he walked straight up to Cassia-bud.

"Look here, Kashie," said the dog, talking with his eyes and his tail, "here is a pretty piece of business! I don't want to wear this beast dangling on my breast all my life night and day. Can't you choke him off?"

Cassia-bud couldn't choke him off, however, but he unloosed the dog's collar; and Bob carried collar, turtle, and all home in his mouth. Strange to say, the beast became as great a pet with the nigger-boy as either the bird or the robber-crab. Nor was the turtle a bit particular as to what he ate, so long as he could swallow it.

The difficulties to be encountered in building a vessel of any size, that should be at all seaworthy, seemed at the first blush almost insurmountable. It was long talked about before anything was done.

Meanwhile the castaways had not been idle, as far as the preparation of wood was concerned. Even the youngest of my readers must be well aware that no ship or boat even can be built of wood that has not been properly seasoned. Here on this strange island timber was certainly not lacking, but the seasoning of it, as experience soon proved to our heroes, was by no means so easy as might be supposed; for it is as much the wind as the sun that dries the wood, and if done too quickly it not only warps but cracks, and is therefore practically useless.

Many different kinds of trees were cut down and sawn up and placed in various situations by way of experiment; some out in the open, others in the woods, while planks were even steeped for a time in salt water and afterwards dried.

It was found that planks of the pandanus tree, first steeped for a week and afterwards dried in the shade, would, as nearly as possible, suit the purpose for which they were required; so with greater hopes now in their hearts they went merrily and earnestly to work.

But many months went by before they had sufficient wood of a reliable nature to fairly commence work with. Wooden pegs had meanwhile been carefully fashioned, and these had all to be fire-hardened, and were, of course, of different sizes; they were stored in the woods under dry fibre from the cocoanut and pandanus trees. The next thing to be done was to build a neat little furnace in which different sized boring-irons could be heated to redness, for Fred laughingly confessed that his plan of making holes with rifle bullets, though eminently practicable in warfare and house building, was inapplicable to the building of ships.

Many and many was the sleepless night that the planning of the yacht gave Fred, or at all events parts of nights, for he would lie and toss about and think till well on in the middle watch, and very often even after he did fall asleep his tired brain kept on working at all kinds of ridiculously impossible vessels, on the stocks and off, till it was time to get up.

Frank did not trouble himself so much about it

"I leave it all to you, Fred," he said; "your head is far longer than mine, and not half so thick, so you must be like Noah of old—master, ship-builder, and engineer all in one."

"Poor Noah," sighed Fred, "I have a higher opinion of him now than ever; my work is nothing compared to what his must have been."

"And I guess, sah," said Quambo, "de tools he hab am not so good as ours, sah."

"No, Quambo, so I mustn't grumble."

"I've been thinking," said Frank one morning as they sat together at breakfast.

"Have you really?" said Fred, pretending to look very much surprised.

"Yes, really and truly, Fred."

"Well then, Frank, will you be pleased to enlighten us all as to the nature and result of your cogitations?"

"Well, Noah the Second, instead of worrying your self into skin and bone over this yacht business, why don't we build a raft and be done with it? If we once embarked on a raft we would get blown somewhere."

"No doubt of it, wise Frank, we might very likely be blown on to a coral rock in mid-ocean, and have to begin life all over again, only in this case it would be the life of a cockroach that has tumbled into a basin of water, very brief but full of excitement."

"Very well," said Frank, "I shan't think any more. I beg leave to descend from the platform. Pass the clams."

"That's better for you, Frank."

But one day an event occurred that gave Fred quite a fresh impulse, and made him determine to proceed with the building of his yacht against every difficulty that could be thought or dreamt of.

This was nothing more nor less than the arrival on the island of a couple of naked savages in a small dug-out.

It had been blowing all night a strong breeze from the direction of the island, that from Beacon Hill could just be seen by the aid of the telescope. Doubtless the savages had been carried out to sea, or they never would have attempted so long a voyage in so small and clumsy a craft as an outriggered dug-out.

As they drew near to the beach—exactly at the spot where the brig went to pieces—the castaways hid themselves in the bush, lest they should frighten them.

They landed at last, and stood wonderingly on the sands, pointing to the ribs of the *Resolute*, that was still visible, black and ghastly in the surf. Tall and noble-looking figures these savages presented. They were entirely naked, with the exception of a kind of cummerbund of fibrous grass around the waist, and each held a long spear in his hand.

The castaways now stalked out.

The savages uttered a yell, threw their spears at them, one glancing close past Fred's head, and made a rush for their boat. But before ever they could get her afloat again our men were upon them and had made them prisoners.

# CHAPTER XXX
## "THERE IS NO GOING BACK NOW," FRANK SAID

Frightened the savages certainly had been at the sudden rush of three white men and one black giant—Quambo—from the bush in what they must have thought an uninhabited island; but cowards they were not. Indeed, as soon as they found themselves captured they submitted to the inevitable with a grace that was highly dignified.

Quambo had sailed in the Southern Pacific for many years, and was not now surprised that he could understand the language of these men. He was very proud, however, at being suddenly raised to the dignity of interpreter. With all the inborn courage of island warriors those savages seemed to possess the simplicity of childhood. They were talking to Quambo, and pointing to Fred, when the latter begged Quambo to translate. "They say," said Quambo, "they not have eat since yes'day; they say, suppose you gib 'em banana now to eat and cocoanut water to drink, the savages will taste yum yum when we cook and eat them."

Quambo laughed, but Fred shuddered. What ghastly humour was hidden in those words!

But the poor savages were at once supplied with food and drink, and told that the white man was their friend, and that, although they must keep them on the island, it was only for the white man's safety, as they did not wish to be discovered.

It is to be presumed that Quambo proved a very faithful interpreter indeed; for the savages seized Fred's hand, and bending low pressed it for a moment to the forehead in a way that was most affectingly dignified.

Very much surprised, indeed, were both Cassia-bud and Hurricane Bob, who had been left as camp keepers, to see the party return in company with two tall and soldiery-looking savages. Bob at first seemed much inclined to resent the intrusion, but as soon as matters were explained to him he walked up to the new-comers and licked their hands, as much as to say, "So long as you're good you won't be touched, but I'm going to keep my eye on you."

That evening the prisoners were allowed to dine on the floor of the cottage, and appeared to adapt themselves at once to their new mode of life. They were afterwards shown their bed under a bush. Their canoe had been drawn up quite close to the garden gate. Quambo and Cassia-bud took it by turns to do sentry duty all night, but the weary savages slept soundly, and awoke happy, hungry, and contented.

After breakfast was over our castaways sat down under the shadow of the trees, and the savages were made to squat near them. They then told their story, and an interesting one it was.

Their home was in a group of islands far, far away to the west. While fishing they had been caught in a squall and blown out to sea. The weather had continued very thick and bad all night, and at daybreak they found themselves near to a strange island, and had therefore landed in quest of food and water. Had they ever seen white men before? they were asked. "Oh, yes!" they answered, holding up both hands, with fingers outspread to indicate the number ten. Ten men had come, many, many moons ago, to their islands in canoes. They were hungry and thin, and were accordingly housed and well fed, because the flesh of white men is so much sweeter than that of black. They had been well fed, better fed than pigs, the savages explained, but would not grow fat. But they began to teach the natives many curious things, and to heal the sick, and staunch blood, and do much good; so instead of being killed and cooked they were permitted to live, and were now slaves to the king on the far-away islands. Where these white men had come from, they were, of course, unable to tell. They had come from the sea, was all they were able to say for certain; and reckoning on their fingers and toes the time, counted by moons, would correspond pretty nearly with the date of the abandonment of the brig *Resolute*. Then Fred got Quambo to enquire what the white men looked like.

Quambo laughed when he received their reply.

"Like de debbil hisself," he explained, "suppose the debbil wore clothes."

Now Fred was a very fair artist in his way, for Eean had taught him the rudiments of drawing, and besides he seemed to have a natural gift for caricature; so on the fly-leaf of a book he sketched a very good likeness of the skipper of the *Resolute*—jacket, hat; hooknose, and goatee beard all complete—in fact as he had last seen him.

When Quambo showed the savages this they roared with delight and astonishment, so much so in fact that Hurricane Bob had to put himself on the defensive.

"If there is much more of that sort of thing," Bob gave them to understand, "I'll be obliged to bring you to your senses."

"Did they ever see that man, Quambo?" asked Fred.

"Oh, yes! They say, sah," replied Quambo, "he de biggest and de cleberest debbil ob all de ten, sah."

This was conclusive enough.

It was evident, therefore, that the ten poor fellows who had landed on one of this unknown but cannibal group of islands were a portion of the crew of the lost brig *Resolute*, and that they still lived there as slaves.

The savages, as soon as they found out that they were to be well fed and treated, instead of being cooked and eaten, became very happy and contented indeed. As a mere matter of precaution their clumsy old dug-out was broken up and used as firewood, and after this it became quite unnecessary to set sentries of a night Hurricane Bob was sentry enough. He tolerated the savages, that was all. He never quite trusted them.

And now the building of the yacht was commenced in earnest.

The first thing to be done was to erect a shed on the beach under which the keel could be laid, and the work carried on pleasantly and as coolly as possible. The dimensions of the yacht were carefully studied and planned out; she was to have a twenty-feet keel, and to be sufficiently narrow in beam to permit of her being easily towed through the gap in the reef. This did not give her quite so much breadth as Fred could have wished, and he determined, therefore, to give her a good deep keel, and a not too high free-board, though the latter must of course be consonant with safety.

The building of the workshed occupied the castaways for the best part of a week, although they were ably assisted by their slaves the savages.

On the particular part of the beach where the shed was erected there was a nice slope towards the water, though it was not too steep; and so determined was Fred that his yacht should take the water like a duck, that he not only laid a slip for her descent, but had a strong railing of stanchions built on each side, so that an accident was simply out of the question.

He was determined also that in building his yacht, beauty and appearance should be sacrificed to safety and strength.

And now came the laying down of the keel. He and Cassia-bud had wandered in the woods for weeks scanning the trees, and at last, half-way up a hill they had been fortunate enough to find a tree, the upper part of whose trunk had been bent by the winds in such a way that it would suit admirably. When trimmed for the keel the bent portion would represent the fore part, that and the keel would be all in one piece. Well knowing that the whole build of a craft greatly depends upon the straightness, strength, and justness of the keel, much time was spent in forming this, and getting it fixed in position. But at long last Fred felt certain he had made a fair beginning. And now came the question of knees and ribs, the general skeleton, including the cross-beams, to keep all in place and to support the decks.

As they proceeded with the making of the skeleton, all hands, including even the savages, began to take an intense interest in the work, and to go at it morn, noon, and evening cheerfully. But until he commenced to plan and make and place the ribs, Fred had had no idea there was so much study and thought required in building even a boat like this. It should be remembered too that he was not only deficient in some most important tools, but in iron and nails as well.

One day he held a regular survey on nails, and finding he had so few he resolved to use pegs of hard wood wherever possible, reserving the iron for the most important parts.

After three weeks of the hardest work and study ever Fred had endured in his life, the whole framework and skeleton of the vessel was completed, and great was the joy of the castaways accordingly. And to give the young man his due as a ship-builder, it must be confessed that though her lines would not be by any means perfection, and would neither rival those of the model yacht *Thistle* or an Aberdeen clipper, they were not so far out by any manner of means. Nor would she be lopsided or in any way askew.

Being quite certain and satisfied on these points, the work of planking the craft was cautiously and carefully commenced. Luckily they had the best of planes, and they had splendid wood, so this part of the work went on smoothly and merrily enough, and every day Fred's men, as he called them, improved in the niceties of their trade of ship-carpentering.

But how genuinely tired and hungry they used to be of an evening!

Ah! well, the dinner that Cassia-bud prepared entirely banished the hunger, and a rest afterwards either in the cottage-ornée as a book was being read, or outside around the camp fire, made them forget all the toils and worries of the day. In fact, every evening the castaways gave themselves up body and soul to the enjoyment of the *dolce far niente*. In plainer language, they had nothing to do, and they did it well.

Reading indoors was all very well, but they enjoyed lazing in the sand by the camp fire far better. The nights at present were nearly always fine. There was the glitter of stars or glimmer of moonlight on the quiet sea.

There were fire-flies and a hundred other phosphorescent things flitting or crawling in garden, trees, or bush; there was the soft whispering of the breeze through the branches; the lulling sound of falling waters on the far-off reef; and above all there was the companionship of the log fire itself, that somehow never failed to talk to Fred and Frank, and tell them tales of their British home.

Songs were never forgotten around the camp fire, and there is no saying how much good they did not effect. Why, those songs used to please even the savages, and it was amusing, if not affecting, to hear them join in singing "Home, Sweet Home," or "Auld Lang Syne."

Before the deck of the vessel was completely planked over, the ballast was carefully adjusted and fastened down to the sturdy boat's bottom.

While digging in the garden Quambo had come upon quite a store of a curious kind of amber-like gum. This was melted and mixed in a cask containing a reddish pigment kind of earth, and lo! a paint of a pitchy nature was formed, and every seam of the yacht, outside and in, was carefully done over with this twice, and they had the satisfaction of finding that it did not become too brittle when dry. The same red earth was mixed with oil and a portion of the gum, and formed an excellent paint to go over all the work with before the vessel was launched.

Two hatches were fitted, each having rough, short ladders descending to the hold, or fore-cabin and saloon, as Fred grandly termed them.

The rudder was next made, and properly and scientifically shipped, and a handy tiller adjusted. Then the mast and a short jibboom were stepped, and after this the vessel was ready for launching, for they longed to prove if she was seaworthy.

Fred could not remember ever having longed for anything half so much as he longed to see the yacht afloat, and if real shipbuilders are as anxious for some days before they succeed in launching their ventures, then they must have a very uneasy time indeed.

But the eventful morning arrived at last, and the vessel was duly christened, not with a bottle of wine it is true, but with the milk of a beautiful green cocoanut, and named the *Island Queen*.

"Let go all now!" cried Fred.

Props were knocked out, the little ship swerved and swayed for a moment, then gently commenced her descent, moving on without a hitch, and finally taking the water just like the perfect duck she was unanimously declared to be. Of course they gave her three times three cheers as she slid into the water, with another little cheer for luck; then everybody crowded round Fred Arundel, the worthy shipbuilder, and shook hands with him in the most approved style; after which all retired to a sumptuous breakfast, quaffing the cocoa-nut of peace, as Frank called it, and wishing jolly good luck to the *Island Queen*.

"I think I can eat to-day," said Fred, with a soft sigh of satisfaction.

"Well, you ought, Fred," said Frank, "for you are positively getting thin."

They had not considered yet what they were going to do with their yacht, or where they should venture to sail to. They were possessed of no chart of the seas around here, but as near as Fred could judge they must be fully a thousand miles from either Auckland or Fiji. Would it or would it not be dangerous to make so long a journey in so small and frail a craft? All agreed, anyhow, that an attempt should be made to rescue the ten men who were still held prisoners, if not even made slaves of, in the cannibal islands from which the two savages had arrived.

Every preparation for the voyage was set about, therefore, without any loss of time.

Luckily they had plenty of spare canvas that had been found in the wreck, so the rigging, &c., of the *Island Queen* was perfected in a few days' time.

Then the first trial trip was made. The boat was sailed and manoeuvred all round the bay at first. Then she was towed with a boat ahead through the gap. It would have been risking too much to have sailed through, for at any moment a sea might have lifted her and carried her against the sharp coral rocks, after which there would have been no more *Island Queen*.

Once away out on the billowy breast of the blue ocean, all sail was set, and the craft was tried in every manner that could occur to a thorough seaman, and behaved herself in everything as a beauty.

"She's a beauty, Fred, a beauty," Frank said, over and over again, "and does you ample credit."

"Does us, you mean."

"No, no, Fred, old man. Honour to whom honour is due. Yours was the working head, ours only the willing hands."

On a bright and beautiful morning, with a gentle breeze blowing from the nor'ard and west, the manned and armed cruiser-yacht *Island Queen* left her anchorage in the bay near which our heroes had resided so long, and sailing easily through the reef gap, hoisted all sail again, and steered to the east away.

The Isle of Good Hope kept receding and receding as the day wore on, till at eventide it was seen but as a green cloud far away on the ocean's horizon.

But higher land was steadily rising ahead. Other green clouds appeared. A whole group of islands stretched out before them, and be their fate what it might they would cast anchor among them early next morning, if the wind but held.

Both Fred and Frank were uneasy in their minds.

"There is no going back now," Frank said.

"Come weal or come woe," replied Fred with great earnestness, "we shall do our duty, and trust all the rest to a Higher Power."

"Amen," said Frank.

# CHAPTER XXXI
## IN CANNIBAL ISLANDS

The crew of the derelict brig *Resolute* had certainly not been idle during the year and a half and over they had been prisoners on the cannibal islands. It was perhaps a lucky day for the natives when their boats drew up upon the beach with the sailors, more dead than alive, without arms or clothes, except what they wore, completely at the mercy of the naked and fierce-looking savages that crowded round them.

Here was a chance for these islanders, such as might not occur again in a score of years. Nothing could be more to their taste than the programme mapped out by their chief, and to be carried out on the following day.

First, Revenge. For they could not forget that long ago a white man's ship had cast anchor in this very bay, and that they had treated the men who landed with kindness and hospitality, albeit they would have preferred picking their bones. They remembered that event, and they did not forget either that in return for their hospitality those white fiends stole their women and their little ones, and put out to sea. Revenge is sweet.

Secondly, a short but bloody massacre of these innocent white men.

And thirdly, a glorious feast of roasted flesh to follow—a feast of white men's flesh, that they should look back to with satisfaction and delight as long as they lived.

So next morning the island had been all *en gala*. Huge fires were built on which to roast the sailors whole, and big round stones made hot to place in their insides, so that both outside and inside they might be done to a turn.

But, lo! when they had dragged the miserable sailors out of the compound, and everybody was itching to club them, they had found they were little more than skin and bone and grief.

This would never do; they must be fed and fattened. So they were penned in the king's own compound. But somehow they couldn't or wouldn't fatten; and besides, the king began to be mightily entertained with them. Seeing that this was the case, not only the Yankee skipper himself, but his nine men—all the rest of his crew, by the way, had been drowned—set themselves to please. They danced, they sang, and they even boxed with each other, all for this sable and savage King Ota's delectation.

Ota soon found out he had drawn a real prize in the lottery of life, and would now no more have consented to kill and eat his prisoners than you, reader, would your pet and expensive pigeons.

But meanwhile another savage king on another island had heard of Ota's luck, and sent to beg for half the white men, that he too might be tickled and amused. Ota replied, saying he would see the other king skinned first.

Well, there was some skinning after this; for that other king invaded Ota's island, and the battle on the beach raged fierce and bloody for many a long hour. The Yankee skipper and his merry men had been obliged to join the fight on Ota's side, and victory was at last obtained. The other king's men fled seaward in their boats, leaving more than a hundred dead and wounded on the beach. But the dreadful cruelties to the prisoners, and the awful orgies that were carried on for many days afterwards, I have no language to describe.

When all the killed were eaten, the bones were taken to "ornament" the kraal of the king, round which the savage soldiers danced and howled for days and nights to the unearthly music of tom-toms and conch-shells, accompanied by rattles made of the dead men's skulls with pebbles in them, and much yelling and brandishing of spears.

This feast, from first to last, was so terrible that the hair of several of the sailors turned white before it ended.

But peace ever since then had reigned in King Ota's island, and he had even become friendly again with the king who lived on the other side of the water. However, Ota would never permit his white men to go on the sea in a boat or canoe. They were too useful to risk. They built him a whole cottage, and taught his people to do many wonderful things. They laid out gardens even, in which yams and sweet potatoes, with cassava root and many other vegetables, flourished most luxuriantly.

But for all the king's kindness to them—and in a savage kind of way he really did treat them well—the poor white men pined, and longed to see a ship appear on the horizon.

Every morning of their lives when they left the huts in which they slept, guarded as prisoners, they betook themselves towards the hill-top.

Two Sailor Lads | 207

They told Ota they went thither to pray. Well, to their credit be it said, they did pray; but many was the wistful glance they cast seawards in hopes of catching sight of the coming ship.

One morning the ship did heave in sight.

That ship was the little *Island Queen*.

Just an hour after she had first been sighted, Ota, the king, called his prisoners before him.

A translation of the speech he made then would read somewhat as follows:

"White men people. King Ota is the biggest king in all the wide world. There is no end to his greatness or his glory. He has destroyed his enemies in many a bloody battle both by sea and land, and cooked and eaten them afterwards. Even the birds of the air fly round the head of King Ota when he takes his walks abroad, and scream their worship in his large and willing ears. And the dark frigate bird, the *eewaoo*, carries the story of King Ota's glory to the utmost regions of the earth. King Ota's arm is very strong, but King Ota's heart is as big and soft as a *jeetee* (the jelly fish). When Ota saw the poor white sailors land on his shore, his first thought was to club and eat them, after smearing his wives and little ones with their bright red blood. But his soft *jeetee* heart forbade; so he has kept them, and is very kind to them. But now behold a white man's ship has appeared in the bay, and they may want to take the king's dear prisoners away. But they must not know they are here. I must hide them in the innermost shades of the forest, and keep them secure until the ship departs. Away with them guards, and if they attempt to escape kill them, and we will feast ourselves on their bodies."

This was a sad sentence, but there was no relenting in King Ota, so they were marched away into the depths of a dark wood, and imprisoned in a bamboo hut, which was guarded by the spearsmen of the savage king.

"Now, Frank," said Fred, "what is to be done first?"

That is what Captain Arundel, of the model yacht *Island Queen* said, as soon as the anchor was let go in the beautiful bay off the Isle of Ota.

"That's what I should like to know, Fred," was Frank's reply. "I'm ready to obey you in everything, and fight for you, and stick by you to the last; but, faith, Fred, I'm a poor hand at giving advice."

"I should say," said Mac, "we'd better first try to make friends with these black beggars."

"They don't look very friendly," said Frank.

This was true; for though many dug-outs had shoved off from the shore, they kept severely aloof from the little yacht.

Quambo was sent down below to question the two captured savages, whom it was thought advisable for the present to keep out of sight.

The savages assured Quambo that this really was Ota's island, but that he would doubtless not permit the white men to appear. If they could lure the crew of the *Island Queen* on shore, they would, said they, kill and eat them, but they would not attack the vessel till nightfall.

This was a rather gloomy outlook, and as no white men could be seen on the beach, Fred could only come to the conclusion that they were hidden away somewhere. He determined, however, that he would not be deterred from landing and seeking an interview with the king on the beach.

So Fred, with Quambo and Mac, lowered the boat, and boldly proceeded to row towards the shore. Quambo was to act as interpreter.

The boat was fully armed with revolvers and rifles, with spears also, lest they might have to come into close quarters with the cannibals.

The canoes certainly did not scatter in all directions at the approach of the white men's boat, but they drew sullenly off.

When within thirty yards of the shore they lay on their oars, and immediately afterwards the beach swarmed with spear-armed, wildly-gesticulating savages. Among them was a personage arrayed in an old pilot jacket, and nothing else, so that with his long black legs sticking out from under he had anything but a very imposing appearance.

He had a spear in his right hand, and by a string in the other was leading along a good-sized pig, of all creatures in the world.

Conversation was at once opened up, and proceeded somewhat as follows:

*Quambo.* "Are you the king of this island?"

*Ota.* "I am King Ota, the greatest king in all the world."

*Quambo.* "And we are poor white men who want food and water."

*Ota.* "I have brought this pig to make you a present of. How much will you pay me for this pig?"

"That's a queer way of making a present," said Fred, when the king's words were interpreted. "Tell him we will give him a beautiful jacket and a pair of white duck trousers to hide his dirty black legs. Hold up the garments."

*Quambo* (holding up the trousers and blue jacket). "Here, O great and good king, we have brought you a coat for your brave body, and a pair of white ducks for your lovely legs!"

*Ota*. "Land and leave them."

*Quambo*. "No, leave the pig, and we will land and exchange; but you must retire."

Fred now determined to bring matters to a crisis. These savages had never seen or heard of fire-arms, so now raising a rifle to his shoulder he took aim and fired, and, lo! Ota's pig dropped dead at his feet. The smoke had hardly cleared away till, with terrible shouts and shrieks, the savages had fled in all directions. For just one brief moment the greatest king in all the world stood looking down at poor piggie weltering in its gore, then with an eldritch scream he too fled away.

"Pull on shore quickly now, lads," cried Fred, and the boat was quickly beached. The pig was lifted on board, the jacket and trousers laid on the sands, and off they shoved again, and were soon once more safely on their own quarter-deck.

In an hour's time, however, they had the satisfaction of seeing King Ota come down to the beach, dress in the new clothes, then stride gallantly away, followed by all his sable suite.

Instead of lying at anchor all night, and probably thus courting an attack, it was thought advisable to put out to sea, where they could bid defiance to a whole fleet of armed canoes.

The king presented himself on the beach next day, but he had no pig. It was noticed too that not a woman or child was permitted to appear; and this Quambo assured Fred was a certain sign that these savages meant to fight.

Now fighting was no part of Fred's policy. With all his courage and daring it would be ruinous not only for his party, but for those he sought to rescue, to go to war with these savages. Against such numbers he could only act on the defensive, and this but for a very short time. So he determined to make friends by every means in his power. He once more, therefore, drew near to the beach and held parley with King Ota, or King Breeches, as Magilvray called him.

Fred informed him that he came now on a friendly mission; that he desired everlasting peace between the white men and the blacks; and that in proof of this if he, King Ota, would venture on board he should be treated kindly and receive many more presents, even a fire-stick such as he, Fred, had slain the pig with the day before.

The offer of a gun was certainly a great temptation, but it evidently was not great enough to induce King Ota to risk his sacred person on board the *Island Queen*.

"Would the white man leave the fire-stick on the beach and go away?" he asked.

"No; the white man would do nothing of the sort."

"Would the white man then kill something else?"

To this Fred made reply, that if the greatest king in all the world wanted a pig for his own dinner, and would bring one to the beach, the white man would kill it.

On this the king seemed suddenly to be struck by a happy thought. He held communication with his dusky warriors; a few of them retired to the bush, and after a while re-appeared dragging along a poor woman. She was stationed on the fore-shore, and stood there with drooping head patiently waiting for the death she expected. The king and his warriors stood aside at a safe distance. Then pointing to the woman Ota hailed the boat. "That is the pig that the greatest king in all the world wants to eat for dinner, make fire, quick, quick."

Fred felt strangely tempted to give the king himself a shot. So inhuman a monster he had never before held communication with.

At this moment a huge black-brown kite came wheeling round his dusky majesty's head; slowly it sailed tack and half tack.

Now Mac had been the best shot in the *San Salvador*. Fred gave him the rifle.

"Bring down that bird," he cried. "Pray don't miss."

Steady was the aim Magilvray now took. Bang went the rifle. The king's eyes were turned towards the poor woman, his face beaming with fiendish delight in the expectation of seeing her fall. Instead of that there alighted on his royal head a huge mass of blood and feathers. He uttered a yell that could have been heard a good mile off, and threw himself struggling on the ground.

It was a rash thing for Fred to do; but there was no help for it now, and almost before Quambo and Magilvray could get way on the boat spears were hurled after them, and a wild rush made towards the canoes.

That was indeed a race for life; but Quambo and Mac made the gig fly and skip across the water, and not only were they aboard, but the boat was hauled up, before the savages in their clumsy canoes could get alongside.

"Shake out the mainsail. Get the anchor up." These were the orders now.

Just one volley was fired at the advancing canoes, which staggered and sent them back, and before they had recovered from their consternation the sails were set, and the *Island Queen* stood steadily out to sea.

But the shooting of that foul bird had ruined everything, as far as peace was concerned.

# CHAPTER XXXII
# THE WHOLE BEACH WAS LINED
# WITH YELLING SAVAGES

Captain Fred Arundel, of the *Island Queen*, now left the island of King Ota far astern, and proceeded to take a quiet survey of the whole group.

The islands were five in all, although one was so small as hardly to be worthy of notice. It is nevertheless the most important of all to our story. This little isle, although well treed, was evidently not inhabited, and had only one landing-place, all the rest of its shore being as inaccessible as the Bass Rock itself.

The other islands were inhabited, as well they might be; for in rugged grandeur of contour, and in beauty of tropical foliage, they exceeded anything that Fred or Frank could have imagined or dreamt about.

Waving cocoa-nut and palm trees, gigantic tree ferns, bananas, pandanus, and bread fruits, and a wealth of waving woods and grasses and flowers, that made them look like veritable fairy-lands afloat, or the fabled islands of the blessed dead we read of in the classics. Yet everyone of them was the abode of savages and cannibals. No boats came off from either, though in one of the bays Fred lay at anchor for very many hours.

He was concocting a bold and daring scheme, which if successful should mean freedom for the white prisoners, whatever might befall them next; but if unsuccessful it would mean death, or a slavery far worse than death, for all concerned.

That the inhabitants of these islands were not really bad at heart was Fred's evident thought, from the kindly way their own two prisoners took to work and civilization.

Could the latter be trusted in a matter of life and death? Fred made up his mind to try them.

So they were now brought on deck and questioned by Quambo, questions and answers being very much as follows:

Why did they—the white men—see nothing of their brothers who were held as slaves by King Ota? King Ota was too clever. He kept them in the forest prison. Did they know the road from the beach to this prison? They knew many roads to it.

Could they and would they be willing to guide a party to this bamboo prison through the forest at the darkest hour of midnight? Yes, they could and would gladly, the white men had been very good to them; but if they guided them to their white brothers they must promise to take them—the guides—away with them, else King Ota would put them to death with much terrible torture.

So far then everything seemed satisfactory, and Fred and Frank resolved to risk all in one bold effort to set the white men free.

"To dare is to do, Frank," said Fred.

"Yes," replied Frank, "and I should never forgive myself if we went away and left these poor fellows prisoners and slaves among these terrible cannibals. I cannot forget, Fred, that the Yankee skipper was kind to me when I was sick, and that he was my captain, you know."

"Well, then, Frank, when does the moon rise, to-night?"

"What, will you venture so soon?"

"Oh, you know what a nervous coward of a chap I am! If I've got to face anything I like to go at it at once. Besides, it is best to strike the iron when it is hot."

"All right," said Frank. "I must say, however, Fred, that your cowardice is of a very peculiar kind, from all the specimens I've had of it lately."

And now the two savages were once more interrogated, and it was soon found that from the back part of the island, where the pandanus forest grew right down to the water's edge, a footpath led up through the woods to the bamboo prison or fort. It would no doubt be well guarded, but nothing venture nothing win.

> "He either fears his fate too much,
>   Or his deserts are small,
> Who dares not put it to the test,
>   To win or lose it all."

These lines are well worth remembering, and everyone who reads British history must be struck with the fact, that nearly all our greatest victories have been won by downright pluck and derring-do.

Well, everything seemed to favour our heroes to-night; for the moon would not rise until nearly two o'clock, a favouring breeze was blowing, and there would be light enough from the stars to creep round to the back of King Ota's island and let go anchor. All the rest must be left.

The sun went down at six o'clock. Then dinner was got through, and preparations at once made for the adventure.

Luckily they had plenty of revolvers on board, saved from the brig, and good ones too, the revolver being a tool as common on board all Yankee foreign-going ships as toothpicks, more or less.

A dozen and a half of these were most carefully loaded with ball cartridges. Ten of these were placed in a hand-bag or grip-sack, and this Quambo was to carry. Fred, Frank, and Quambo, with one of the savages, were to take part in this cutting-out expedition; little Cassia-bud, all by himself, was to remain with the other savage as ship-keeper; while Mac would come along to take charge of the boat.

Cassia-bud would be captain of the *Island Queen* therefore for once in a way, and Hurricane Bob assured the boy that he would keep his eagle eye on the remaining black fellow.

"Would it not, sir," said Mac, "be as well to handcuff the darkie we leave behind?"

"No," said Fred boldly. "I have told these men I trust them, and trust them now I must and will."

About ten o'clock the *Island Queen* quietly got up anchor and sail, and began her dangerous voyage.

It was indeed in every way an expedition fraught with the greatest danger. To begin with, they were in an unknown sea, where they must trust to Providence to keep them off rocks and shoals. Secondly, after they landed their lives were in the hands of the guide, who might, if he chose, lead them into the very midst of the enemy; and even if he proved true, they had the guards to silence, if nothing worse.

All hands were armed to the teeth, and the boat's oars were muffled.

It still wanted half an hour of midnight when the yacht crept slowly in towards the darkling shore, and the anchor was let silently down.

Finally the boat was lowered, and everything being ready, she was shoved off and silently rowed towards the shore.

Stars were all out and shining, but the woods lay still and quiet under their feeble light. Not a word was spoken by any one on board; but just before the boat was run upon the soft white sand Fred felt for Frank's hand and pressed it.

Frank well knew what was meant.

Then the landing was effected, Fred whispering some words in Mac's ear just before the three brave men headed by their savage guide, dipped into the dark woods and commenced the march.

Silently, and in single file, they followed on and on. It seemed a very, very long mile, and more than once Fred suspected treachery. So too did Frank. If treachery it was going to be, they at all events had resolved to sell their lives as dearly as possible; and it was satisfactory to remember they were venturing those lives in a worthy cause.

"Hist!" It was a signal from the guide.

All stopped, then cautiously advanced again. In a minute more they came in view of the bamboo prison. And yonder were the guards, seated by a blazing log fire—a fire that revealed their fiercely-savage faces, but left all else in Rembrandtesque darkness.

Savoo, the guide, pointed to a spot just behind them, and whispered to Quambo.

Quambo in his turn conferred with Fred and Frank, and in a moment a plan of action was agreed to.

Quambo was to rush on, and throwing his huge bulk against the door, burst it open, while the other three settled matters with the spear-armed sentries.

For that matter they might have shot them where they sat; but Fred was averse to using firearms before it was absolutely necessary.

Savoo was armed with a huge club. Fred and Frank, in addition to their revolvers, had each a sword.

"Are we all ready?"

"All ready."

"Then dash on."

Quambo was first. He thrust at one of the guards with his spear as he passed; but, rushing on and heeding nothing, hurled his whole gigantic force against the frail bamboo door.

It gave way at once. It flew into flinders in fact. Meanwhile, Savoo, club in hand, had followed Quambo to the fire.

Thud! thud! Two awful blows; and the two remaining sentries were disposed of, and stretched beside the one Quambo had speared.

There was nothing left for Fred or Frank to do.

"Friends," cried Quambo as soon as the door flew open, "are you all here, men?"

"The Lord's name be praised!" cried the Yankee skipper, "whoever you are. But we're all tied and trussed like fowls goin' to the market."

Frank was beside his old captain in a minute, and Fred showed a light from his bull's-eye lantern.

What a fearful sight! Every man was tied up in a bundle, as it were; and when the cords were cut, for a few moments they scarce could stand.

Here was a new danger that had not even been thought of. They could not carry the men, and what if they could not walk?

But the odour of their prison was like that of some vile charnel-house; and it was as much this as their cramped position that rendered them so helpless.

They revived very soon after they were brought into the open air, and were able to receive each a revolver from Quambo's grip-sack. Then the return journey was at once commenced.

They reached the beach in safety, and half the party were at once rowed off to the vessel. Fred, Frank, and Quambo remained behind with two men—one being the Yankee skipper himself. This was the most anxious time of all for Fred and Frank, and the longest too, apparently.

Do what Fred would, he could not keep that Yankee skipper's tongue silent.

To be sure he talked in a kind of half whisper, but the night was so terribly still that even this could be heard a good long way off.

"What I'm terribly vexed about," was one of the skipper's remarks, "is that I didn't have it out wi' that rascal, King Ota."

"Hush, hush!" whispered Frank. "Not so loud please, captain."

"The skunk," he continued, "to truss us all up like fowls."

Fred lost his temper now. "Look here, sir," he said, "I'm in command here, and if you say another word I'll gag you—there!"

"I say, youngster," whispered the Yankee in a kind of wheedling tone, "gag me with a lump o' baccy. I'd give ten years of my sinful life for a chew."

In spite of the extreme danger they were in Fred could not keep from smiling.

But Quambo stuck a big lump of tobacco in the skipper's hand, and he was silent after this. "Hist!" It was the voice of the guide again. He had clutched Fred's arm and was pointing away to the woods.

Fred could hear nothing for a time. At last, however, a confused noise of tom-tom beating, couch blowing, and yelling, was borne to his ears on the night breeze. It was only too evident that the escape of the prisoners had already been discovered, that the whole island was alarmed, and that the savages had found their trail.

Again and again Fred flashed his light towards the *Island Queen*, to induce the speedy return of the boat. But seawards all was silent.

And every minute the shouting and yelling in the woods drew nearer and nearer.

Both Frank and Fred did feel fear now. They stood almost face to face with a terrible death, knowing well too that if caught alive they would be put to the torture.

Nearer and nearer! Would the boat never come?

At last, oh, joy! a black spot suddenly appeared among the surf, and they made a dash towards it.

None too soon, for hardly had they left the shore ere the whole beach was lined by the howling savages. Spears whirled past them in the darkness, and shots were returned from the boat.

Fred presently heard a dull thud close beside him in the boat.

"Oh!" groaned the Yankee skipper. "That's got me. Poor Silas is to be sewed up at last."

"Has the spear hit you?" said Frank anxiously.

"Gone clean through and through me. Oh, don't attempt to draw it out! Blood will flow in bucketfuls if you do. No, let me just collect my thoughts and try to pray a bit. Oh! ain't got nary a cigar about you, 'ave you?"

Meanwhile the boat was speeding across the water towards the *Island Queen*.

"Oh, be careful now!" cried Silas. "I tell you I'm pinned clean through the body on to the gunwale of the boat."

Fred showed his light. The spear certainly appeared to be sticking right through Silas like a pin through a moth. But more minute investigation showed it had only gone through his jacket and shirt, grazing his skin.

"Oh," he said coolly, "well shiver me if I didn't think I was a gone coon!"

In less than ten minutes after, all were on board, the sails were filled, and the *Island Queen* was standing rapidly out to sea.

# CHAPTER XXXIII
# SOUTH AND SOUTH SAILED
# THE GOOD BARQUE

The word "Sarpinto" kept ringing in the old fisherman bard's ears as he retired to bed that night.

I believe the last words he said to himself as he laid his head on the pillow were "Sarpinto, Sarpinto, where on earth have I heard the name! Sar——"

He was asleep before he could finish the word, but when he awoke next morning he did finish it. "Pinto," he muttered to himself, "Pinto, yes, now I have it. That was part of the word that I read on the bill of lading that came on shore with dear Toddie, and that Bunko afterwards found in the log of wood. Pinto! I have it. How singular now if this Señor Sarpinto turned out to be nobody else but Toddie's wicked uncle."

Captain Cawdor was not an early riser, as the term is understood by the fisherfolks of Methlin, but on this particular morning he was up and out by seven o'clock.

He found Eean anxiously waiting for him.

"Come with me for a stroll," said Eean, "as far as a cave I have here. Ah! Toddy darling, here you are."

Toddie, who was quite a tall and very pretty girl, now threw her arms about the old bard's neck to give him a morning kiss, and receive his blessing. Then she shyly gave a hand to Captain Cawdor.

"Yes, you can come with us, pet," said the bard. "It is about you we are going to talk."

So the three walked along the cliff-top, and finally descended to the cave.

And there Eean, with the paper in his hand, told Captain Cawdor the whole of Toddie's strange story, as far as he himself knew it.

It was a strange story certainly, but simple enough in the main. There surely was nothing in it to strike so sturdy and hardy an old seafarer as Captain Cawdor speechless. But that is precisely the effect it had on this ancient mariner.

His eyes had got bigger and bigger as Eean proceeded, and as he finished his jaw had actually dropped.

He found his tongue at last, however. Then three times in succession he thumped his red round fist on the deal table in front of him, and three times in succession he muttered the words:

"Bless my soul, sir! Bless my soul!"

"Why, what is it?" said Eean. "Do you know anything?"

"Do I know *any* thing, man? Bless you and me both, I know *every* thing. I declare I'm half afraid wonders will never cease."

"Well," said Eean, "it is all very wonderful, but tell us all you know; for I am certain my little girl here is quite as anxious to hear about her early history as I am. And I pray God this moment, Captain Cawdor, that you will tell us nothing that can result in parting me and my more than child."

"Nay, nay," cried Captain Cawdor, earnestly and thoughtfully, as Toddie had thrown herself on old Eean's lap, and was nestling close to his breast.

"I'm certain sure you won't be parted; for Señor Sarpinto—and he really is Toddie's uncle—is one of the kindest men that ever breathed, and an ill-used man he has been."

"But," said Eean, "the paper here calls him a villain. See! Read for yourself."

Captain Cawdor adjusted his glasses, and glanced at the frayed and worn manuscript Eean placed in his hands.

"Nay, nay, sir, here you have made a great mistake. You will note, sir, that the words 'uncle'—'villain'—and 'malediction' are widely separated, and that a deal that has been written between them has been frayed out and obliterated. The word 'villain' doesn't refer to my dear, kind-hearted friend Sarpinto, nor the word 'malediction' either."

"You relieve my mind considerably, Captain Cawdor, but pray proceed."

"Well, sir, on our passage back from the southern seas, Sarpinto and I got very chummy indeed. Although he is a Spaniard, he is a man nobody could help loving. He told me all his life story. But I need tell you no more at present than what refers to the dear wee lady there.

"They were twins, sir, the brothers Sarpinto, and loved each other as dearly as brothers should. The only misfortune in their lives was their both falling deeply in love with the same young lady. No fault of hers, mind you. By all accounts that child's mother was an angel. She loved the sailor brother best, however, and she married him, and sailed with him wherever he went. And never, mind you, did this sailor know his brother's secret. But, between you and me, it broke this brother's heart, though he still lives. And while he lives he'll roam and rove around the wide world in quest of adventures, for, alas! he cannot rest.

"Now, sir," continued Captain Cawdor, "do you begin to see how the land lies?"

"I do," said Eean.

"Señor Sarpinto's sailor brother, on his last voyage, carried with him much specie, and it was not till long after he had sailed that the Señor found out there had sailed with him in disguise one of the blackest-hearted villains that ever drew a knife. The ship was the *Santa Maria* sure enough, and the very commonness of the name threw the Señor off the scent, and he does not know now, of course, that his niece here is alive and well, and in such fatherly arms."

The captain ceased to speak, and after a moment's pause Eean rose slowly from his seat and held out his hand, which the sailor grasped right heartily.

"You are a good man," he said, "and God has sent you."

"And now," he added, as he reseated himself, "my duty lies before me more clearly than before."

"And that is?" — —

"That is to return with you to America, and see this Señor Sarpinto for myself."

"Oh, daddy," cried Toddie, "you will not leave me."

"Nay, child, you too shall go. I feel we will not be separated."

"That you won't, sir."

"So cheer up, darling, you shall see a little of the world yet."

"And, oh, daddy, I feel sure of one thing."

"What, dear?"

"That we shall find Fred and Frank too."

"The Lord send that your words may come true," said Eean piously.

Then all three returned slowly along the cliff-top.

There was much talk and wonderment in the wee village of Methlin, when it got bruited abroad that Eean and his daughter, as Toddie was always called, were going off with the strange sailor gentleman to America.

And almost the first to hear of it was Bunko, the herd.

Now of late years, through the earnest and indefatigable teaching of Eean, a very great change had come over this strange lad. Simple he might still have been called, but half-witted no longer. He went straight away now and sought audience of Eean.

"I hear," he said, "you're going off to the lands o' America. Well, sir, I've saved ten golden pounds, and I'm goin' too to tak' care o' Toddie. No, no, you canna shake me off."

Eean smiled, and Bunko won.

So it came to pass that when Captain Cawdor, with Eean and Toddie, took passage at Liverpool for Baltimore, Bunko was booked also.

"Heigho," said Bunko, as soon as they were embarked, "I can hardly believe I'm no' dreaming. And we really *are* going down to the sea in ships, to behold the wonders o' the Lord in the mighty deep."


Just one month after the sailing of the steamer that bore old Eean and his party to the new world, and early on a beautiful forenoon, Señor Sarpinto was lounging in the gardens of a splendid hotel in San Francisco. At such a time of day as this very few people are to be found lounging anywhere, in this great busy, bustling city, for those who are not engrossed in the work of their lives are intent on pleasure.

But Sarpinto was an idler to-day, and a dreamer as well—that is, if so restless a spirit as his ever could be idle.

He had smoked two or three cigarettes, and lit a fourth, but presently he threw this away, and throwing himself back in his chair, allowed his eyes to rest on a fleecy cloud that was speeding across the blue sky on the wings of a western breeze. There was not another morsel of cloudlet to be seen anywhere.

"All alone! All alone!" he was saying half aloud, "alone like a ship at sea, or like my own time-tossed barque of life. How different, how very different it would all have been had Helena loved me! Ay, it is just seventeen years to-day since I dared my fate, and in these very gardens too, and not very far from this spot. Heigho! how the time flies! How——."

He had not heard the sound of light footsteps advancing, nor noted that anyone was near him, till a sweet soft voice said:

"Oh, please sir, can you tell me which is the path that leads to the gate? I——."

She ceased speaking, and stood before Señor Sarpinto, shy, half-frightened, but wholly surprised. And well she might be. For Sarpinto had clutched the arms of the chair with both hands, and was bending forward, gazing into her face as one might who has suddenly awakened from a strange dream.

"Good heavens! girl," he cried. "Tell me what or who you are, and how you came here."

"Oh, sir!" Toddie began, "I'm sorry—I didn't know, Pray forgive me, sir—but, ah! here come father and Captain Cawdor."

"O, Daddy!" she shouted, running towards the group, and forgetting all about Sarpinto. "I'm so glad you have come. I had lost you."

"But, my dear child," cried the jolly old captain, "I do declare you've found your uncle before us."

"My uncle? My uncle Sarpinto, Captain Cawdor!"

"Ay, ay, lass, and nobody else. Señor Sarpinto, you got my letters explaining all; and here, my dear sir, stands your little niece."

The Señor took a step forward with half-open arms, and next moment Toddie's head was pillowed on his breast. He kissed her brow, then held her at arm's length, that he might feast his eyes on her rare young beauty. The tears came welling up. He struggled to suppress them.

"How like your mother!" he sighed.

Then he kissed her again, and smiled.

"We shall all be very happy," he said. "How pleased I am to meet you, Mr. Arundel," he continued, turning now to Eean and shaking hands right heartily. "But, sir, you are to me no stranger. Many and many a night, when frozen up in the southern sea of ice, I have heard about you, and about Fred Arundel too."

"Yes," he added, looking at Toddie, "and about you, my dear, also, and your *Water Baby*, and all about your adventures on your desert island. Oh, I assure you, Carissima, Frank was never tired talking about you."

"Oh, sir! oh, uncle! do you think we shall ever see Fred and Frank again?"

"I dreamt we should, mia Carissima, and I have chartered the sturdy old *San Salvador* for a cruise in southern seas to look for them—for I cannot, will not, believe them dead—and to look also for survivors, if any there be, of my good ship *Resolute*."

Señor paused for a moment. Then, once more turning to Eean and extending his hand, he said with a pleasant smile:

"Come with me as my guest, friend Arundel, and bring my niece as well. There, I will not be denied."

"In that case I will not refuse," said Eean, "and I shall write to my wife to-night."

"Oh, your wife shall know all about it in an hour! I shall cable."


Very much surprised indeed was honest, kindly Eppie to receive that cablegram all the way from San Francisco—over three thousand miles of land, across three thousand miles and more of ocean. And the reply was paid for; so that Eean and Toddie had that very evening the pleasure of reading Eppie's message back, and her blessing.

And thus then it happened that, when the *San Salvador* left the Pacific slope, and once more spread her canvas wings out before the ocean breeze, on her ivory-white quarter-deck sat old Eean, the bard, and Toddie, the latter dressed in the most bewitchingly yachty costume it is possible to imagine, and looking every inch a sailor.

And not very far off, leaning over the bulwarks, was Bunko himself, not looking very like a sailor, it must be confessed, but a well-dressed and interesting figure nevertheless.

Captain Cawdor was in uniform now, and he had not only the same mate, but pretty much the same men, as he had sailed into port with more than a year and a half ago.

One other person deserves a word of introduction. Yonder he is, talking now to Bunko, a Scottish missionary, one of those fearless young men who take life in the left hand, the Bible in the other, and carry the gospel of peace and goodwill to the most savage tribes on earth.

South and south sailed the good barque *San Salvador*, and every day a new life seemed to be opening out before Toddie. Her young heart was full of hope; it was therefore full of joy, and she seemed to be part and parcel of all the beauty she saw around her—beauty of sea, beauty of sky, beauty of wild wheeling birds of the ocean wave, and beauty of green islands that seemed to move and float and flit on the world of waters, as the ship sailed past them and away—south, south, ever south.

# CHAPTER XXXIV
# FIGHTING IN EARNEST

"And now Frank," said Fred, as the *Island Queen* stretched away out into the more open sea, and the round moon was rising and casting its silvery rays athwart the waves, "everything depends upon the wind holding. If we get becalmed we'll be boarded by swarms of those savages, in spite of all we can do."

"I don't think," replied Frank, "that there is much fear of a calm taking place. Why, the wind seems to increase every minute since we have left the shore."

"How thankful I am though that we dared all! Ah, Frank, old man! there is nothing like a bit of dash."

"No; dash does it. I've always thought so. First feel yourself fit, and then do a dash."

"That's it, Frank."

The poor fellows who had been delivered from slavery on the island of savages had eaten a hearty supper, and were now one and all fast asleep. Even the Yankee skipper had gone to sleep, with a quid in his mouth.

The breeze in two hours' time had increased to quite half a gale, and Fred began to grow seriously uneasy. The little craft was very much deeper in the water now, for the addition of ten men made a vast difference in so small a ship.

She pitched and rolled to a tremendous extent—she took in water over the bows, she shivered and shook like an old clothes basket when on the top of a wave, and wallowed when in the trough of the seas. In fact she did not behave at all prettily now she was put fairly on her mettle.

By-and-by Fred found it necessary to batten down, although he had to leave a portion of one hatchway open, in order to let those below have a sufficiency of fresh air.

Frank relieved Fred about four o'clock, or eight bells in the middle watch, and feeling completely exhausted, Fred lashed himself to the mast, covered himself up as well he could with a piece of canvas, and was soon fast asleep.

He never stirred, nor, knowing his condition, did Fred permit him to be disturbed until two bells in the forenoon watch.

Though he pretended to be cross with Frank for having allowed him to oversleep himself, he knew that his friend Had done all for the best.

The wind was still roaring through the rigging; but had veered round several points, and the yacht was now close hauled. Far away astern were the green islands they had left on the previous night.

"Whither away, mate?" said Fred.

"'Pon my honour, captain, I haven't the ghost of a notion."

"But you've been steering for the east?"

"Yes, all the watch."

"And I guess that's about as near right as a toucher," said Silas the skipper. "'Cause don't you see we're bound to come among islands o' some kind, and shiver me if they can be a bit worse than those we've left."

"True enough," said Frank.

About five bells that forenoon a heavy sea struck the *Island Queen* on the weather quarter, and almost laid her on her beam ends.

She slowly righted, however, but hardly was she once more on an even keel than there was a shout from the men below.

"We've sprung a leak!"

Fred handed the tiller to Silas, and rushed down. It was only too true. The water was coming pouring in, in three different places at the bows.

"All hands to bail her out," cried Fred.

And the men set merrily enough to work. Those below filled calabashes, and handed them to others on deck to be emptied overboard.

They kept the water under for a while. But it was soon evident enough she could not float for any length of time.

The question now arose, What was best to be done? and a consultation was held.

"I see nothing for it, young men, except put about and just run back for them same islands," said Silas.

"And beach her?"

"Aye, aye, but look you here, Frank," continued Silas. "I've no great inclination to be crucified alive, and eaten afterwards. I'd rather drown, and be done with it. So we better beach her at the little island to the nor'ard. There is only one landing, and we can hold that again' all the savages in creation."

The skipper's advice was certainly good. So the *Island Queen* was put about.

It was sad, disheartening work, but there was no other chance of life, so Fred never uttered one single complaining word, and "Heigho!" was all that Frank said.

Towards sundown the savages in Ota's isle must have been considerably surprised to see the white man's little ship standing in again towards the land. But she disappeared all at once, and in all probability they imagined she had sunk with all hands.

The fact is the *Island Queen* had got in behind the island, and was now in comparatively calm water. But the poor wee ship that our castaways had been so proud of was settling down fast.

It was an anxious half hour.

Every minute they expected she would take the fatal plunge, and the boat was all ready on deck to launch, if indeed they were not sucked down with the yacht. The land had almost taken the wind out of their sails.

But at long last the clear sandy bottom became visible all around them, and a big rolling wave carried them far up on the beach, receded, and left them almost high and dry.

They were safe for one night. That at least was certain, for no canoe could live in the sea that was running outside.

Safe for a night. Yes, perhaps safe for a week; but as soon as the wind should change, and the waves dash into the little land-locked bay, the *Island Queen* would break up.

So no one thought of sleep to-night. They worked in the dark by pandanus torch and lantern light, and even before the moon rose they had landed all the arms and ammunition, and all the stores as well.

The boat was now hauled well up, and the shipwrecked crew at once set about fortifying their position. It was a curious little bay, and a curious little beach, not thirty yards in width, and flanked at each side by dark frowning rocks, fifty feet high at least. Away into the interior the island was densely wooded, and the land rose into quite a mountain peak, while all around, with the exception of the little bay, the cliffs rose sheer up out of the deep, dark sea.

A barrier of sand and gravel was speedily thrown up across the bay just beyond reach of the waves, and over this they commenced to build a rampart, with a front that was almost inaccessible towards the sea.

Well those poor fellows knew they were working for dear life, so on they toiled all night long, and far into the next forenoon, emulating each other in their feats of strife, and never thinking of either food or drink.

But the barricade was completed at last, and little Cassia-bud, with his friend Hurricane Bob, were set to watch, while the others retired under the shade of the trees to obtain rest and enjoy some refreshment.

Being entirely worn out by their terrible hardships and exertions, nearly all slept till far into the day, when, after another slight meal, a party was detailed to spy out the resources of the island.

It was far better provisioned than they could have believed possible. That it had been at one time inhabited was also evident, for yams were still found growing, and several wild pigs were seen in the woods. The wind continued to blow high all that day and next; but towards night it fell dead calm, and early on the following morning the enemy's fleet was reported in sight, and in full force. This was signalled by a man on the outlook to those below.

By the time breakfast was finished the canoes were in sight. Quite a cloud of them there were, with King Ota himself leading.

Now it suddenly occurred to Fred that the enemy could easily possess itself of the *Island Queen*, and thus have a coign of vantage from which to hurl their spears and other missiles at the fort. So he called for volunteers to help him to fire the craft.

There were hardly twenty minutes to spare. Indeed, they were not sure of even this time. Quambo sprang forward; but little Cassia-bud was before him.

"You no go," he cried to Fred, "you no go, sah. Nobody go. Cassia-bud fire de ship all by hisse'f."

"You can, boy?"

"Yes," he cried energetically, "I can, plenty quick." He quickly made up a parcel of combustibles, which he tied knapsack-fashion over his shoulders. Then, almost before they could have counted six, the brave little fellow had scaled the ramparts and disappeared towards the beach.

They next saw him boldly paddling through the surf, then climbing cat-like over the vessel's bows, and so along the deck and down the main-hatchway.

It was an anxious time now for those on the ramparts. Every eye was turned at one moment towards the enemy's quickly approaching fleet, that seemed to near the bay with startling rapidity, and next towards the deck of the *Island Queen*, in momentary expectation of seeing Cassia-bud re-appear.

It appeared a lifetime to Fred since he had gone below.

"Stand by now, lads, to give the foremost boats a volley!" he cried presently. "Don't throw away a single shot."

Onwards swept the boats. They were not seventy yards from the stern of the *Island Queen* now; but look, smoke comes curling up from both the fore and main hatchways, and then Cassia-bud himself appears. But instead of coming straight over the bows again he rushes aft, and waves his jacket in proud defiance at the savage fleet.

Those on the ramparts shout to him to come on. A shower of spears flies over the decks, and Kashie is seen leaping forward. He falls! He is killed!

No; up again, and bounding along through smoke and flames and flying spears. Over he leaps, on through the surf, and next moment he is on the barricade. A dozen arms are stretched towards him, and next moment he is safe and sound.

"Thank God!" says Fred right fervently.

From stem to stern the *Island Queen* is soon sheeted in flames, and through the smoke which rolls slowly seaward the canoes appear.

"Give it to them now," cries Fred, "to show them we're not dead!"

A single volley had a startling effect on those sable warriors. Instead of advancing with shouts of terror the foremost rowers threw themselves pell-mell into the sea, and the other canoes beat a hasty retreat.

With a rifle each, Fred, Frank, Quambo, and Mac now betake themselves to the cliff top. They want to prove to those savages that it will be best in future not to venture within a radius of half a mile at least. And this they do in the most satisfactory manner imaginable.

Baffled and defeated where he had expected an easy victory, the greatest king in all the world retires to his island home, and the coast is once more clear.

For five days the savages made no sign, and the beleaguered garrison occupied itself in strengthening the position.

The main anxiety would soon be want of water. Not a drop was to be found in the island except one little trickling rill, that hardly supplied them with a pint a day each. And even this might dry up.

There was now no moonlight, but every night sentries were placed all along the ramparts.

Early on the morning of the sixth day there was not a canoe to be seen anywhere on the sea, and so the men sat down to breakfast cheerfully enough, and even the sentries, completely off their guard, were chatting gaily together on the ramparts.

Suddenly, without a moment's warning, the whole front of the barricade was found to be alive with swarming spear-armed savages.

Luckily every man's revolver was by his side, but the fight that now ensued was terrific. Hand to hand they fought, savages and whites, till the former disappeared at last in the same mysterious way they had come, leaving their dead behind them, and spearing or clubbing all the wounded lest the whites should torture them.

But where had they come from? This was easily explained. They had approached the island under cover of the darkness, and arranged their canoes close under the rocks, and thus out of sight. As soon as this was discovered they were speedily dislodged by the simple expedient of hurling down stones, and as soon as they had put out to sea rifles were once more brought to bear on them.

But by placing sentinels at night here and there on the cliff top no such ruse was again possible.

In this battle the garrison lost two men killed, and had three wounded.

One day Cassia-bud returned from the rock with an empty calibash. The water had given out. Then the sufferings of those unhappy men began in earnest.

The cocoanut supply still held out, however, but the water at last failed to quench the thirst, and the men began to fall sick.

The three wounded men died, and so weak were the others that they could not bury them. All they could do was to drag them to the cliff top and let them roll over into the sea—unknelled, uncoffined, and unknown.

# CHAPTER XXXV
## "WOULD SHE SEE THEIR SIGNALS?"

With the exception of Quambo, Cassia-bud, and Fred himself, not a soul could walk or even creep at last. Their tongues, their very faces, were swollen, their voices were reduced to the hoarsest of whispers, and their red eye-balls burned like fire.

Death was staring everyone in the face, when one morning Hurricane Bob, the faithful dog, was seen coming bounding joyfully from the bush.

He shook himself, and water flew in a shower from his jacket.

"Get the calabash," cried Fred. "Quick, Quambo, quick. Go on, good dog. Find it, boy. Find the water, lad."

The honest fellow gave one quick sharp bark and trotted off in front, the rest following as quickly as they could. He led them straight to a rock in the midst of a wood, and here, pushing a bush aside, he disappeared entirely. It was a cave, and in the centre thereof was a large pool, clear, cool, and sparkling.

Then down beside the cave's mouth knelt Fred, his arm across the great dog's neck, and there and then, with uplifted, tearful eyes, returned thanks to heaven.

The garrison was now snatched from the very brink of the grave.

But greater joy was to come, for on the very next day, behold, bearing down towards their island, a stately barque under full sail.

Would she see their signals, their frantic signals? Yes, she does, and seems to understand them too. She alters her course, and bears right down towards the bay, and lets go her anchor. And not till then did they discover that the vessel was none other than the good ship *San Salvador*.

Surely such joy as those poor fellows exhibited when the boat landed on the beach, and honest Captain Cawdor and Señor Sarpinto leapt on shore, was never before, witnessed.

You see they were all in a very weak and exhausted condition, so they wept and laughed by turns, and even sang and danced for joy, till the tears rose up in Captain Cawdor's eyes, and even Sarpinto was fain to turn away his head to hide his emotion.

But when Fred and Frank got on board at last, and found Eean and Toddie there, to say nothing of Bunko, then indeed their cup of joy was full, and in the bliss of that meeting they felt rewarded for all the dangers, trials, and sufferings they had gone through.

In less than a week both Frank and Fred had recovered their strength, and so had all the others.

All this time they had lain at anchor in the bay off King Ota's island, endeavouring to re-establish friendly relations with that mighty potentate.

He was dead set against them, however. He would not trust the white man, nor would he receive any presents or favours from him. When boats' crews were landed, they found only a deserted shore, with no one to hold a palaver with; for King Ota and his fierce spearmen, afraid that revenge was sought for, and dreading the terrible fire-sticks of the pale warriors, had sought the deepest shades of their forests, and climbed for safety into the highest hills.

So the ship left Ota's shores, and sailed away to another island some miles to the westward. This was a very much larger one, and looked even more prolific and beautiful than Ota's.

Here they were more successful. Although the canoes held aloof for a time, yet by a display of kindness, and by sending them presents, which had first to be left on the beach, the savages became gradually more and more bold. At last the king himself paid the ship a visit. He came unarmed and almost alone, explaining to the captain through Quambo that he knew the white men were all-powerful, and that if they chose to slay him they could find him wherever he happened to hide.

His majesty marvelled very much at all he saw, especially at the firearms and the telescope. When invited to look through this at his distant palace on the hills, he did so with fear and even superstitious dread. Why yonder squatted his favourite wife in front of the palace door, so very near that he could apparently almost touch her and talk to her!

And Captain Cawdor made him a gift of one of these telescopes, or magic glasses as he called them, fixing it for him at the right focus.

The king got even chatty and garrulous at last; and when Fred made him look through the glass with the wrong end towards him, and he saw his wife reduced in size to a mere midget, and so very far away, his merriment was as boisterous as that of an infant-school-boy.

He had plenty to eat and drink on board, and went away at last dressed in a scarlet robe—it really was a spare dressing-gown of Señor Sarpinto's—and loaded with presents. I do not believe there was a happier king in all the South Pacific Ocean.

The men of the *San Salvador* could now go on shore without fear of molestation, and all but unarmed.

One day the king brought his queen on board, and Toddie presided at the tea-table on the quarter-deck. There was chocolate as well as tea, and it was a good thing there was, for as soon as the queen had taken a huge gulp of tea she found she did not like the flavour of it; so she simply gaped, and it all ran out again over her robe of cocoa-fibre. But she liked the cocoa, and passed her cup fifteen times in succession, for Cassia-bud assured Fred he had counted every cup.

And Toddie, with an armed escort under the charge of Frank and Fred, went next day to visit the king's kraal. The view from the doorway was truly superb. All the rich and fertile island, with its flowering trees, with its orange groves and waving cocoa-nut and banana plantations, its woods and waters, its silvery shores and the bright blue sea itself, patched here and there with opal or green, lay down below at their feet; and up here, so high was the hill, a cool and delightful breeze was blowing.

"Oh," cried Toddie, "I think I should like to stay here for ever and ever!"

When Quambo translated this remark of Toddie's to the king, that potentate gallantly offered to club, cook, and eat his queen that Toddie might reign in her stead. And Toddie, the little witch, nodded smilingly to him, and assured him, through the interpreter, that she would "ask mamma."

This king was asked his opinion of Ota. He gave it very brusquely indeed, and in two or three words.

"He is an old woman, only fit to pound bread-fruit."

On the beach a day or two after this Toddie and her guard were assembled to see a review of the cannibal warriors, and a very fearful sight she thought it. The review was followed by a warrior dance, with wild, unearthly music from tom-toms and conch-shells, and then there was a great bonfire at night, with another dance around this.

Toddie dreamt about what she had seen all night long.

However, complete amity was secured with these people, and so much were they trusted that when the ship sailed away on a visit to the Isle of Good Hope, Quambo, the missionary, Bunko, and a party of whites were left with the king to show him how to build better huts or houses.

Toddie's delight on arriving at the Isle of Good Hope knew no bounds.

When she stood on the beach and gazed around her at the bay with its peaceful waters, the waves breaking with low and mournful boom on the reef outside, the feathery cocoanut palms stirred by the breeze, the flowery pandanus groves, the little cottage, with its rustic porch and its walks of silvery sand, across which the wild flowers were now trailing, she smiled and sighed, and tears filled her eyes.

"Oh, how romantic!" she said, "and yet how mournful!" "Still," she added, "I think I should have liked the life."

"Had you been here," said Frank gallantly, "had you been here, Toddie, perhaps we should not have been in such a hurry to leave."

They spent the whole day in wandering through the forest, and on their return they found dinner ready in the little cottage, cooked by little Cassia-bud, just as it used to be when Fred and Frank were Crusoes.

When the sun began to get very low in the western horizon, they left the island in the *Salvador's* boat, and were rowed towards the gap.

During a lull in the conversation, and as the boat was speeding over the placid lake, "Oh, Miss Toddie," said Cassia-bud, "hab massa Fred told you ob de big debbil-fish that fly ober de boat, and hab nuffin on but his head?"

Fred had not told her, and very much puzzled she was; but when Frank explained all about this debbil-fish, and the fright they had when it flew over the reef, she laughed right merrily.

"I think," said Eean, "there must have been a good deal of mystery as well as romance about this island of yours, Frank and Fred. I suppose you are half sorry you are leaving it."

"Not quite half, sir," said Frank, "and yet we spent some very pleasant days here. Didn't we, Fred?"

The party next visited the little coral reef island and once again Toddie was told the story of the strange and wonderful mirage, which had so nearly cost our heroes their lives.

When, after an absence of some days, they returned to the islands, they found that matters had progressed very pleasantly indeed. The king was delighted with the huts which the white men had thrown up for him, and still more delighted with a little church which had been built.

This king, savage though he certainly was, possessed a good deal of common-sense, and over and over again he had asked the missionary to explain why he seemed to take so much interest in his people. What did he expect in return?

He could understand, he said, white men coming to his island to trade. They brought one thing and they took away another. But this man, this missionary, wanted to do all for the islanders, yet receive nothing in return. Was he a true man, or did he harbour some deep-laid scheme against the king and his people, which he was skilfully trying to hide?

The answer to all this was not easily understood by this savage people. But to the best of his ability, and with the aid of the two savages who had been so faithful and so true all along, he told them all the gospel story, and then he in his turn put a question to the king. "If," said the missionary, "the Saviour of mankind, and Son of the Lord of all, could give his life for us, was it any marvel that he—the missionary—a mere human being and mortal, should humbly try to follow in the great Master's footsteps, and do all he could for the salvation of these islanders?" The missionary triumphed.

That which never, never, could have been effected by the sword and force, was easily accomplished by one man, Bible in hand.

When the *San Salvador* was ready to start away on her homeward voyage it did not seem at all strange that the missionary should express his desire to remain here, or that Quambo, Magilvray, and five other white men resolved to keep him company. But when Bunko came up to Eean on the quarter-deck, and said:

"This is my home now, kind master. There's many and many a poor, dark soul in this island I can do some good for. Bunko hasna the gift o' tongues. He canna preach the Word, but he can act it."

Then, I say, the old bard marvelled not a little, but he took the young man's hand kindly in his, and replied:

"Yes, lad, you can act it, and example is better than precept. Stay, my friend, stay. We are sorry to lose you; but as you think you can do good we will not gainsay you. Farewell, and God bless you, Bunko."

And as the ship sailed away from the island the last figure seen was Bunko's, standing on a knoll, waving his bonnet in the air, till the *San Salvador* passed round a wooded cape, and they saw him no more.

Five years have passed away. Five years! What changes a space of time, even of this brief span, may work in the lives of all! Think of it, boys of fifteen. Why, in five years' time you will be men, and must ere then have chosen your career in life for better or for worse.

Five years! But they have been busy ones with Fred and Frank. They have not been at home all that time, you may be sure. No, for Señor Sarpinto, restless ever, saw fit to return to those islands, and in a much larger and finer ship, of which the young sailors were chief officers.

From San Francisco he took out with him a colony of busy bees of Americans, with everything necessary to develop the resources of those cannibal islands. They are cannibal islands now no longer. A church stands on the largest, where once dreadful orgies used to take place, that are too revolting even to think of. There is a busy and prosperous little village near the sea, and fields of rice and roots and sugar-cane stretch over the rolling hills far away to the woodlands. The islands are rich too in spices and in gums, as well as some forms of mineral wealth, and ships call many times during the year to buy and barter goods.

The black population is industrious, the white men and their families are well-to-do. Fred is governor, and honest Bunko is his overseer.

But of all professions in the world what should Frank adopt in the end but farming?

I will tell you how it turned out. Señor Sarpinto, after a visit to the little village of Methlin, was so enamoured with the quiet peace and repose that reign around it, and with the simple ways of the fisher population, that he determined to make it his home. He was growing old, he said, and he should like to be near to Toddie. He had plenty of money, he told Eean. What was the good of money if it did not bring happiness? So he set about "building himself happiness" — these are his own words.

First and foremost he found out his old friend, Captain Cawdor, who had retired, and was living in the city of Glasgow.

"My good captain," he said, "I cannot understand why you should like to live among stones and mortar, quite away from the sound of the sea."

"Ah! my friend, I'd fain spend my life, or what remains of it, where I could hear and see the waves; but I am not wealthy enough to do as I please."

"But the rent you pay for this house," said the Señor, "would, I think, get you a charming villa surrounded by pretty gardens, close to the woods, and close to the western ocean."

"When you find such a place, my friend, come and tell me, and I will rejoicingly take it," the captain said, laughing.

Now there was land to be sold at Methlin, and around it, and the Señor quickly became the purchaser, and in six months' time not only did a lovely mansion spring up in the glen behind the village, but a pretty cottage close to the sea.

In the former soon dwelt the Señor Sarpinto, and in the latter, who but Captain Cawdor; and one of the largest wings of the Señor's house was given to Frank, on condition that he should farm the Señor's land on a handsome salary.

Frank was very happy now, and his altered circumstances in life gave him an opportunity of taking care of his mother, who still resided in town, but was getting old.

Yes, it was a strange freak of Fortune to make Frank a farmer. After this no one would be surprised to know that Cassia-bud left the sea also, after officiating as steward for some years, and became butler to Señor Sarpinto at Helena House.

One day, about the end of the five years, Frank and Toddie might have been seen walking together on the beach near the igloo, or the house that Bunko had built with the skeleton of the Johnnie Whale. They seem in very earnest conversation indeed. It would be obviously unkind, however, for me to play the eaves-dropper; but one thing I do know, and must tell the reader. Just six weeks after that earnest conversation at the igloo a very interesting event was the subject of general conversation among the villagers—the marriage of Miss Arundel. And every one confessed that a more beautiful bride than Toddie never was seen, nor a more handsome and manly bridegroom than Frank Fielding.

Fred happened to be at home at the time, and the marriage was celebrated in the fisherman's humble cot.

Before stepping into the carriage that awaited the happy pair at the door, Frank held out his hand, and right heartily did Fred Arundel grasp and press it.

"Brothers yet," said Frank.

"Brothers ever," said Fred.

And so they parted.


Alone in his romantic cave Eean, the bard, still writes his charming verses, still sings his wild lays, soothed by moan of wind and murmur of sea; there has come a peace and repose to the mind of the Señor Sarpinto he had never known before; old Captain Cawdor is very contented, and very jolly too, in his cottage by the sea. And oftentimes, on summer evenings, may the trio be seen strolling together on the beach, or when the wild wintry winds are raving through the woods, seated perhaps round Eean's cottage hearth with Eppie near by, birr-birr-ing at her wheel.

And many a reminiscence is theirs to tell of their strange eventful lives, and of dangers gone through by sea and land.

Thus calmly pass their peaceful lives away.